Life Weaver

Sandra Taylor

Life Weaver
Copyright © 2020 by Sandra Taylor

All rights reserved. No part of this publication may be reproduced, distributed, or transmitted in any form or by any means, including photocopying, recording, or other electronic or mechanical methods, without the prior written permission of the author, except in the case of brief quotations embodied in critical reviews and certain other non-commercial uses permitted by copyright law.

Tellwell Talent
www.tellwell.ca

ISBN
978-0-2288-4307-8 (Hardcover)
978-0-2288-4306-1 (Paperback)

I remember being young, when I thought getting grounded was the worst thing in the world. . . . . . I was WRONG!

Things aren't always what they seem. Sometimes fantasy and fairytales are the true reality and what we perceive as reality is just wishful thinking from naïve minds...

We can go our entire lives thinking one direction is up then have someone come by only to show us that up is in a complete different direction.

No. this is not a story about the direction up. Sadly, it is a story about me, Louanna Marie Teelf, (aka Lou) and how I came to realize nothing in my life was, is, or ever will be what I thought.

Lou

Remembering

"Not every time that phone rings, it's for you, ya know!" I was already mad, even before she spoke.

"Why would anyone call *you*?" Lucy snapped. "*I*, unlike **you**, have a little thing called friends. Somehow I doubt those *flea infested primates* you run with have enough smarts to use a phone, let alone possess the necessary skills to dial and speak." She laughed at her dig to my buds.

I simply glared at her and continued with my chores. Arguing with Lucy was useless; we'd never see eye to eye about our taste in friends. I thought hers were too snobby and she simply thought mine were beneath her.

We used to be close sisters . . . Things were changing though.

"Bu-bye." She said and hung the receiver back on its rest.

Honestly, some days just looking at that, *oh so perfect* face of hers, set my teeth on edge. This was just such a day!

"Ya know, Luc, I have several really good friends. Why you always dis on 'em, I'll never get." I said exasperated.

"Friends? Geez, Lou**anna**, every time I watch **America's Most Wanted**, I half expect to see one of them on it and the rest of them will no doubt end up on **World's Dumbest Criminals**." She chuckled again, gathering her things to leave.

"My buds never bother anyone. Least of all you, Luc. Why do you always have to act so haughty?" I was so upset it felt like wind was blowing around the kitchen, upsetting the stillness.

"**DON'T. BOTHER. ME**!?. . . . Did you really just say that to me, Lou**anna**? Those Cretans go out of their way to *bother* me. I'm sure they sit up at night thinking of ways to torment me!"

"Oh for goodness sake, Luc, they like to joke and have a good time. Try to grow a personality; one that has a sense of humor with it . . . and don't call me *Louanna*. You say it wrong." I sneered at her.

"It's your name, so I *will* call you Lou**anna** . . . *Louanna*. As for your precious *buds*, all I can say is, I hope you have had your shots."

She said it like they were all animals. I hated how she looked at my buds. I simply avoided her group of high and mighty friends so I hardly ever had to deal with them. She seemed to go out of her way to find mine. I think she liked seeing me cringe when we would walk up on her. She knew exactly which buttons to push on me and my buds, and boy did she push them.

I don't like confrontation. It always feels like someone could get really hurt if I lost my temper and the someone would most likely be **ME!**

I know, I know. Silly, right? But it just feels that way: (*More often here lately . . . hormones!? Yuck! Teen time is too emotional and I want it gone!!)* It seemed like there were times when Lucy was trying to get me mad or angry; well too bad for her!

The silence in the kitchen was once again broken by the ringing of the phone. Lucy darted for the receiver and gave her chirpiest tone a go at the caller.

"Hullo?" Lucy smiled, leaning a hip against the wall, twiddling with the phone cord. The smile left her face and she looked at me. "Oh, it's for you; it's that *Leah* girl." It was all she said as she laid the receiver on the counter and left the kitchen, nose held high.

"Sup, Leah?" I asked.

"Sup, Girlie head? What's wrong with Princess Lucy tonight? She seemed even more *snotty* than usual." Leah laughed.

"Who knows, girl. She's been acting weird for, well . . . Every since she was born basically." I laughed, looking up the stairs where Lucy had just gone. She had been acting strange lately. I couldn't put my finger on what the change was, but it was there.

"So, why the ring; what's going on out in the land of the free?" I laughed.

"Oh, man!" Leah began. "I nearly forgot why I called. Can you get out? Make it down town?"

"I wish!" I sighed as I finished my kitchen work. "But the warden has **Alcatraz** locked down tight. There's no way of escape. The last time I went out after curfew, mom flipped a script. You'd of thought some alien was gonna *beam me up* or something. Why the third degree?" I asked.

"Well, the 3-D is because that new hottie is here. I think he's putting in an app. If he gets a job at Burger Boy, that place will be crawling with lil flip tails, all trying to make a play for him."

. . . Let me tell you about "The new hottie." So you'll know what all the fuss is about. He just moved here a few weeks ago, keeps to himself and seems quiet and *secretive*. His chocolate brown hair is wavy and long. He almost always keeps it tied with a strap of leather. (It lies between his shoulder blades.) There is almost always a runaway strip that hangs over one of his eyes . . . His iceberg blue eyes make you want to jump in them and swim. His face reminds you of the Greek God statues in the museums. DeLainey Landon is **_one hot cookie_**! . . . swoon!

"I **soo** wish I could get out, but I guess I'll just have to eye molest him with the masses at school tomorrow." I joked.

"Well, if you're sure you can't." Leah said, sounding disappointed. "I'll drop it, but I will remind you that with your birthday coming up, as per Ms. Leona's rules, you will be old enough…"

"I know that Mom said I can start dating once I turn 16. But ya kinda need a mate to date. And the last time I looked Chickadee, I am tragically and most likely *permanently*, single; therefore, **dateless**."

I cannot tell you the <u>thousands </u>of times Leah and I have had this conversation. Believe me, checking off my, *ever so many* faults and flaws is usually a "**good time had by all**" ((***NOT***)) but I didn't want that to be the way I ended my day.

"All of Louanna's faults and flaws brought to you live. Film at 11:00"

I see that show *WAY* too much!

"Well, **dateless,** doesn't mean **UN**datable." Leah went on. "So you need to let guys know that you "can" date. When the time comes, there will be "options" and not just a few, "ok, I settled." She laughed.

"That's true enough. But, date or no date the age 16 is coming either way. We'll just have to wait and see what happens." I said

A subtle clearing of her throat was Mom's way to say, ***"Get off the phone."*** So I took my cue.

"Listen, I gotta get ready for bed." Mom just cleared her throat." Meet at the usual place in the A.M.?" I asked

"You know it. See ya on the flip side."

That was Leah, no long good bye, just a "click" and the call was ended.

Entering the living room, I saw Mom sitting, cross-legged, in her chair listening to the radio. She had a strange look on her face. Not worry, but perhaps concern.

"I'm done in the kitchen, Mom. Sorry 'bout the long call."

Mom looked at me and smiled. "That's fine, baby. I just think you need to get some sleep, don't *you*? It's getting late." She reached her hand out and pulled me into a big hug.

Her hugs always made me feel better. Mom just seemed to have a way of making things right. Only one other person had those "magic" hugs. It was Mom's dad, my Papa. Their hugs both seemed to yield safety and comfort.

I took a deep breath and inhaled her unique smell. Fresh spring flowers, was how she always smelled. "Do you need anything before I go to bed?" I asked and kissed her forehead.

"No, Baby. I'm fine." She said. "You head on up and get ready for bed. I'll see you in the morning. I love you, Louanna." She smiled up at me again. But the smile seemed strained and didn't light her eyes like usual. She looked sad and worn. I wanted to ask what was wrong but she closed her eyes and began to hum the song playing on the radio.

The music was barely above a whisper as a reached the top stair. I never quite got the music mom listened to. I'm sure she feels the same about what I listen to; but honestly, who are the **Bee Gees** anyway?

As I entered my room, something nearly knocked me down, striking me in the stomach area with a punch like blow. Lykie, my large black dog, came bounding out from the shadows to happily greet me and get his evening treat.

"Well, hey there, handsome." I said, scratching his head. Looking around I found some leftover pizza crust and tossed it to him. "How's my special man, Huh? How's my baby tonight?" Lykie was wagging his tail so hard he was shaking all over and nearly bending into.

"I missed you today!"

I looked up to see who had spoken but only Lykie and I were in the room. It seemed I was more tired than I first thought.

I looked around, Mom fussed at me all the time about, "cleaning up this PIG STY", but honestly I don't see where a sty, pig or otherwise, is! I mean four or five pair of jeans lying about, *some were clean (ish),* and a few (dozen) dirty socks, random shoes, (Hey, the missing ones could show up!) And let's face it, in a pinch; that bowl of green-grey furry stuff, could make a good science project. See, no sty! Face it, not *EVERYONE* makes their bed! (You're only gonna mess it up again!)

After scavenging for my pjs and quite a few *not so friendly* comments to my room about why it should be self-cleaning, I scratched Lykie's ears and headed for the bathroom to end this night with a long shower.

I wondered if I could invent a *"self-cleaning"* room where *"I"* wasn't the *"self"* doing the cleaning. I reached for the bathroom door only to find it *locked.*

BAM! . . . BAM! . . . BAM! I banged on the door.

"Go awaaaay!" Lucy chirped with that "Ha!" tone in her voice.

"Awwwww! Come on, Luc! I have to use this bathroom too, ya know!" I whined, hating the pleading tone my voice had adopted.

"I said go away, Lou**anna**. I just got in and I'll be *in* until I'm not *in*." She had way too much joy in her voice at my inconvenience.

BAM! I just had to get one more in.

"And *that* won't make it happen any faster." She snipped.

I just never seemed to be able to get into that shower first! I must be predestined to an endless life of warm/cold bath time schedules.

"NOTE TO SELF: Along with self-cleaning rooms, I also need to invent a forever hot water additive." I mumbled as I stood outside the *hot shower promise land*, clearly dismissed, when Lucy began to torture a cat . . . or sing. I'm sure they both sound the same so it could have been either one.

I stood and listened to the defenseless cat, or helpless song, being slowly and painfully killed by Lucy on the other side of the door as long as I could take it then I made the Catholic cross sign and whispered. "Poor cat/song . . . your suffering will end soon." I then turned and headed back to my room.

'That hurts my ears.'

"It hurts my head." I said looking for who had spoken. I was alone in my room, only Lykie and I were in here. "You're losin' it ole girl, talking to oneself is a sure sign that you are going Bonkers gazoo."

Everyone hears voices in their head, "Don't eat that green thing." or "You should slow down." You know . . . that sorta thing. But when you start talking back to them, it's white coat and *Jell-O* time.

There was little light in my room. Just the moon's blue hue could be seen. I lay there on my bed, mindlessly stroking Lykie's head. My gaze went to the window box, where it often did when I found myself needing to think.

The window box was the only place in my room that Mom ever deemed clean. I never allowed it to go askew. All my stuffed animals were placed just so; each showing years of long nights, whispered secrets, and hugs that were far too tight following nightmares I never could quite recall, simply the feeling of fore-boding they left in their wake. Each pair of eyes danced brightly in the moons light, shinning with an almost intelligence at my Jequota.

Moon light always seemed to find the Jequota, even on cloudy or rainy nights. A small beam of moon hue would somehow find its way to caress it.

Jequota is a small, hand carved, wooden box about the size of a child's shoe box, given to me by my Papa on my fourth birthday. He said it is a special box, given to special people like me. It was mine to care for and it would care for me. The wood that Jequota is made of is the color of a brindle dog. Papa had carved different symbols and swirls into the outside. The inside was laced with a strange blue/silver cloth that always looked like flowing water. When I was younger, I often pretended that I had captured water's essence and was holding it to use in a pool . . . if we ever got one . . . (*We didn't!* ☹)

Papa said the *spirit box or Jequota* had chosen me. He always told such great stories, making each one seem true and somehow majestic. He just had a way of making you believe in things that seemed impossible.

"Remember, Louanna, even impossible has possible in it. Always believe with your heart, your mind is taught to doubt and disbelieve but the heart will almost always lead you true." He often said to me.

I always listened to Papa. Even when he was joking you had the feeling you should still pay close attention.

I lay there on my bed, mindlessly stroking Lykie, and looked at the Jequota and its cotton stuffed band of sentinels setting around guarding it.

....

"Where's my girl? Where's my beautiful, Louanna Marie? Papa called out to me as he looked up from the bottom stair.

"**You came!!! Papa, you really came!**" I squealed as I bound down the steps into his arms for a *grizzle hug*; which is what we called them. Seeing as they were more special than any regular, plain ole bear hug. Papa's hugs were the ***best***!

"Came? Louanna, you hurt me." He joked. "Of course I came. It's your fourth birthday, Lemoya; I'd like to see anyone try to keep me away."

I loved when he called me ***Lemoya***; it sounded so much sweeter than "Little one." Papa often called me things from his native tongue; **which he never told me where that was,** just that I'd know when it was time for me to know.

Papa kissed the back of my hand "Every year you get more beautiful; you **do** remember our pact, don't you?" he smiled mischievously.

"Yes, Papa, you stop getting older and I catch up with you; then we run off and have an adventure!" I said eagerly.

"HA! HA! HA!! That's right! That's exactly right, Lemoya." He said cheerfully, as he hoisted me onto his shoulders and rode me into the living room.

The house was full of the smiling faces of family and friends. Balloons, streamers, and other party decorations were hanging all around the room. Music played softly in the background. Papa danced me into the center of the room where all eyes could see the "birthday girl."

Gifts were stacked neatly on the coffee table; at the age of four, the stack looked to be about fifty feet tall, holding a thousand gifts. (I know it wasn't, but like I said... I was four.)

Everyone sang "happy birthday" to me and I opened my gifts. There were dolls, clothes, cards bearing money, plastic dishes, and other various toys. After the last box was opened, thank you and hugs were given out. The room fell eerily quiet and Papa said

"And now, Louanna, one last gift, a gift from me." He held out a small package, no bow, no fancy wrappings, just plain brown paper, like a paper bag. He smiled at me and gestured to the couch. I walked over and sat down, eager to get my "grizzle gift."

Papa handed me the gift and took a step back, smiling down at me. All eyes had now settled on me, causing my hands to tremble; at least I *think* that's what made my hands tremble. Slowly I began unwrapping, that seemingly ordinary brown paper from the package; careful not to rip or tear it; where before all the other paper had been torn and discarded quickly, this paper seemed more important. There was no tape holding the paper in place, only a leather strap binding it in place.

I opened a small cardboard box and took out the hand carved wooden box that lay inside.

"Thank you Papa! Now I have a jewelry box like Mom and Lucy, all I need is some earrings and stuff to put in it." I sad happily

I opened the box, to see how big the inside of the box was, and heard the sound of wind blowing softly. Several people gasped but I didn't look up at them. I seemed to be mesmerized by the inside of the box. The cloth inside seemed to flow like water when I touched it. It felt cool to my touch yet somehow still warm; like I was touching a dream, I knew it was there but couldn't feel it properly.

"It's a Jequota, Louanna, a very special box. It chose you, asked me to make it so it could be with you always.' Papa said "Jequota; it sounds so mysterious, what is it Papa?" I asked but couldn't seem to take my eyes from the box. I felt like it was trying to speak to me...

"A Jequota is a spirit box, Lemoya. Each one is specially made for an individual. Your Jequota is as special as you are." Papa beamed a smile at me.

"Jequota is a spirit box." I repeated thoughtfully. "Well, I'm not gonna put some silly ole earrings in a box with a fancy name like that." I ran my fingers over the elaborate carvings and symbols on the box.

"When she wants something inside her, Louanna, she will tell you. In time you will find that she is a great friend to you, Lemoya." Papa smiled at me then turned and smiled at Mom. Her smile was wide in return, but I noticed that her eyes seemed shadowed and troubled.

....

Bright light flooded into my room blinding me and causing Lykie to jump and growl.

"I'm out of the bathroom, Lou**anna**." Lucy said, not even slowing to see if I had heard her. She simply went to her room and closed the door.

After a shower of, not so hot water, I combed out the tangled mass that is my hair, brushed my teeth, and stared at the reflection in the mirror. "Where is the beauty you see in me, Papa? The person I always see looking back at me . . . is *no* beauty." I sighed

The reflection of the mirror seemed to quiver, like water kissed by a slight breeze. I squeezed my eyes tightly, stretched and left the bathroom.

"Hearing and talking to voices in your head; and now seeing things? Louanna, your brain is in **serious** need of an overhaul. All you need now is to grow an extra arm or other appendage and you can star in the circus. You can share a space with "Bucky, the half chicken boy." I scolded myself, and then I went to bed.

"Night Lykie, at least you're normal, me? . . . Not so much.

Glass and Mirrors

"Get up! I mean it, Louanna Marie! I'm not going to tell you again. Do you hear me?" Mom yelled at me from the kitchen for the third time. What can I say; I'm not a morning person.

Didn't I just go to bed like five minutes ago!? I don't even think my pillow has gotten warm yet. Why oh why does the start of the day come so stinking early!?

"I'm up, Mom." I grumbled; have I mentioned that I am *NOT* a morning person?

Lykie had already gone down and was, no doubt, chasing a squirrel or digging up mom's plants again. I on the other hand was still asleep; regardless of the fact my body was in motion.

I threw on a pair of jeans and a shirt that I was 85% . . . no, 82% sure were cleanish, gathered my things and brushed out my hair as I went down for breakfast.

Mom, Lucy and our neighbor, Mrs. Wolff, were sitting in the kitchen talking when I came in.

"Well, I just thought you should know, Leona." Mrs. Wolff was saying. "I think we should all try to attend, a neighborhood watch program would be a great thing for this community. With crime being what it is; it's a wonder we haven't been burglarized already, or worst."

"I'll try to make it Carrol, but if I can't, please be my voice. I agree. A neighborhood watch is a great idea. We need to look out for one another," Mom said as she refilled their coffee cups. "Your breakfast is getting cold, Louanna." She said, looking up at me as I entered the kitchen.

"Thanks, I'm gonna have lunch at school today, I'll need lunch money." I said as I scooped up eggs and sausage then downed my orange juice in one gulp.

Lucy sat in her usual spot at the kitchen table, eating a grapefruit and eyeing me like a bird does a bug. She never had to rush to meet the bus like I did. Her snobby friends would pick up the *princess* and drive her to school.

I opened my mouth and showed her the chewed up food then swallowed it and smiled at her.

"That's very mature, Lou**anna**. Everyone needs to see your partially chewed breakfast first thing in the morning." She griped.

I bat my eyes at her in fake innocence, kissed Mom, said good bye to Mrs. Wolff, and headed for the bus stop; feeling good that I had gotten in the first dig of the day and Lucy hadn't.

"I wish you could just stay here today!"

"I'd love to stay home today but I have to go to school."

I looked around but saw no one. Lykie had stopped his digging, beneath the trees, to look at me. He looked like he was smiling; with his tongue hanging out, head turned sideways, and his one lopsided ear flopped down, he appeared to be enjoying himself. He sneezed at me sending dust from his nose into the air and went back to digging up Mom's plants. I love that dog. He is one of my best buds but mom is gonna kill him over her plants one of these days.

Several people were already standing around the bus stop when I arrived. Most of them looked sleepy and like me, not morning people. A few were cheery and perky; I wanted to poke 'em with a stick, a sharp stick possibly with a point on the end.

(I may not have mentioned this, but, I'm NOT a morning person!)

I don't really make eye contact or speak to any of these people. We have to ride the bus together; I don't have to converse with them. I usually just stand off to the side and then join the *'bus lemmings'* as we all file onto *the big yellow taxi* and head off for seven hours of tortuous learning.

"Hey there!" Travis Traviene said, looking my way.

I was puzzled at his addressing me. "Hey" I said, just as someone behind me said it too. I turned only to find myself staring at the broad expanse of someone's chest. Slowly I looked up into the ice blue eyes of . . . DeLainey Landon.

Ok, see, I don't do the whole; "girlie girl" thing. I don't wear makeup, flirt, or giggle ridiculously when a boy is near; but a squeak, *far too close to a nervous giggle,* escaped my mouth. I wondered if that odd noise had just come out of me.

DeLainey just stood there, with that band of hair hanging down covering his right eye, his head leaning slightly to the left, staring at me.

Now; I've heard the phrase "time stood still" before, but I swear to you that the world stopped moving at that very moment. I'm not sure, but I think I forgot how to breathe because I stopped *that* too.

"Travis Traviene." Travis said, holding out his hand as an introduction. "It seems we're neighbors, DeLainey." He smiled.

"De" DeLainey said

"What?" Travis asked, sounding a bit puzzled.

"Call me De, most people do."

"Trav, my friends all call me Trav. Don't they, Lou?" Travis asked, dragging me into his conversation.

"Sure, *Trav*" I said, like we were friends . . . how 'bout NOT!! I can count on one hand the amount of times we have spoken to each other and including this one that rounds up to a womping big ONE.

"Nice to meet you, *Lou*, is it?" DeLainey asked

"Yes." Was all I could get to squeak out. My voice had apparently taken a vacation at that very moment; leaving me looking stupid and girlie girlish.

"Here, De," Travis said, taking Delainey's arm "let me introduce you to everyone." Then he walked DeLainey to the other side of the group of people. I was grateful to good ole 'Trav' for saving me from further embarrassment.

"Way to go, Lou, you just made a fool of yourself in front of a Greek god." I mumbled to myself. DeLainey looked over the group of heads, straight at me and smiled. I felt like a deer caught in the headlights of a train . . . a train going 180 mph.

I was soon saved however by the arrival of the bus. The familiar "shhhhhhh" of the breaks and the "whoosh" of the door opening was the starting bell for the *'bus lemmings'* to climb aboard. Our bus driver, Mr. Ford, is the absolute coolest adult ever! He listens to loud music, and really seems to like his job, and us kids, he always has a kind word and an ear if you just need to talk. ☺

"This is De, Mr. Ford. He'll be riding from here on." Travis said as way of introducing DeLainey.

"Welcome aboard, De. Grab a seat and hang on. I'll get you to school; just don't know in what condition." Mr. Ford laughed and winked at him.

"K." De said and took a seat in my usual spot.

Travis stopped and looked at DeLainey, "Come on back here De, meet the rest of the gang."

DeLainey didn't respond, he simply stood up and followed Travis to the back of the bus and sat down.

Now I have to ask: Why do you only seem to have things happen to you on days when you feel like hot barf and look like one of the zombies from a horror movie? DeLainey Landon is a mysterious, handsome, well put together, guy. (Guys always seem to have it easy in that department!) But not me! . . . Oh no! All the glam makers in *Hollywood* could not do me any good.

I sat there on that hot, over crowded bus, thinking why I even cared.

I don't care . . .

Well, maybe I care a little . . .

Or more than a little; but I won't admit it . . . out loud!

The ride to school seemed to drag on forever. It might just be because we were returning from Fall break but it seemed to be just dragging on and on. Time was defiantly NOT my friend this morning. I could feel DeLainey's eyes boring into the back of my head, making it hot and uncomfortable.

I won't look . . .

I won't look . . .

I. Won't. Look! . . .

Ok, I looked. Casually of course; but dang it, **I looked!** Even telling myself not to, *I did*.

His gaze locked with mine. Those eyes, those incredibly, dreamy eyes were looking at me. I could spend a lot of hours just gazing into those all too knowing eyes of DeLainey Landon. At that thought I noticed he raised an eyebrow and the corner of his mouth drew up in an almost one sided grin. If I had thought he was gorgeous before; that grin made him even more so. A full grin now covered his oh so kissable lips like he'd heard what I had just thought.

He looked away to respond to something someone had said to him; like a scared rabbit, I took flight and turned around to stare out the window. My reflection grew blurry and the window seemed to ripple like water kissed by a breeze. I rubbed my eyes and looked back to a clear reflection. This bus must be hotter than I thought.

The bus slowed down and stopped. Mr. Ford turned and yelled his morning message; "Everybody out, Time to get some learnin' on!"

I jumped to my feet and headed for the big Oak tree. I knew my buds would already be at waiting. I was not just trying to get away from DeLainey Landon.

Well, I wasn't!!

We always met at *sanctuary* before the start of our academic day. The tree was close to the school but still secluded enough that we had privacy. So, we called it sanctuary. It's sort of the meeting place for all the weirdoes, rejects, and misfits . . . like me. ☺

As I came around the corner of the school, I saw my buds were already there. I could see Dixie Styxx or Pixie as I called her; not only because she loved the candy, but also because of her small size. She is just above four and a half feet; her long, platinum blonde hair, hangs nearly to her waist; giving the allusion of a pixie or sprite from a fairytale. Despite her size; she is strong and doesn't have the good sense to back down from anything. She is very touchy about her size and won't hesitate to let you know your place.

Allen and Andee Farmer: no, not twins, but look so much alike that they could be. They are related by marriage. Allen's uncle; who he lives with, is married to Andee's mom. They are like a pair of pit-bull pups, always rolling around trying to *best* each other. They are fiercely loyal; not only to each other, but to anyone they deem a friend or care deeply about. (P.S. don't dis on the UFC around them, just sayin')

Then there is lil Frankie Hylt, or Squeaks, *my baby*. I'm not sure that Frankie would know how to raise her voice. What? Frankie can't be a girl's name? Well, it is. She is uber smart. At only 13 years old she could have already graduated and gone on to college but she has chosen to stay in the same grade as the gang. Her short red hair, huge blue-green eyes, and timid manor of speech make her appear older. But if you spend a few short minutes with her you'll know that she is only 13; books can only teach us so much.

Next we have Devaine Johnson, or DJ to all of us. DJ is the clown of the group. He is always up to some shenanigan or the other. He is also the least likely *outcast* of the bunch. He is a jock; played in every sport the school offers, and even some they didn't. DJ is a star athlete at, football, basketball, track, soccer, fencing, wrestling, and swimming; I could go on but I think you get where I'm going with this... I could name them all but I do have to move on otherwise we'd be here on "D.J. is great at" all day! Now I know I told you that sanctuary is a place where misfits meet and hang out. DJ *chooses* to hang with us; he rarely ever hangs out with his fellow jocks. He's very good looking and really built; but he is tragically shy around people. He once told us the only reason he plays sports is because he *has* to or his mind would go Bonkers gazoo on him if he didn't stay busy and physical.

Next in the line of buds is Leah Armstrong, by far the **bff** of all my bfs. She and I have been friends since kindergarten. (She stole my snack then pushed me down at recess. You know; how all true friendships start.) Leah is headstrong and tough. She has to be, she has practically raised herself since she was about four or five. I'd like to tell you that violence doesn't touch a small town, and living in one is all rainbows and picnics, like you see on TV. I'm sorry to pop that delusion bubble for you; but, drugs, abuse, and alcoholism is as real here as it is in the big cities; a fact that Leah knows all too well. *Don't look like that.* Leah **hates** people to show pity on her. She says, life throws curve balls at everyone and she is no different than the rest of the billions of people, young and old, who get hurt each day.

Now you have a rough idea of the people in my life I call buds. These people are so much more than friends to me. Each one of them is true and honest in their own way. I trust them with my life.

"I had him pinned down that time didn't I, DJ?" Andee said breathlessly as he and Allen got up off the ground.

"Pinned? . . . Is **that** what you did?" DJ said with a mischievous look in his eyes.

Before either Farmer could blink, DJ had pounced on both of them, was sitting on their backs, and grinning like a baboon. "Are you sure you know what a pin *is* there short stuff?"

"HEY!" Pixie groused. "Lose the 'short stuff' comments or I'll show you a thing or two 'bout a thing or two, Muscle head!"

"No Ma'am!" DJ said as he helped the Farmers off the ground. "Last time you went all *Ramboette* on me, you gave me a black eye! I had to tell people I's mugged by a gang just to save face. Getting your can kicked by a Pixie, when you're 6-6 isn't something you come back from easily." He looked down at his hand. "Look, I scraped my pinky. Who wants to kiss my, boo boo?" He held his hand up and wiggled his pinky at Pixie, batted his eyes, and pooched his lips out, trying hard to look pitiful.

"I ortta break the darn thing for you!" Pixie said as she muffed up DJ's hair.

"Look, there's Lou! Bout time there girl." Leah said as she got up to greet me.

I smiled at my buds, "Mornin' guys, what's going on this early in the day?" I asked, knowing the answer.

"Ha, Same as every morning. Tweedle Re and Tweedle Re Re were wrestling and *Conan* there sat on 'em and hurt him wittle self. Ya know, typical Tuesday for us." Leah said

Everyone laughed, DJ held up his wound, Pixie rolled her eyes, and everyone started jabbering to each other about this and that.

"So, what's on the menu for the day, fearless leader?" Leah asked

"I just wanna make it through the day, Leah. No fuss, no drama, no . . ." I hesitated, "Weird stuff to make me go, bonkers gazoo!"

"I hear ya, sister! Come on guys, bell's bout to ring." Leah said to all of us.

All shenanigans ended and everyone gathered their things. When all had gotten packed and ready; we started for the school, leaving sanctuary and the serenity we found there behind.

We walked along talking about random things, enjoying each other's company. As we came around the corner by the big entrance doors, I nearly stumbled into someone. A huge group of students were all standing by the entrance waiting to be allowed to go in. Leah looked up to see what had caused me to stop.

"What's goin' on here?" Leah asked, looking around at the crowd.

Inching closer to the school, we could see there were new security doors at the entrance. Teachers and officers were stationed at the doors, guiding students through.

"Someone broke all the doors, mirrors, and half the windows over the break." Some unknown voice said from in the crowd.

Slowly one by one, the students were all ushered into the school. I felt like a criminal. The atmosphere inside school was tense to say the least.

"That was different." Allen said.

"Scary." Squeaks whispered.

"Don't worry, Squeaks." Leah said as she patted her shoulder. "It's to keep the bad stuff out. You know we won't let anything happen to you." She smiled.

"Thank you, Leah." She whispered, and then she walked off towards her first class.

The rest of the day, "*the security doors*" seemed to be all anyone could talk about. Teachers went over and over how these doors could keep us safe, stop vandalism, keep out people who wanted to otherwise deface the premises, provide needed protection. Yada. . Yada . . . Yada . . .

I have to admit, I did wonder why someone would break into a school and break glass and mirrors. Why not break in and change grades, or make it mandatory for teachers to **not** bore us to sleep then fuss and gripe because we fell asleep. Ya know . . . important stuff.

I hate trying to listen to a teacher go on and on when I'm sleepy. It's hard enough when I'm wide awake, but throw in the heavy eye lids, and in desperate need of some Z's; it's darn near impossible. My brain; the part that has the reasoning, tells me to: "Take notes"... "Pay attention." But my *mind;* see how I split them up? Tells me: "Come on! ... What's a five little minute, cat nap, gonna hurt?"

Now, being the good student that I am, with good grades and a good level head on my shoulders, I obviously did the right thing. ☺ Go me!

"Ms. Teelf? Would you like to answer the next problem please?" My eyes snapped open at Mrs. Sensing saying my name. I stared down in horror at the large pool of drool on my desk. There were giggles all around me as I was caught, red handed, listening to my treacherous mind... Sleeping in class. "Well, Ms. Teelf? Are you in there?" Ms. Sensing prodded.

Slowly I rose my head, spun the rolodex; I called my brain, and blurted out the first thing that came to my fog covered mind. "I think you add the remainder."

Giggles and snorts broke out everywhere.

"I'm sure that is the answer to some question; however Ms. Teelf, you are in Biology, not Algebra, please wake up and pay attention." Ms. Sensing said to me as she smiled and called on someone who was awake and knew the answer to the question.

That is the last time I listen to my mind when I'm at school! I still had this huge pool of drool to try to 'discreetly' dispose of.

(I won't even tell you how I did it. Let's keep some mystery between us, shall we?)

Last class of the day had finally come around. "Thank Goodness." I was *soo* ready to get out of this place. Seeing as I was now, the proud owner of a ton of homework and expecting two tests later in the week.

I walked into art, unpacked my things, and moved my canvas near the window to start my day of painting. In a painting you are the one in control. You decide who lives where and how they will survive. I love art class!

Ms. Rhone is a very gifted artist. She has had pieces in museums and has sold countless pieces to big name buyers. She just prefers teaching though. She tells us to: "Go deep, find who lives there, and set them free on canvas." She is a really laid back sort of teacher, she doesn't freak if you have out your phone or a music player of some kind. "I don't want to see your phone or hear your music." She says. One kid was dumb enough to ask "Does that mean that we can play with our phone or jam to music?" she looked at him very seriously then said to the rest of us, "Since all of you did not ask that question; I will not punish the rest of you, but you, I am afraid I have to say; no, *you* may **not** have out your phone or any type of music." We all learned a valid lesson that day. Sometimes what is **not** said is the more important information.

I stood there in the sunlight by the window, music in my ears, and paintbrush in my hand. I never just *painted*. I waited for the feel of the brush then followed where it led. Ms. Rhone says that I am gifted and show signs of someone living deep inside who wants to get out. I don't know about all that, but I do love to draw and paint. When I paint I feel electric, I don't know how else to describe it. I sometimes don't even remember painting, just sorta snap out of my "art trance" and there is a painting in front of me.

Ok: art class, unpacked, by window, music in ears; there, you're caught back up. I had just dipped my brush into the paint and was about to begin, when Ms. Rhone came up beside me and tapped me on the shoulder. I took the ear bud out and looked at her, puzzled. She asked if I'd help with a new student.

Now here is where I have to steal one of Papa's funny lil sayings; he always said he was gonna write a book someday and all of the titles were: **much to do about**, whatever he was talking about. So when Ms. Rhone asked me to help, I should have said:

"Much to do about, No, Ms. Rhone!"

I smiled, *like the ignoramus I am*, and said, "Sure, Ms. Rhone." Then followed her to retrieve the poor kid; who was to be saddled with the class weirdo, who paints by the window... Me! I stopped at the desk as she went into the hall to get the kid. I had a weird feeling, not my *"henky feeling"* which is the feeling that I get when something bad is about to happen, but a *weird* feeling none the less.

When Ms. Rhone came back into the room I instantly knew what the odd feeling was. Strolling behind her was none other than, Mr. Hottie, DeLainey Landon himself. Tall, dark and handsome was invading my day for a second time.

He looked all brooding and mysterious; enough to melt a gal's heart. I was sure that the Spirits that-be would not be so cruel as to have me look at this Adonis every day and still try to paint!?

How does he get his hair to look like that? Like a melted chocolate bar hot in the sun, all shiny and dark. Not to mention his eyes, *OH MY*, his eyes... (Swoon)

He looked up, as they reached the desk, with the look of shock on his face. **What? A weirdo can't have a talent like art?** I thought and began to get a bit flustered.

Then he unleashed his secret weapon; that lethal half grin he has and the hair covering that one adorable eye. 'He should have to wear a mask, to protect people from those eyes and that grin.' I decided. Come to think of it; a bag over his entire head to cover that, too perfect hair of his as well, yep… that would help a lot.

DeLainey turned his head to look at the class but not before I saw a hint of humor and a telling twinkle in his eye.

"Much to do about, not thinking around, DeLainey Landon."

"Louanna, this is our new student, DeLainey Landon. He just moved here a short time ago. We just got his transcripts so he is now able to join our advanced class." Ms. Rhone said "I hoped you would show him around and guide him through our schedule; seeing as you are one of my top artists." She beamed a huge smile at me.

"Call me, De." He said quietly. "Everyone does."

I made the vast mistake of looking him in the eye. It felt like time stood still again; like I was swimming in a deep clear pool. It was a welcome feeling in the heat of this stuffy art room.

Once again; he looked away from me, breaking the semi trance I had fallen in. The humor now evident on his face was like he knew the childish thoughts I had had of him.

"Ok then." Ms. Rhone said. "Go deep,"

"Find who lives there," the class said in unison. "And set them free on canvas." We all finished together.

DeLainey looked at the class then stared at me. *I'm almost positive I didn't have a zit, but ya never know when a zit is involved,* I mean why else would he keep looking at me?

I walked DeLainey back to the window where this nightmare had started and I wondered how I was gonna talk to him when I couldn't even look at him without going comatose. Then there was the spastic way I've starting to act.

This was not going to be one of my finer moments I could already tell.

"I usually paint alone by the window." I started, giving him an out to go and paint elsewhere. "There are extra supplies, over there." I pointed to the storage lockers across from us. "All she asks is that you replace what you take."

There; that should do it. He'd see that I am a total spaz and use getting his supplies as an excuse to move to a better place and life would go back to normal.

Yea . . . Right! 'Cause that's how life goes here in the real world of Louanna Teelf.

"Much to do about, not in this lifetime!"

"Do you mind if I paint here by you?" he asked quietly.

Did he really think that Ms. Rhone had meant for him to be chained to me? "She's not like that, DeLainey—"I started

"De." He sighed.

"Ok. She's not like that, *De*. You can paint anywhere you want to. I'm just here to help you if you have a question. But you can paint anywhere in the room . . . Anywhere! She didn't mean you have to stay with me.' I tried to smile and *not* look at him.

"If you don't want me over here I understand." He said whispery, and even had the nerve to look like *I'd* hurt *his* feelings . . .

AS IF!

"That's not it. I don't care *where* you paint. I won't even know you're here. I get *lost in the zone,* as Ms. Rhone calls it. I was just letting you know." I said as honestly as I could.

"Ok, I'll get some stuff and paint, umm . . . there." He pointed to the spot directly in front of me.

Suddenly the room was too hot and way too noisy. Blah... blah... blah... was being said all around the room. Girls were looking at me; most of them were *mean mugging* me, and **who** was banging that drum so loud!? I thought.

Exasperated, I looked around; only to discover that the phantom drummer... was **_me!_** My stinking heart was pounding in my chest so hard; I was sure people around me could hear it banging away in there.

After a few minutes, DeLainey... I mean "De" made his way back and set up his painting station. It was obvious that he was no stranger to the world of art. I couldn't help but admire his technique; like a jungle cat, no wasted movement. Each stroke of the brush was precise and planned. I told him the "Music/cell phone rule" he simply smiled and nod his head at me.

"So now you know all the rules in Ms. Rhone's room. Tomorrow you won't need a sitter and can go where ya want." Again, I offered him an out.

"This is fine." He mumbled, leaning his head to the side to peer around that band of runaway stray hair, which dominated the right side of his face. "Unless you don't want me here; then I'll move.

Ok; you treacherous heart. Heel! Down Boy! Or whatever you say to a stupid runaway organ. Stop acting like you don't know how to function properly! I was fast losing any measure of control I had on my out of control heart.

"Like I said, I don't care *where* you are. This is your art class too. So you can paint wherever you want... *I do*." I think I sounded calm... cool. I'd even say I sounded casual. I think he bought it. I sounded sincere enough when I... *Lied through my teeth.*

Art class was a total bust for me. My entire rhythm was off.

I mean really; how is a girl supposed to paint when every time she looks up, there is a pair of blue eyes peeking around a canvas at her? It was like he was staring at me every time I looked. And not that there were a lot of times that I looked at him mind you, but *every* time I *glanced* his way, he would have the most concentrated look on his face. I felt like a bug under a very hot microscope.

Arriving home was uneventful; thank goodness.

I sat on my bed doing homework, listening to music and giving Lykie the occasional ear scratch and kiss on his nose.

I couldn't help but think that besides all the craziness that is associated with teenage life; I had to throw in *bonkers gazoo* and hit the blend button on my "mixer of life". Then to top off the whole thing; all the sadistic teachers seem to band together to plan test and quizzes for the same day.

(By the way; you're not fooling any one by saying *quiz*. We know they are just tests that have been disguised. The name change doesn't fool anyone, ya know!)

Mom was in the kitchen and Lucy was at one of her after school clubs or meetings, so the house was really quiet.

I put down my homework and went to the bathroom for a drink; that and to stretch my legs. When I came back to my room Lykie had moved to the area by the window box. His hackles were raised, head cocked to the side, and he was growling at the mirror standing in the corner.

"It's just your reflection, you silly thing." I laughed and started for my bed and the mound of homework still waiting there.

Lykie barked and jumped between me and the mirror; blocking the path to my bed.

"What is wrong with you boy? You never bark at me." I looked in his eyes; eyes that looked as if they were filled with knowledge, and I saw concern. "It's ok baby." I cooed at him. "There is no strange dog in here. It's just your reflection, sweetie."

I looked at the mirror and for a bleak second, thought I saw it shimmer or move; when mom's voice caused me to look away.

"What's Lykie barking at, Louanna?" she asked, walking into the room.

"He has finally gone bonkers gazoo, Mom. He saw his reflection in the mirror and had a hissy about the strange dog in here." I laughed.

"He barked at the mirror?" she asked, putting her hand to her throat. "Has he done this before, baby? Has he done it to anything *mirror like*?" She sounded far too concerned about my dog acting like a dog and barking at something he saw.

"No, I took the throw off of it earlier to cover up in while I did my homework. I honestly think this is the first time he has seen the strange dog in here." I joked

Mom looked around my room. I knew the "pig sty" talk was coming. She was mumbling under her breath.

"Well I'll just take it out so he won't be so upset." She said

I looked at the mirror and saw Mom's reflection. I could see her moving her arms around like she was swatting at gnats or flies. Now honestly! My room isn't white glove testable, but there are no bugs in it! Her swatting her arms around at the **imagined** bugs was just going too far.

She took it out without a word about the "pig sty" so I suppose the bug invasion was her newest tactic at getting me to clean. I picked up a few things and flung them to a new pile. Cleaning is such hard work.

I took Lykie's head in my hands and looked in his eyes. "Good boy! You ran that mean ole dog away, didn't you baby? Yes you did."

"Gone."

"He's gone now baby. " I piled up on the bed and patted it for him to join me and went back to my homework. My henky feeling seemed to be flirting with the out skirts of my thoughts; keeping me from studying at 100%.

Mom seemed so disorganized at dinner; not at all like her usual self. She didn't seem to be able to stay on track and appeared jumpy.

Lucy came in the back door and let the screen slam behind her. Mom jumped and dropped the salad bowl she held in her hands.

"Lucyenda Nicole, how many times do I have to remind you to **not** slam that door!?" mom fussed.

"I'm sorry, Mom." Lucy replied. "My arms were full and I couldn't catch it." She looked taken aback by Mom's harsh tone and attitude.

"I'm sorry girls. I'm tired I suppose. Forgive me, Lucy." Mom said quietly. "Let's eat and forget the whole thing, shall we?"

We all sat at the table and ate our food in near silence. The atmosphere seemed off and made me uncomfortable. We looked at each other; each hoping that the other would be the one to speak first.

"So how was school today, girls? Is there anything new or exciting in the world of academics?" Mom asked.

"Not a lot. We did get new security doors at school; otherwise, same ole, same ole." I replied.

"Why on earth would they put in new security doors; were the others faulty?" Mom asked.

"Vandalism is what I heard." Lucy said. "Someone broke in and done some sort of vandalizing at the school."

"How odd that someone would break into the school." Mom said.

"Not as odd as what they chose to vandalize." I remarked, scooping up more green beans.

"What do you mean, Louanna?" mom asked me then turned to Lucy in puzzlement.

"Don't look at me; all I heard was that there was some stuff broken or broke." Lucy snipped.

"Some girl was talking this morning outside the school. She said that all of the mirrors and half of the glass were smashed or broken. I didn't get any details and don't know who it was. My buds and I had just come up behind the mob waiting to get into school." I said.

Mom dropped her fork and nearly choked on the bite she was chewing on. "Are you certain, Louanna; mirrors and glass?"

"I can only say what I heard. And even as goofy as that is; it's what I heard." I replied.

"Please excuse me, girls. There is something I need to do." Mom said then got to her feet and . . . Poof! She was out the door.

"Yea, 'cause that wasn't weird or anything. I wonder what that was about." I mused aloud.

"Obviously she had something to take care of; nothing more to it." Lucy replied.

"Oh, sure it is; first Lykie has a hissy fit, then Mom does her pop up and leave routine. I tell ya, everybody's going Bonkers Gazoo around here. It's only a matter of time before; we too are plowing fields down on the funny farm." I grumbled.

"How on earth can a dog have a hissy fit, Lou**anna**? You act like that mongrel is human sometimes." Lucy made a face at Lykie. He simply turned his head like she was amusing him in some way.

I told her the whole story about the phantom dog in my room and how Lykie had reacted, and that Mom had taken the mirror out of my room.

"Mom took the mirror out of your room?" she asked, getting to her feet.

"Yea, Lykie didn't like that strange dog. Mom said taking out the mirror would calm him down. She shooed off flies; *that weren't there,* and she took it out of my room." I grumbled at the memory of the phantom flies in my pig sty room.

"I'm done." Lucy said, gathering her things and leaving me sitting alone at the kitchen table.

"I'm not cleaning this up alone, Luc!" I yelled after her.

Lykie looked at me and sneezed then curled up to take a nap. "Gee thanks." I laughed and rubbed his head.

No one showed up to help clean the kitchen. I grumbled and griped about the unfairness of the whole thing and slammed dishes around. Maybe I slammed them harder than I should have. My complaints fell on the ears of . . . NO ONE! If I gripe enough maybe the dishes will hear and clean themselves . . . yea, cause that's how my life goes.

Later, I lay on my bed wondering how far down the rabbit hole one had to fall before the nice people in white coats came to give you a soft room to live in. I don't know the exact distance but I had to be close to that point.

"Can't I have one day; just one day that's quiet and normal and no one goes bonkers gazoo?" I grumbled as I gathered my things to take a shower. Lykie came into our room wagging his tail and plopped down turned to me expecting his evening treat. I tossed him a half-eaten biscuit from a few days ago . . . (I think it was a few days anyway)

I entered the bathroom and almost giggled. I had beaten Lucy in and she'd be the one to have the "not so hot" shower. This was gonna be sweet!

I stood under the hot spray enjoying the feeling on my sore muscles. It's strange how such a simple thing had been so important to me. What can I say? I like hot showers; I'm just funny that way. It was amazing the difference in the way it felt.

Tap . . . Tap . . . Tap . . . a small knock came and I couldn't hide the smile on my face.

"Go away, Luc! I got in here first fair and square." My, how good it felt to get to say that.

Tap . . . tap . . . tap . . . the taps were very light this time. Lucy would just have to wait. "Knock all you want to, Luc. I'm not getting out any quicker." I said.

She stopped knocking, no fussing or griping; she just walked away.

"Ha! How's it feel?" I thought

I took a long shower. Heaven only knows when I'd get in here first again. When I got out the bathroom was full of hot steam. It felt almost as good as the shower had.

I did a good job hair, teeth, face, and lotion on my dry scaly knees; then laughed at the condensation lines on the mirror that looked like small hand prints. "It'd take a really small person to make a hand print that size." I said holding my hand up and seeing mine was two times larger than the ones on the mirror. "Maybe one of Santa's elves came by to see if I was naughty or nice" I laughed and cleaned the mirror.

In the corner of the mirror, behind me, I saw something small and brown move quickly by. I turned around to see if a rat or mouse had found its way into the bathroom. A thorough search turned up neither a mouse nor rat; simply my tiredness catching up with me, causing me to see things.

"Much to do about, I need sleep!"

I left the bathroom to tell Lucy she could now have the shower but I found her room empty.

"Humm, gone to tell mom that I wouldn't get out of there for you I guess." Thinking about all the times I'd been the one trying to gain entrance. I went down stairs only to find it was still vacant as well.

"That's weird, why would she knock on the door for the shower then just leave?" I wondered aloud.

Back in my room I lay on my bed and finished my homework, repacked my backpack for school and turned out the light.

"No drool pools for me tomorrow." I said to Lykie as he did his three turn, stretch and sigh. "I got busted by Ms. Sensing today. I soo fell asleep in class; then made a spaz outta myself by drooling all over the place and then calling out an algebra answer." I told Lykie

Lykie yawned and put his head on my stomach looking at me like he knew what I was saying and he felt my pain.

As always my gaze went to the window box where a dozen pair of shinning eyes looked down on Jequota. With heavy eyes I looked at my special box and slowly drifted into a much needed sleep.

The sound of the doorbell caused my eyes to pop open. Rubbing them clear of sleep, I looked at the clock, (11:03)

"Now who on earth goes visiting at this hour?" I wondered aloud.

I could hear voices downstairs, muffled and seemingly urgent. There were at least four different voices; I couldn't make out what they were saying or what could warrant such a late night visit.

Half afraid to open my door; but too curious not to, I made up my mind and cracked it open. The voices all sounded jumbled and hushed. Importance hung in the air like a tangible substance. I stepped into the hall and began to ease closer to the sounds.

A man's inaudible voice spoke then clearly said, "We're sorry, but yes, we are positive."

Mom gasped then said, "NO!" barely more than a whisper, yet ringing deep into my soul. "You're wrong, you have to be wrong!"

The heart wrenching sorrow embedded in her voice cut through my heart. I had to get to her; somehow, I had to get to Mom. In my head there was that single thought; however, my legs had been turned into Jell-O. They quivered but simply refused to move.

When I finally started running to her, everything seemed to move in freeze frame motion. A trip that should take 30 seconds seemed to take an eternity. Even taking the stairs three at a time wasn't help.

The crowd of nameless faces stretched on forever. Mom was sitting in her chair; large silent tears streamed down her beautiful face; crying harder than I had ever seen her do.

She looked up and saw me and somehow found her voice. "Oh, Baby!" was all she could manage as she reached out for me.

"What's happened, Mom?"

"I can't believe this has happened" she began, and then lost her voice as another wave of uncontrollable sobs rolled over her.

"Mom, Please! What has you so upset? What has happened?" I pleaded. Looking around the room of sad faces I asked: "Where's Lucy? Where is my sister?"

"It' a real shame." Someone said

"Death at this stage of life." Said another

"I never heard how they found the body, did you?" whispered yet another.

The room started spinning; I screamed for answers, looked into each pair of eyes pleading for the truth but no one seemed to hear me.

Lucy came running into the room, knelt down beside Mom and began to cry.

My heart pounded in my throat. I knew something bad had happened but no one wanted to give me answers. The smell of pipe tobacco and cedar came out from the crowd, calming me instantly. Looking over the room; I found him . . . Papa. He stood just outside of the crowd looking at me smiling; taking all worries I had away. I came to my feet and was about to go to him when he held up his hand and mouthed ""no" at me. It wasn't like Papa to stay so far away from me; especially when I needed him so much.

He winked at me and mouthed "I love you" and blew me a kiss. I was in desperate need of a grizzle hug but the room was now crowded and I couldn't get to him. He once again smiled at me with the shine in his eye and turned to leave.

"PAPA!" I yelled. "Mom, make him stay, I need him! . . . PAAAPAAA!"

I tried to get through the crowd. How could he just leave me? He didn't give me a grizzle hug, kiss me, or didn't even try to find out why Mom was so distraught.

"He'll make it better, he always makes things better! Please Mom, make him stay!" I pleaded, pulling at the arms that were now holding me.

"Make who stay, baby?" mom asked as she tried to keep me from running.

"Papa!" I yelled in her face. I knew she was upset but he was standing in plain sight! She had to help me make him stay. "He's leaving! Make him come back!" I gave up the fight for freedom and fell to the floor, exhausted.

"He isn't here, Louanna." She whispered.

"He was!" I snapped, now exasperated that he'd left. "He stood just over there." I pointed to where he'd stood. "He blew me a kiss and whispered I love you, can't you smell his pipe!?"

The room fell silent and all eyes turned to stare at me. "Baby, Papa isn't here; he's gone. Papa is dead."

"PAPA!" I screamed as I woke from the nightmare that had plagued my nights and waking thoughts for the past few years.

Lykie whimpered and crawled closer to me; licking my hand and looking worried about me.

"I'm ok boy, it happens all the time; a lot more lately." I snuggled deep into my covers hoping to erase some of the bone deep chill. I looked at the window box and for a bleak second; it hurt to look at Jequota. "I miss you so much, Papa. Why'd you leave me?" I whispered

I closed my eyes and silently cried myself to sleep.

Reflections

The days after the dream passed uneventfully. There were no special happenings, home, school, home, bed. Life had regained its mundane style and all seemed to be as it should be.

My sweet sixteen birthday was tomorrow and to be honest; I was more excited than I let on. In olden days; turning 16 was a rite of passage of sorts, there were a lot more things allowed to you; once you turned that magical age.

Mom had planned double parties for me. One would take place at midnight, oddly enough; it was the exact time I was born. All my family would be there for that party, it was the *la-tee-da* one. Later that night I'd get to have the *real* party; the one with all my friends. It would be my first "girl/boy" party. My buds were all going to come and we had invited the kids at school that we could all tolerate; it should be a good party.

Yea, that's how my life goes . . . everything all neat and going just as it should.

"Much to do about, not in my world, sister!"

When I woke the day before my party, I was glad it was Friday. One day of "Breezer" classes. (Breezer: Days at school; or anywhere, that are easy and one can "breeze" through.) All week had been jammed full of tests, lectures, and a lot of pop quizzes. (Again; it's just a test in disguise! We are not fooled by the name change.)

My buds and I had left sanctuary and were all going our different ways. The halls were filled with the same mundane chatter that always seemed to be here. Leah walked beside me going on about how the Farmers were yet again trying to "best" DJ at arm wrestling; at the same time, when the window beside me seemed to quiver, causing the reflections to look odd and disoriented. Looking at it I thought I saw . . . something.

"Did you see that?" I asked

"Well, yea! They were using all four of their arms trying to pull DJ's down. He didn't even seem to notice them, just flexed his muscles at Pixie; then winked at her and flipped them both over the table winning "Tag-team-arm wrestling" as they call it." She laughed. "We all nearly died laughing at the look of shock on their faces."

"Not those Looney tunes we hang out with; did you see that . . . that . . . I've gone bonkers gazoo!" I sighed and looked at her.

"What'd ya see, Chickadee, to send you to bonkers gazoo?" she patted her jacket pocket. "I have a sedative for just such an occasion."

"Ha! Ha!" I smirked "You're soo funny Leah, I may have to take you up on that though. I think I saw a little man in the window."

Looking at the window she laughed. "You see Mr. Olive all the time, he works here, remember?"

"Not Mr. Olive." I grumbled but started down the hall to homeroom. "The window kinda went all "clear Jell-O" and for a half a second I saw this lil' man. He looked kinda garden gnomish but had on all green colored clothes. And so help me if you laugh; its foot to shin time my friend."

"Maybe you want a trip for your birthday. You seeing that traveling gnome thing is your mind's way of saying: "Take your frieeeennnndddd!" she giggled as we started into the room.

"Maybe you're right." I joked but wondered just what I *had* seen.

The TV was pulled out when we got inside; Ms. Hickerson stood in the hall like a buzzard, waiting for a student to die as they ran late for class or had the audacity to chew gum near her. It was the high light of her day to slam the door in your face so you had to trudge off to the office for a tardy slip. She was like some creepy ole spider just waiting for prey so she could pounce on it. Believe me, I know how it feels; I have been pounced on too many times. The sound of the whoosh as the door closed in your face; the look of triumph in her eyes peeking at you through that little window in the door . . .

"Much to do about, all over body quivers."

Ms. Hickerson took roll and turned to write on the board. "If I write; then you write." She grumbled and the sound of nineteen kids; scrounging for paper and pencils, was the only sound that could be heard. In other classes when the teacher turned her back the students would talk or get up . . . not in this class; Oh no! The spider would get you and we all knew it.

The movie started an we all settled in. I sat there trying to concentrate on life science, but my mind kept returning to the little man in green. I know I didn't imagine him, he was there, and the more I tried to remember him the more clear his image became.

He was around two and a half feet tall, bright orange hair with red tips. His eyes were a glowing yellow and he had on a small pair of glasses. His clothes were in different shades of green and looked well cared for. He had on a tall pointed hat; giving him a Christmas elf look. His tiny little feet wore brown leather looking shoes that resembled moccasins, without beads.

I couldn't have pulled up such a detailed image unless I had seen the little man . . . right!?

"Much to do about, going bonkers gazoo."

I looked at Leah and she held her hands up gesturing "what?" I drew a little stick man with a pointed hat on and showed it to her.

Leah looked at the picture and gave herself a fake shot. I made a rude face at her and took down some notes on the movie. I knew the spider was aching to pounce and I wasn't gonna be her victim.

I had an uneasy feeling that I couldn't place. I didn't think "lil man" was the cause of it. Maybe I'd dreamed him up or saw him in a book or something. There is no telling where my warped mind dug up that little gnome dude.

The bell rang and we were finally able to leave the spider's lair. We could breathe again. Leah walked with me until we had to split and go to our next class.

"See ya at sanctuary." She said and trotted off down the hall in the opposite direction.

I walked into Biology; Ms. Sensing greeted everyone as they came into the room. She gave out instructions and spoke to a few students who owed work or papers needed for grades. The room seemed unnaturally hot; as I went to my desk and began to unpack. I felt a hot wave wash over me and saw the windows wiggle like Jell-O that had been struck.

The air caught in my throat and I was unable to swallow. The noise all around me seemed muffled and my vision became blurry. I tried to stand; to ask Ms. Sensing if I could go wash my face or something but my legs refused to cooperate. My head began to pound and sweat started to bead on my forehead.

I looked at the Jell-O glass and thought I saw the little man again. The edges of my vision grew dark and began to close in like an old TV screen shutting off. I could hear gasps and saw Ms. Sensing kneeling over me. A squeaky voice said "I'm here to help you." And everything went black.

My head throbbed, my mouth was dry, and my tongue felt like it was too big for my mouth. I was laying on my back when the memory of my "blackout" came flooding in. "Man!" I thought. "I'm on my butt, in the classroom and everyone is probably taking pictures of this." I tried not to move so no one would know I was awake; suddenly it dawned on me, the surface beneath me was soft. "I must not be in class." I peeked open my right eye and was instantly blinded by the overhead light.

"Welcome back, Louanna." Someone said. I heard a "click" and behind my eyes I could tell that the light had been shut off. Braving another try I again opened my eyes and was forced to squint. "You banged your head pretty hard when you passed out, dear." Nurse Ann said handing me a glass of ice water. "I'm sure your mouth is dry." She took my wrist and stared at her watch then scratched on a note pad. "Everything seems fine, Louanna. Are you on your cycle by chance?" she asked and looked at me.

"No ma'am." I said. (FYI: I hate this subject and try to never talk about it.)

She looked at the chart, mumbled to herself, scrunched up her face, and looked at me. "Humm, maybe you got too hot or stood up too quickly."

"I did get really hot and then dizzy right before everything went black. (And I saw a little man)" I added quietly.

"Well, that's probably it then dear." She said, pleased she had a plausible answer for my blackout.

I had one too: Louanna Teelf has gone bonkers gazoo! My cheese has slid way off of my cracker on this one.

"We called your mother, Louanna. She's on her way to get you." Again she smiled and scratched more notes down.

Well now, that is just great! They called mom and now she's gonna be all worried about me getting hot . . . or having a gnome fetish.

"Can I use the restroom?" I sat up and found the dizziness and blurry vision had gone.

"Let me help you." She said, taking my arm and raising me to my feet.

"I actually feel fine, Ms. Ann. You can call Mom and tell her there is no need to come." It was just a suggestion, but I knew she wouldn't do it.

"I'm afraid it's school policy, dear. And besides; she is already on her way, Sweetie. She seemed very concerned when I called her." She led me to the bathroom door. "Please don't lock it; okay Hun; just in case you fall again."

"Okay." I said and closed the door.

I stood in front of the sink; filling my hands with cool water and splashing it on my face.

"You're such a spaz!" I said to my reflection, wondering how my day had gone all loony on me.

I always knew I'd be the first to go bonkers gazoo for real; but somehow I thought I'd be much older' living in a house full of stray animals. But NO! It's gonna happen the day before my sixteenth birthday; at school, in front of all my classmates, brought on by an orange haired, yellow eyed, green wearing runt thing. (That's probably a piece of undigested food.) I thought bitterly.

"Much to do about, being in denial."

Drying my face I glanced at myself in the mirror. Behind me I saw what looked like thin rainbow colored spider webs shimmering all around me. I quickly turned around to find the source and saw . . . nothing. Looking back at the mirror I saw once again the miniscule lines all around me. Glistening like wet spider webs, caught in the evening sunshine. I reached my hand towards the mirror then Nurse Ann knocked on the door.

"Are you ok in there, Louanna?" She asked; as she stuck her head in; obviously looking for my unconscious body sprawled out on the floor.

"Yes Ma'am." I answered and wiped down the sink.

"Good; your mother is here when you're ready." She said and left me standing alone once more.

"Thank you." I looked back at the mirror and saw only my clear reflection looking back at me.

Mom was quiet on the ride home; saying few words and only in response to something I had said.

"Are you hungry, Louanna?" she finally asked.

"Kinda." I said and found I was indeed hungry.

"Where would you like to eat; do you have a preference or do you just want to wait until we get home and eat there?" She turned to face me and smiled.

"I can wait 'til we get home. I won't starve between now and then." I laughed.

"If you're sure; ok, we'll wait 'til we get home." She sighed and turned back to the road; throwing the car into an uncomfortable silence again.

Once we got home I felt ten times better. I felt . . . sane again; and more like myself.

Lykie came bounding across the yard and pounced on me; slamming both front paws on my shoulders and began to lick my face.

"Good to see you too, boy." I laughed.

"I was so worried"

Lykie wined and seemed to be trying to get as close to me as he could, almost climbing me.

"Ok, boy, let's go inside baby. I'm hungry." I said and took his paws from my shoulders; putting them on the ground and kissing his head.

We went into the house and found Mom was already making vegetable beef soup and grilled cheese sandwiches. I grabbed a can of juice from the fridge and downed it quickly. Retrieving another, I asked if Mom wanted one as well.

"Thanks, yes I do." She smiled, taking the juice and putting the food on the table. "Let's eat." She said.

I sat eating in silence; barely giving my spoon time to leave my mouth until it was returned to the bowl for the next bite. After my second bowl of soup, third grilled cheese, and third can of juice; I slowed my eating down and even remembered Lykie. I gave him half of a grilled cheese sandwich. I'm not sure he even chewed it; just swallowed it whole and sat there looking for the next bite.

"You're such a spoiled baby, Lykie . . . Yes you are . . . Yes you are!" I cooed at him, scratching his head. I got up and kissed him on nose; then put my dishes in the sink.

"How are you feeling, Louanna?" Mom asked as she finished the last of her lunch.

"Better. I still feel kinda tired though. Do you think it would be ok if I went up to my room and took a little nap?" I found that I was suddenly sleepy.

Lykie stood up, stretched and trotted off towards our room; like he'd understood what I had said and where I was about to go.

"I think it's probably a good idea. I'll come up and check on you in a little while."

"Thanks Mom." I said, kissing her on the cheek. "I love you."

"I love you too, Louanna." She said as I started to leave.

"Oh, and Louanna?" I stopped and looked at her.

"Yes Mom?"

"I do want to know what happened today; *EVERYTHING* that happened."

With a nod of my head; I left and headed to my room. *Yeah. Sure! I'll tell you all about; little men, strange voices in my head, Jell-O reflections, and seeing things that are not there.* I thought.

"Much to do about, Not gonna happen, Mom!"

Lykie lay sprawled out on my bed; head lying on his paws, pretending to be asleep. He was lying on the new outfit that Mom had gotten me for the "family party" tonight.

"Hey!" I said and snatched the dress, (Yes . . . I said dress . . . you read it right.) out from under him. "I'm not wearing "Fashions by: *Sir Lyke*, ya know." I grumbled then retrieved the hose and shoes. "I don't think Mom put that there for you to sleep on."

Lykie looked at me, sneezed, sighed, and returned to his sleep.

I took the outfit to the closet and hung it up neatly then returned to the bed and joined Lykie for a nap. Looking at the window box; seeing my Jequota, I closed my eyes and let sleep wrap its arms around me and take me away.

I felt so warm and relaxed; I didn't want to move. "Mmmmmmm" I moaned. I felt a slight breeze and with it there was the smell of pipe tobacco and cedar. My eyes snapped open. I sat in the middle of an open field; the sun was shining brightly; warming everything it touched.

"Papa!?" I whispered looking to the edge of the field and surrounding forest. The grass seemed to have found a hidden melody and was happily dancing to the beat. A doe and fawn eased into the meadow, just beyond of the safety of the trees; eyeing me with curious gazes.

Startled by a sudden movement; the two deer ran back into the safety of the thick trees and were quickly out of sight. The smell reached my nose before I could turn and see what had spooked the deer; pipe tobacco and cedar could mean only one thing . . .

I turned and saw him, running at full speed I threw myself into his waiting arms. "Papa!" I screamed and buried myself deep within his open arms.

"Louanna, my sweet mia noja." He said as he tightened his grizzle hug.

"Papa, I have missed you **soo** much." I cried as tears streaked down my face.

"As I have you, Lemoya." He wiped the tears from my face. "But I am never truly away from you. I live within your heart." He held me back away from his body and looked at me. "You have gotten so big; I thought you could get no more beautiful yet here you stand; proving what a foolish old man I am."

His smile was deep and genuine. His eyes gleamed with more knowledge than one person should be allowed to have.

"I'm asleep, aren't I Papa?" I asked

"Not exactly *sleep*, little one. But yes; your physical shell does slumber in the other realm. This is Xela, the spirit plane; each being creates his or her own version of Xela and can travel freely within its boundaries. Here in this open plane." He gestured to the field around us. "I will be able to come to you and give guidance should you have need; or want, of it."

"So, this isn't just a wonderful dream then.' I mused

"No Lemoya – little one, it is very real. Unlike an ordinary dream; if you were to be hurt here, it would affect your physical body. We are always watchful and diligent at keeping the passage to Xela guarded and safe. There are those who would wish to enter someone else's Xela in order to influence or control them."

"So how are you here, Papa; if other people cannot come into others' Xela?"

"I am your spirit guide, Louanna. You brought me here." He smiled "You can bring me to you here any time you have need."

A loud bang had me sitting upright in my bed. My eyes were still wet from the tears I had cried and my skin was still warm from the sun in Xela. I looked around and saw that Lucy had dropped my school books on my desk; knocking over a pile of . . . well, a pile of stuff. That is what had woken me from my dream place . . . and Papa.

"Here are your things from school." She said, eyeing me suspiciously. "Mom called and asked if I'd pick up your work so you wouldn't fall behind. . . . Are you ok? You were crying when I came in. if you are hurting I can get Mom." There was genuine concern laced in her voice.

"No, I'm fine." I said "Just had another one of my weird-ish dreams again. But thanks anyway, Luc." I had to fight hard to keep the bite out of my tone. Lucy had no way of knowing how horrid my day had been; or how desperately I had wanted to stay in that place. (With Papa)

"Weird-ish dream huh?" She sat on the edge of my bed and mindlessly stroked Lykie. "Do you wanna talk about it?"

"No, not really." I lied "it's just one of those bonkers gazoo dreams I have; no biggie, but thanks though."

"One of? . . . You have weird dreams a lot, Louanna? Have you told Mom?"

I laughed "Tell Mom, no, I haven't. They're just silly dreams, Luc. Everybody has them. We can't always be riding a unicorn on the beach with some hunky guy following us around."

"Riding a unicorn on the beach, huh?" she laughed. "Well, that's a new one for me; but I still think you should tell Mom."

"Let's go help Mom with dinner; she looked tired when she came and picked me up." I said and we headed down to the kitchen.

Music and delicious aromas wafted up in greeting as we descended the stairs to the kitchen. I couldn't help but breathe deeply and savor the smell. Mom had made her lasagna, garlic cheese bread, and a fresh garden salad. She smiled in greeting as we entered the kitchen.

"You're just in time." She said, munching on a cucumber slice. "I was just about to call you down for dinner."

"Something smells great Mom." I said

I grabbed a plate and started fixing it. I hadn't realized that I was hungry until I smelled the food. Now I found myself hurrying to get to the meal.

"This is delicious, Mom" Lucy chirped as she munched on some cheese bread. "I love Italian food."

"I do too." I said as I shoveled in a huge bite of the lasagna. "I . . . lub . . . it . . ." I mumbled with a mouth full of cheesy goodness,

I tossed Lykie a chunk of food; he caught it in midair and swallowed the whole thing without chewing. We all laughed at him; he merely licked his lips, wagged his tail and waited for his next piece.

"You have to chew your food baby. You're gonna get a tummy ache and have me up all night." I laughed and tossed him a smaller piece; which he gobbled down in the same manor.

"I'm hungry"

I looked at Mom and Lucy but neither had spoken so I just continued to eat, ignoring the voice.

The meal was great. There was so much love and laughter in the house; I had forgotten about all the craziness from earlier in the day.

"So." Mom began.

I swallowed my lasagna and sat back in my chair; waiting for "the talk".

"I'd like to talk to you about what happened to Louanna at school this morning." She sighed heavily "I got the call early in the day; so it has given me plenty of time to think about how I want to approach this and talk about it." She looked at us and smiled.

"Do you want me to leave; so you can talk to Lou**anna**?" Lucy asked.

"No. I want you to stay Lucyenda. There are several things that I need to talk about and some of them involve you as well."

"Me? How does something happening to Lou**anna** at school; have anything to do with me?" Lucy asked.

Mom took a deep breath and let it out slowly. She looked at both of us and sighed. "It actually has to do with all of us." She said, cleaning her dishes away and putting them in the sink. She retrieved a gallon of ice-cream from the freezer and placed it and bowls on the table. (Even a bowl for Lykie) "I have put off telling you this for as long as I could. I'm afraid I may have waited to tell you this too long; a mistake that may prove to be." She hesitated, "Dangerous."

"Dangerous!? How could Lou**anna** passing out at school; be dangerous, especially to me?" Lucy asked.

"Yea, what she said." I replied.

Lykie looked at me and Lucy; the alarmed tone in our voice had him looking around the room for the danger that had caused it. He came closer to me and I pat his head genially.

"Well, I should have been more specific; it has to do with all of us, *"me"* included." Mom said

"So don't keep us in suspense." I laughed nervously. "Tell us what kind of danger we are in." I looked at Lucy, raised one eyebrow, and smiled nervously.

"I know no other way to tell this than to just blurt it out. The truth of this is we are a family of Weavers; magical and telepathic. Weavers are really rare." She turned to look at me, "And you, my sweet Louanna, you are a True Weaver; a much anticipated and very much longed for Weaver."

The room fell eerily silent. We sat staring at each other. Mom never told fairytales so for her first attempt . . . it was a good one.

"Much to do about, Mom's gone Bonkers gazoo."

"What are you talking about, Mom?" Lucy asked "Magic, Weavers, telepathy, and you said danger as well. What does it have to do with us and what happen to Lou**anna** at school?"

They both looked at me.

"Much to do about, being in the hot seat."

"Our family is the descendants of a magical race of people. There are different branches of magic. We are known as "Life Weavers". Weavers in general, carry their own special magic. A True Weaver," She looked at me. "As I suspect Louanna to be; is the rarest of all Weavers."

"What on earth makes you think that I am a "True Weaver" anyway?" I asked, putting quotation marks when I said True Weaver.

"Jequota." She said simply "Your Jequota, baby."

I laughed nervously and looked around. "Lucy has a Jequota too Mom." I stammered.

"Yes she does, as do I: but ours didn't react to us at the presenting day or fourth birthday. Your Jequota's spirit was awakened by Adnama; it is a living cloth now more Adnama like herself than just a spirit cloth. It isn't the only sign of a True Weaver but it is one of the most important ones." Mom said.

"My Jequota cloth looks different than Lou**anna**'s does." Lucy said quietly. "I thought Papa just liked Lou**anna** more than he did Me." she finished and looked at me.

"The cloth is the same in all Jequota. The difference is that Louanna woke the cloth in hers; again, as I said before, due to her being the True Weaver. Yours; as well as mine, remains a spirit cloth."

"You're saying things that sound like they came from Mars or something; and you expect us to know what you mean." I said, sounding exasperated. "Don't get me wrong or take this the wrong way Mom but I think you've gone Bonkers Gazoo on us."

Mom leaned back in her chair and laughed . . . Truly, deeply, laughed from the heart.

"It's a lot of information to take in. I know this has come at you from out of the blue. But you need this information and you need it before midnight when Louanna turns 16."

"Why midnight?" Lucy and I said in unison.

"You were born at midnight, Louanna; another sign of the True Weaver, and at the stroke of midnight you will receive most or all of your special gifts." She smiled at me reassuringly. "I'm not really sure what is going to happen; to you or Lucy and I. There hasn't been a True Weaver in . . ."

"2,000 years."

We looked at one another; acknowledgement was plain to see. They had heard the strange voice the same as I had.

"Ok, I know I'm not Bonkers Gazoo. I can see that you both heard that voice the same as I did." I said "I hear it; or something like it, a lot here lately."

"I do too." Lucy said quietly.

I looked at her and saw the same confusion in her eyes that I was feeling. This was hard to try and understand; hearing voices wasn't helping and I was apparently not the only one to be hearing it.

"We are Weavers, babies." Mom said, smiling at us. "We are telepathic. Do you want to tell them or should I?"

Lucy and I looked at each other, confused more than ever.

Lykie put his paw in my lap and whined.

"It's me, Lou! I'm who you and . . ." He turned and looked at Lucy. "Lucy have been hearing. I'm your Guardian."

Sweet 16

I felt numb. I looked at Lucy and Mom; who had both clearly heard Lykie . . . my dog . . . speak to me telepathically.

"Much to do about, being far down the rabbit hole. Volume 2"

"When I wake up," I stammered. "I hope I can remember all of this. I'd like to tell you about it because I'm having one cur-azy dream!"

"You're not dreaming, Lou. I am really talking to you. I have tried to communicate with you for so long and had nearly given up hope; I was afraid I'd have to leave and seek out the True Weaver. But I **knew** I was right about you. . . . I just knew it."

"*SEE*! Like that! My dog was just talking to me again. He just informed me that he has been thinking about running away from home." I laughed nervously "Looks like I'm gonna have to get a chain for him or he'll be gone. This whole dream is going to make me go . . ."

"Bonkers Gazoo?" the voice asked. "Well, you're not going to. And I'm not a dog; I'm a Lydian, and the guardian to the True Weaver, to *you*, Louanna. My ancestor, Lyden, served the last True Weaver. At her death Lyden grieved himself to death. He felt he had failed her and could not live in a world that she was not in. His death left me next in line as the senior guardian and the next True Weaver's protector. **Your** protector, Lou."

"This isn't really happening." I mumbled to myself.

"Yes baby, I'm afraid it is. I know this is a lot for you to have to take in; but as I said, you need to know as much as we can tell you between now and midnight."

"Grundals seek the power of Adnama. Your Jequota has been touched by her magic; when you have your Tresstel, its location will no longer be concealed. Your magic; the three of you, your magic will be stronger and the flow of power will be an irresistible treasure for anyone seeking to gain power."

Lykie jumped up in the chair beside me and looked me in the eyes.

"I always knew you were smart boy . . . I mean, Lykie . . . I mean . . . I can't do this! I can't even talk to my dog; who's not a dog, who's a guardian, that's really a Lydian. And I don't even know what in the name of a three legged chicken that is!" My voice steadily rose as I spoke; veins were bulging in my neck and forehead. My face felt hot and my skin was clammy. I closed my eyes and took a calming breath. I then turned and looked at my dog . . . who's not-a-dog.

"Lou, you can still think of me as your dog. I have loved having that role in your life. And for the record; you have **never** treated me like a dog. You treat me just as you do your buds; and that is an honor in itself."

He licked my hand. I had to hug him, he was right; he had always been one of my buds, ever since right after my fourth birthday . . . when I found him in the back yard.

"I found you, Lou. Your Jequota's magic called to me; it drew me to you. I felt the shift, the awakening of Adnama. I knew that you were mine to protect. I was born to serve and protect you. Only the True Weaver can awaken Adnama. You are the real deal, Lou." He sounded so excited. "When you get your powers; I will be able to once again shift into Lydian form."

I looked at Lykie; once again he had the silly look on his face like he was laughing. I couldn't help but giggle a little.

"You make me want to laugh, Lou." He wagged his tail happily.

"Ok." Mom said "Back to the information that you need to know girls. Grundals, as Lykie has mentioned, are vial, evil, little buggers. They can appear anywhere there is a reflective surface; like mirrors, glass, and certain medal objects, you get the picture. If you can see your reflection in it . . . they can use it; and they **will** use it. Don't fall for their trickery. They are small, fast, and cunning; they have existed for centuries and will know things to use against you."

"You sound like we are at war or something, Mom." I said

"In essence we are. As Weavers, we are bound to the Jequota and its safety is ours to uphold." Mom responded.

"What did you mean when you said they are small? Do you mean they are skinny small or more like an insect kind of thing?" Lucy asked.

I looked over at Mom for the answer that I already knew. My little traveling gnome dude had to be one.

"No Lucyenda, they are about two and a half to three feet tall with red hair and eyes. They wear brown clothes because their sour soul emanates a charge that will turn anything that touches the skin, brown; clothes wise anyway. They are very powerful in their magic." Mom smiled at us. "I'm no expert on much of this; but luckily we have a guardian here to fill in the gaps in the information."

She placed a bowl of ice cream on the table. "You are not a dog Lykie; you should sit at the table with the rest of the family."

"Thank you Leona."

"You are very welcome."

"I just heard you think talking to each other. It was just like you had said it out loud but inside my head." I was still having a hard time believing any of this.

"I can talk to you as well as to Lykie, Louanna; we all can do it. It is part of the Weaver gifts. Try to do it, both of you." Mom projected her thoughts in my head.

"I don't know how to think inside someone else's mind, Mom! This whole thing is-"

"Please don't say **Bonkers Gazoo**" I beg you Lou**anna**. You say that so much it makes me want to hurl."

I slowly turned my head and looked at Lucy. She winked at Mom and beamed a big smile at me.

"This is just all too much." I sighed. "Think talking and little evil Grunts; I think I saw one of the little Grunting things, by the way." I had to get the subject off of think talking.

All eyes fell on me, pinning me to my seat. I'm not sure what I had said but whatever it was had captured everyone's immediate attention.

"What do you mean, Louanna? Where did you see a Grundal?" Mom asked.

"Here in the house was one time: I didn't actually see it though. I was taking a hot (I looked at Lucy) shower and Luc banged on the door to get in. When I got out; I saw little hand prints on the mirror in the condensation. Then today at school, I saw a glimpse of one early on the day then again when I umm, "blacked out", it talked to me and I think he said he was here to help me." I laughed nervously.

"If it spoke to you it most likely wasn't a Grundal. They don't like to be noticed. Well, unless they think you can be used. Hate or deep rooted anger is like a magnet to them; I doubt that's what you saw. It was most likely a . . . Darn; I've been out of the magic loop for so long I can't think straight. What is it they are called, Lykie?" Mom asked.

"Speritalz: friends to all Weavers and those who serve them." Lykie answered.

"Speritalz? I thought you said they were Grunts or something." I was getting more confused by the minute.

"**Grundals**, not Grunts, and no; Speritalz are like the wood gnomes in fairytales, to use a phrase you would understand. They are friendly and helpful; holding life sacred. That is why they honor Jequota. They take from nature, only what she gives willingly. They are always in shades of green because their clothes or made from natural things. A Grundal is; I'm sorry to say, a Speritalz that has turned on nature. They become hungry for power. Being close to Weavers exposes them to the power of Adnama and if their soul is weak, they turn evil with the drive and obsession for having Jequota."

Lykie sounded all business when he spoke. I laughed to myself that I had thought of him as a pet for so long.

"A power such as that, in a Jequota, can only be directed in the hands of a Weaver. Even a guardian; as powerful as they are, cannot yield Jequota's magic. It would be dangerous on an epic scale for a Grundal to get their hands on one. Even a Jequota with a slumbering spirit cloth; holds power that they could harness. It's why we are so secretive about who we are." Mom said

Ok, I have to try to crawl myself out of this rabbit hole and get back to reality! Grunts, Spurts, gnomes and a mind talking not-a-dog . . . this whole thing was giving me a serious migraine! I knew that hearing voices, seeing those little green elves, (not to mention the wiggly mirrors) would lead me nowhere but Bonkers Gazoo. (X-infinity)

I have gone absolutely white coat and Jell-O crazy! And here's the rub; it happened the night before my sixteenth birthday! Now I will never date. Who wants to date the crazy girl with the "think talking not-a-dog?" NO ONE! . . . THAT'S WHO!

"Much to do about, alone and dateless."

(I really don't like the titles of these books here lately!) ☹

Lucy spoke up and brought me out of the stupor I had fallen in. "How many Weavers are there, Mom? Where do we come from?"

"There aren't as many of us as there once was, I'm afraid. As I understand it; our magic has been almost nonexistent since Lisdom Teelfel's death; that was the name of the last True Weaver. The Jequota everywhere sort of went into a hibernation mode; still very magical, yet unable to be where it should be. I'm not sure what your Tresstel will mean to us. No one that will be here tonight was alive when the last True Weaver came into her power."

"I was only a foundling when Lisdom had her Tresstel; so I do not know what will take place here tonight either." Lykie said . . . thought . . . You know what I mean!!

"Do you know anything about the last True Weaver, Lykie? " Lucy asked

"I do remember the True Weaver; however she was well into her reign at the time. She was a great warrior, noble and true. The Grundal who took her life is named Logton; he was her second, which is high ranking in the Court of Brethren; the True Weavers army of sorts. He was respected and feared by all. He was an honorable Speritalz. He made no secret that he would protect Lisdom, she loved him and trusted him with her life; trust that I fear, was her undoing. She could only see "good" in life. Regardless of the pain; she would find the silver lining. No one noticed Logton's hair and eyes' turning red until it was too late. Her death was mourned by all." Lykie dropped his head.

No one spoke as we allowed him to morn. The pain in his voice as he told this story seemed as fresh as if it had just happened. I couldn't resist the impulse to wrap my arms around him; he seemed so helpless and alone. Waves of sorrow rolled off of him and it seemed like he was crying.

"I'm sorry Lykie." It was all I could think of to say. I'm not really good with emotions and this was still too far out of reach for me to feel like I'd be of help.

"Louanna, you are more help than you can possibly know. You are the True Weaver and at your Tresstel we will once again gain power. We will be able to fight and protect Jequota and the elements inside."

"Tresstel . . . you've said that word before. Am I going to grow some big horn out of the top of my head or grow wings or something?" It was looking more and more like Bucky the half chicken boy would soon have a roommate; Louanna the un-dateable flying horned freak.

"No baby." Mom laughed "A Tresstel is the name of the ceremony where you will receive the Weaver gifts; it will happen in the back yard."

"Do many people know about all this Weaver stuff?" I asked

"Very few, we usually attract people who are intended to know. That's how we know they are supposed to be in our lives. They are drawn to us, kind of like a magnet only pulls to it what it's meant to be attracted to. If you feel like you should tell someone; then it is most likely meant for them to know. The same goes for if you have an odd feeling or feel off in some way about sharing the information with anyone; you should go with your gut and avoid that person and be on your guard." Mom explained.

"I call the ones that I get, my "henky feeling". Sometimes it makes me sick to my stomach. It feels like I have my hand on one of those electrical conductor balls at a science museum. It doesn't hurt, but I can feel it."

It was hard to describe how my henky feeling felt. I don't know myself how it feels. I just feel it and know something bad is about to happen. I guess my Weaver skills were active all along.

"What is going to happen to us; you and me, Mom? If this is all about Lou**anna**, what does it have to do with us?" Lucy asked.

I could be wrong. I mean, I am crazier than a bat turd now; but there seemed to be a snip in Lucy's tone when she asked that question. She wouldn't look at me like I wasn't in the room with them.

"I'm not sure exactly Lucyenda." Mom answered. "There has not been a True Weaver in more than two millennia. It's been difficult keeping the whole thing quiet. But a Jequota with an awakened Adnama spirit cloth inside; it was bound to leak out. Now with the Tresstel tonight, every Weaver within a hundred miles will be here to witness it."

My head hurt. I felt sick to my stomach and knew I'd never get all of this junk straight. Now I find out that a bunch of strangers will be here to watch what happens. My mind was a jumbled up mess. I can't be a True Weaver . . . I can't be anything but a True Spaz! I excel at that.

I went to my room. There had been so much stuff thrown at me; I had to go to my own personal space and try to make sense of it all. Lykie trotted along with me, wagging his tail and looking content. I on the other hand felt like a haggle or horde of creatures was trying to claw their way out my brain from the inside.

"Do you want to talk about it Lou?"

"Don't do that Lykie!" I snapped. "Stop doing that Vulcan mind thingy. It's really weird to have someone talk inside my head. So stop!"

Lykie didn't respond. He simply drooped his ears and looked hurt.

"I'm sorry boy . . . I mean . . . Man; this is impossible! I don't even know how to talk to you now." I had hurt his feelings and was whining and feeling sorry for myself. How pathetic is that?

He didn't respond, just lay in the corner by Jequota, sighed, and closed his eyes.

Great, I hurt his feelings **again**. I can't seem to win here. I didn't mean to snap at him. I was feeling more and more like an ogre and I probably looked like it too.

"You're beautiful. You could not be an ogre; your heart is too good."

"Thanks, but I'm not either of those; beautiful or good."

I looked at Lykie as the thought left my head; he wagged his tail in approval.

"I am incapable of telling untruths . . . You are beautiful; and your soul is good, True Weaver."

He's just too sweet, I thought. "I like talking and not Vulcan mind thingying ok? It just feels less . . . weird for me. And please, call me Lou." I said aloud

"In time you will be more at ease with all of this, Lou"

"I'm scared Lykie; I mean really, **really** scared. All of this magic/evil stuff is things you read about in books. It isn't supposed to be real. And it most definitely isn't supposed to be happening to me!" I said and plopped down on my bed. "I think Lucy is the T-Weave, I'm just not the kind of person that this happens to. Lucy is the better choice for this than I am; she's smarter, more popular, and really a better choice. I think everyone got it wrong when they said it was me." I *hoped* that everyone had gotten it wrong.

"You woke the Adnama; you are **the** "T-Weave." He laughed at the phrase I'd used. "Adnama chose you, **we** didn't, and she does not make mistakes, Lou."

"I need to talk to my buds; I think they need to know that one of us has gone-"

"Bonkers Gazoo." We said together and both burst out laughing.

My buds came to the house when I said I needed them. That's one of the things I love about them, there were no questions when we needed each other. If it was important we were there for each other and we always just seemed to know when it was really important.

"You had us worried, Chickadee." Leah said as she plopped down on my bed.

"We went to sanctuary and waited for you. After the second time Andee pinned Allen and you still weren't there; we knew that something was wrong." DJ said as he grabbed a seat on the floor by Pixie.

Squeaks and the Farmers came in and found spots to sit down. It was a good thing I don't care what people think about how "tidy" my room is. If this was anyone but my buds I might feel anxious about them being in here . . . might.

"I have a lot of stuff I want to tell you guys." I began, looking into each pair of eyes; hoping this wouldn't be the last time they looked at me as normal.

"They will not change how they feel about you. Of this I am sure."

"Get outta my head Lykie! This is gonna be weird enough without that, ok?"

He wagged his tail and jumped up on the bed, putting his head in Squeaks' lap.

"I know no other way to tell you this than to just tell you." I began

My friends all sat in silence, listening as I told the strange tale of what my life had become. I was grateful for the Vulcan mind thingy when I got lost or stuck on something, Lykie could help me and no one knew.

I paced the room as I told them everything. It felt strangely like I was telling something that I already knew but was just getting around to reveling it to them. When I finished everyone sat quietly, looking at each other. For a brief moment I thought I'd made a mistake in telling them.

"Whew!" Leah finally said. "I thought I'd gone over the edge there for a while."

"What do ya mean?" I looked around the room as my buds started to mumble to each other.

"Well, Chickadee, I have heard voices in my head and seen things that I couldn't quite explain. I thought I'd taken one too many blows to the head. I thought I was going crazy."

She pretended to knock herself out and fell back on the bed laughing.

"This is way cooler than going crazy!" DJ said and winked at Pixie.

"Are you supposed to tell people this? Will it get you in some kind of trouble?" Squeaks asked, sounding her young age and looking timid.

"I was told I could tell this to who I felt I could and I called you guys." I looked at her and smiled.

"If you're the big cheese, that will make us the Scooby gang or something." Andee and Allen gave each other a high five

"This is cooler than cool, Lou. Oh man, this is awesome." Pixie chimed in.

"I was afraid you'd think I had slid too far down the rabbit hole to hang out with me anymore." I laughed nervously.

"Are you kidding!?" DJ asked. "We all live down the rabbit hole. I often wondered why you guys hung out with me. I'm the real weird one Lou, not you."

"You're the only normal one of us." Pixie said.

DJ smiled at her, got to his feet, and walked over to the bed. He looked down at me, Leah, Squeaks, and Lykie all sitting there. He stuck out two fingers, one on each hand, bent over and picked up the bed . . . with two fingers . . . with three people and a large dog on it.

"NO FLIPPIN' WAY!" The Farmers looked at each other, grinning like two baboons.

"So, that's not so special." Pixie said "Watch this, Muscles!" She walked over to the corner, looked over her shoulder at the rest of us, blew on her fingertips, and climbed up the wall. When she got to the top she shimmied across the ceiling then down the opposite wall. She stood up, turned around and said "Ta-da!"

Everyone clapped and DJ picked her up and twirled her around.

"Oh yea?" The Farmers said in unison.

Andee was humming pop goes the Wiesel but they were nowhere to be seen; when he got to the "pop" part of the song, he and Allen just sort of poofed into view. They were standing back to back in (really bad) Charlie's Angels poses.

"See, we're all weirdoes." Allen laughed

"Maybe that's how we found each other." Andee mused. "Maybe we were meant to find each other. We were destined to be Lou's gang or some junk like that."

"T-Weaves." I laughed

"It has a nice ring to it. What do ya think guys, T-Weaves?" Pixie asked

"T-Weaves!" Everyone said. We all held our hands up and gave a group high five then burst into laughter.

It felt great sitting around with my buds; the newly formed T-Weaves, and laughing about all the weirdness in our lives. It made it seem less strange to know that I wasn't alone in this craziness. One by one they all left, each promising they'd be here for the party tomorrow.

"That went really well, don't you think so, Lykie?" I asked after the last one had left.

"I told you it would be, Lou. I do need to go out for a bit before your Tresstel; I have a few things that I need to take care of."

"You'll be back though . . . right?" I sounded like a toddler whining about being left by my mommy.

Lykie came to the side of the bed and laid his head on my lap. "I'd never miss your Tresstel Lou. You're who I have looked for for over two thousand years."

"Thank you Lykie." I hugged him tightly then watched as he left the room, tail wagging happily.

This going to be interesting to say the lease; but with my buds, the newly formed 'T-Weaves' I knew I could get through anything life was going to throw my way.

Tresstel Trouble

Ok. Nerves or no nerves . . . I look awesome in this dress that mom picked out for me. I actually look like a girl. I don't do dresses or the whole girlie girl thing in general; but I have to admit, I look good in it. H.O.T spells:
"Much to do about, how I look!"
I walked over to the window box and picked up my Jequota. It was warm from the sunlight yet it felt cool as always. Its smooth surface with the raised symbols on it felt like brail under my fingers; like words I could not yet read. I opened the box and looked at it with new eyes.
"Adnama." I whispered, running my fingers over the water-like cloth inside. "I always knew you were special; maybe not *how* special, but I knew you were special. I think you made a mistake choosing me though"
Jequota got warm in my hands and seemed to vibrate.
"You are the True Weaver, Louanna Marie Teelf. There has been no mistake. I have waited over two millennia for you. Your power can not be mistaken."
The voice was spoken aloud, soft and majestic. There was a compulsion imbedded in it that made me want to hear it and do anything it took to please the speaker. I looked at the cloth inside Jequota and saw shapes dance in its depths. No matter how hard I stared, I could not make out what the shapes were.
"Are you alive?" I whispered

Life Weaver

"All of life is alive, True Weaver. Your concept of life is very limited. Life has many levels in many realms. Your eyes will open to many things, young one."

"This is all happening so fast. I'm nobody special; I'm just Lou, the weird girl with the weird friends." I sounded like a toddler again.

"There can be no other than you, True Weaver. There has been no mistake. The light that shines in you woke the slumbering spirit cloth, only the True Weaver can accomplish such an act. Have faith sweet Louanna, you are the True Weaver."

The voice faded and Jequota became still once again, only the silver/blue cloth could be seen. I had loved this box since the day Papa gave it to me. With all of this new stuff going on; it made my Jequota even more wonderful than before.

I looked at the window box; it looked lonely without its centerpiece. It may have been my imagination but even the stuffed animals seemed to have lost their sparkle. "Jequota will be back soon guys, don't worry." I patted the bears on the head and left my room.

It was the first time since I was four years old that Jequota had left my room. I clung to it tightly as I walked down the stairs to the kitchen.

The back yard had been totally transformed. Tiki torches lined its edge, a pathway fell between two rows of logs; cut in half and made to resemble benches. The backs of the benches were vines that had been woven into symbols from the Jequota. There were log-like stumps sitting along the front of the benches, giving each setting its own little table.

At the end of the path in the center of the benches; stood a hand carved pulpit. Candles stood all around it and tiki torches had been placed on the front two corners.

People were standing all around the open areas. Nameless faces all dressed in their Sunday best clothes. Several people sat in the front corner playing strange wooden instruments throwing quiet music over the whole scene creating a warm loving atmosphere.

Voices all fell silent as I exited the house and every eye fell sole on me. Suddenly I felt uncomfortable in this dress. I think there is too much *me* showing in this thing.

"Louanna." I heard Mom's voice say

I scanned the crowd and found her, talking to a group of people. I quickly made my way to her side.

"I was about to come and get you baby." She whispered.

"Who are all of these people Mom?" I asked.

"They are all Weavers. News of your Tresstel has apparently gotten out. They are here to witness the birth of the True Weaver's powers." She explained

"This is embarrassing enough without all these strangers watching it, Mom." I whined.

"Louanna, this is an historical event for our people. A True Weaver is very rare; of course they want to be here for the Tresstel that she receives her gifts from Adnama. Come, I'll introduce you to some of them. Mom grabbed my elbow and guided me into the crowd.

The next thirty minutes flew by in a blur. A line of faces passed in front of me with curious smiles as they greeted me. I felt like a spring pig at the county fair. (FYI: not a good look for any girl to have.) I thought the conga line would never end Ms. So-in-so... Mr. what's-his-name... old who's-it-again? But the line did finally thin out and I was no longer required to smile and pretend to be important.

"There are still a few people coming but we need to get this started." A man said to Mom.

"Yes, of course Jeph." Mom replied then escorted me to the back of the yard.

"Much to do about, I wish this was over already."

Everyone filed into the bench seats. I noticed that each one had a Jequota with them. They placed their spirit boxes on the little wood stump tables and turned to face Mom and me.

"Lykie, you said you'd be here. You promised me!" I felt lost somehow without the comfort of my life long companion.

"I am here Lou, you will see me soon, and you have nothing to fear."

I felt more at ease knowing he was close by. I'm not sure why it did; think talking to my not-a-dog should have made me feel even weirder but somehow his vulca-voice; however strange it was to me, made me feel comforted.

"You think the strangest things, Lou." I could hear laughter embedded in his words and it felt like a hand brushed along the side of my jaw.

As we reached the end of the path, I was asked to place my Jequota on the Altar of Life. (I guess I was wrong about it being a pulpit.) I stroked the symbols carved on its top and placed it on the altar. The Jequota began to vibrate and glow looking like a lightning bug in the spring.

The people standing around began to mumble softly, it was more like some kind of chant, but was low and I couldn't hear the words being said.

Mom placed a gold chain around my neck; it had a small locket attached to it and on it I saw the same symbols that were on the Jequota. Then she took a string of flowers, woven together, and placed them on my head like a crown. She dipped her pinky into a silver bowl of water and placed a drop between my eyes. An identical bowl of oil was next;

she dipped her pinky into the oil and placed droplets on the inner side of both my wrists. In a third bowl she took a hand full of dirt from the ground and put it in the last silver bowl then added the unused water and oil. Mixing it all together; she dipped her pinky yet again in the mud and smeared mud on each of my heels. The chanting fell silent as she stood up and moved to my side.

"Jequota has chosen a True Weaver." She said to the crowd. "At the stroke of midnight of her sixteenth year of life; Adnama will bestow on her the gifts she is due."

The crowd all clapped and repeated, "Adnama"

"We have waited long; and suffered many losses awaiting the True Weaver's return to our people. Now our wait is over." Mom looked at me. "Our power and magic will be as it once was. Weavers will be able to once again yield the magic of the Jequota; to protect our beloved Adnama and the life that has been ours to enjoy."

"It is time." Jeph said

"Five . . . Four . . . Three . . . Two . . . One . . . Tresstel is here!" Mom said and all eyes fell on me. I looked back at the crowd. Dumbfounded as to what I was supposed to do. (See, I knew that I wasn't the person they were all looking for!) The thought had barely left my head when I doubled over in pain.

I tried to scream but I found I had lost my voice. Air rushed all around me, trapping me in a vortex; picking my body up and holding me in midair. There was an electrical charge building up around me and the sound of crackling became loud in my ears. A bright light fell on me like a huge spotlight.

"LOU!" It was Lykie's voice that pulled me out of the mind trap I had fallen into.

"Lou, you must not fight. Adnama is filling you with power that belongs to the True Weaver, you must not fight, Lemoya."

"Lykie, it hurts! It hurts so bad: help me, Please!"

"I will come to you True Weaver; you will not suffer the transfer alone."

I felt arms embrace me, holding me tight. Some of the pain lessoned instantly. The light that surrounded me became blinding, opening my eyes was not an option. The wind blew in such frenzy that it tore at my clothes and skin. I felt weightless yet grounded by the arms that held me close.

"I'm the wrong choice! I'm not strong enough to do this!" I thought

"You are the True Weaver! I have waited for over two thousand years Lou. You are mine to protect. I will not fail you!"

I felt lips touch mine. Soft and loving; the briefest of kisses, then silence fell and everything went black.

I woke lying on the ground, surrounded by worried faces. My hand went to my lips; the feel of the kiss still lingering there. I wondered who had given me the kiss, if it really was a kiss. . .

"Thank Goodness, you're awake." Mom said, kissing my forehead. "We thought we'd lost you baby."

"What happened?" I looked around, still puzzled about what had happened. (And tingling from a mystery kiss)

"We're not sure exactly. You started floating as the wind started blowing really hard. Then you started screaming but we were unable to get to you. Lightning was striking the ground all around you, then you stopped screaming and everything grew quiet. We thought you had died, the wind stopped blowing and the light went out. You were lying on the ground and Lykie refused to let any of us near you" Mom's voice was filled with worry.

I looked over my shoulder and saw Lykie lying on the ground behind me. "Are you ok boy?"

"Yes Lou, I will always protect you. It is my duty . . . my honor." He didn't open his eyes, merely wagged his tail.

"Look at her hair." Someone whispered.

"What's wrong with my hair? I asked, wondering why my choice of hair fashion could be so important at a moment like this one.

"Nothing is wrong with your hair baby." Mom said, handing me a mirror.

I took the mirror and looked at my reflection. My dark brown hair was streaked with golden highlights and silver streaks woven in and out. I now had brindle colored hair that matched the color of my Jequota.

Mom ran her hand down the length of my hair. "It's beautiful Louanna."

"Thanks Mom," I said looking in the mirror. It really was beautiful to see.

Lykie came over to my side. "I have someone I'd like you to meet, Lou." He said

Movement caught my attention. At the edge of the tree line emerged two little men, both dressed in shades of green and wearing huge grins.

"Hello, True Weaver. I am Leafkin, a humble Speritalz, tis an honor to be in your presence." The small man, around two and a half feet tall with bright orange hair, red tips and little round glasses said.

"I am Leafkon, Speritalz as well, and the honor or meeting you will be with me always, True Weaver." The other little man with flaming orange hair and black tips said.

"The True weaver, I can't believe this." They said in Unison

"Please, call me Lou, okay? True Weaver just seems weird."

The two little men looked at each other with puzzled expressions. "Begging your pardon; but, you are the True Weaver, are you not?" The little one named Leafkin asked.

"I have been told that I am; however, I'd like you to call me Lou, it is my name. Well, Louanna is my name but most people call me Lou." I smiled at them both "If Lou seems too informal, just call me Louanna."

"As you wish, My Lady, we live to serve the True Weaver. If it is your wish that we call you Lou or Louanna and not True Weaver, then so be it . . . Lou." He bowed low.

"Thank you." I said "You don't have to bow down, either. I'm just a sixteen year old kid. We can be friends who help each other, not you serving me; ok guys?"

"As you wish . . . Louanna." Leafkin said. He smiled brightly at Leafkon.

"This is my Mom, Leona Teelf. Mom, this is Leafkin and Leafkon." I introduced them.

"Tis an honor to meet the mother of the True Weaver. We are grateful to you as well, My Lady." He took mom's hand and kissed the back of it.

"You are Speritalz?" Mom asked.

"Indeed, My Lady, we are. We served the True Weaver, Lisdom Teelfel. Her death is still a source of sadness for us all." Leafkin dropped his head in a show of sorrow.

"It is the dream of all Speritalz to be in the service of the True Weaver. We hope that Louanna will accept us and allow one or more of us to be in her Court of Brethren." He reached in his pocket and took out a small green cloth bag. "I have a gift for the True Weaver, if you will accept it."

He placed the small bag in my hands. It was closed with a draw string. I slowly opened the bag and took out a small stick. There was nothing special about it; yet it held a mystery within. It was the same color as my Jequota.

I took the stick out of the small bag and looked at it. . . . A stick, twig even, I guess it is a great gift where they are from. I smiled at the little man; not knowing what to say. I put it on the altar beside Jequota and it sorta vibrated or quivered; then fell silent and still.

Leafkin looked at the twig then back at me; a great deal of satisfaction on his face.

"I mean no disrespect, but what exactly is it?" I asked

"A Weaving Wand, My Lady; it will be essential in your use of magic." He looked at Leafkon and beamed a huge smile.

"Wait, just a hot little minute, here. I am no True Weaver. I keep telling you people. **I. AM. THE. WRONG. PERSON!!!!!!!**" It felt like I was talking in a language that I alone could understand.

Something that sounded like the crackling or snapping of a campfire came from behind me. I turned to find the cause of the noise, only to find myself looking at one of the most handsome faces I had ever seen.

Midnight black hair shrouded a face that could not be real. His eyes were the color of spring grass with a silver sheen that was evident in the hue of the moons glow. He was in a pair of snug fitting jeans and no shirt and he just stood there smiling at me.

"You are the True Weaver, Lou. We have already discussed this." His voice boomed all around seemingly soaking into my skin or deeper. He reached out and took my hand.

"WHO. ARE. YOU?" Was all I could squeak out. I was so mesmerized by this strange man. His eyes held me captive; looking deep within them I felt like we had known each other for several lifetimes.

"I am your guardian, Lou. You named me Lykie when you took me in; I am your Lydian protector." He leaned in close to my ear causing my heart to skip *several* beats and whispered, "I told you that I would be able to shift at your Tresstel if you were the True Weaver; and it would seem that you *are*, My Lady." He kissed the back of my hand and sent flames licking down my spine.

"Wow, you really are not-a-dog, Lykie. Soo **not-a-dog!**" It slipped out of my mouth before I had the good sense to sensor it.

Everyone around us laughed at my childish reaction and Lykie pulled me into a hug.

"I have waited for over two thousand years for you Louanna. You are such a gift to me; to us all." He said.

People all around cheered and clapped their hands. Everyone was happy and smiles were on every face, every face except Lucy's. She stood in the far back of the crowd with a look of distain etched on her face. Waves of hatred rolled off of her; straight at me.

"The True Weaver will now speak to Adnama, with the help of the Weaving Wand she should be able to communicate with her Jequota's spirit." Mom said, causing everyone to go silent.

"I already spoke to the spirit inside my Jequota." I said

"What?" Mom asked and looked at Lykie.

"Before I came down tonight, she has a beautiful voice. There were shapes swimming in the cloth, but I couldn't make out what they were. Jequota kind of vibrated then glowed.

The voice was out loud but inside my head as well. Why, is there a problem?" I was suddenly worried.

"No one . . . has ever been able to speak to Adnama without the use of the Weaving Wands. Are you sure it was Adnama, My Lady Louanna?" Leafkin asked.

"Sure I'm sure. She said my concept of life was limited and there are different realms of life. I felt like I *had* to listen to the voice. I was holding my Jequota and when she spoke, Jequota grew warm. Is there something wrong?" I looked over at my Jequota. The seam of the box cracked open a small bit, a silver light emanated from inside causing instant silence.

"The True Weaver has power far greater than those before her. This small child holds the key to all we have longed for. The power she yields will be our salvation . . . . Hold on to your faith in the days to come; danger lurks closer than we would wish it. You are my children and I hold you each in my arms. Do not let hate or anger be your guide; it will lead to your destruction"

The sweet voice faded and took with it the silver glow. I could feel every eye on me so I kept my gaze locked on my Jequota.

"This is astounding Louanna. Thanks to you we all just heard the majestic voice of our beloved Adnama. You did this for us." Lykie had not spoken aloud but I knew it was his voice in my head.

Leafkin brought over the little wooden rod and placed it in my hands. There was no "Whoosh" or an electrical "zap" it simply lay there in my palm, unmoving.

"Much to do about, I wish people would stop staring at me!"

I rolled the rod between my fingers . . . Nothing. I turned it over and shook it like can of paint . . . Again, nothing!

"What am I supposed to do? Flick it around?" I asked, letting my hand move of its own accord. My hand had adopted a mind of its own, circles, swirls, zigzags, and loops. Each movement brought on a sparkling rainbow spider web. My hands continued to dance and weave; the tiny rainbow webs began to connect and spread, soon there was a hole in the air. It seemed to just hang there, outlined by the shiny webs.

The moon light seemed to cause the rainbow colors to glow. Inside the hole I saw an old tattered book lying on a rock shelf. Dust, at least an inch thick, lay on top of the book. I reached in and gingerly took the book from its apparent long time resting place.

"You have found the Nivlem; you created a portal to the Nivlem to be more precise." Lykie: the man, not my not-a-dog, said "How, How on earth did you do that, Lou?"

"I don't know. It's like when I paint, my hands just moved. It happened without my knowing how; I don't even know what I did." I explained

"It is said that only an Elder can be granted access to the book of knowledge. The Nivlem is a sacred book; protected and guarded, not even a True Weaver should have access to this book." Leafkin said, awe in his voice. "You should not have been able to get through the spells set around it; did you see how to do this . . . in a dream, perhaps?"

"I don't think so." I said, feeling a bit defensive. "I just waved my hands around like this."

Again I let my hands flick and jump around; the hole in the air disappeared like it had never been there.

"SEE! Like that, I don't even know what I just did and that hole "poofed" away." I said

Lykie stepped to my side and put his hand on my shoulder. "It is obvious that you are meant to have this book or you could not have found it." He said happily.

Leafkon walked over to me shyly and placed another stick in my hand. "Here is the Weaving Wand's twain. You umm, are supposed to need two of them to weave magic." He laughed.

The rest of the ceremony went by in a blur; food was eaten, drinks were drank; people all seemed to want me to touch their Jequota and shake my hand or hug me. I felt very out of place; I never liked being the center of attention so this was very uncomfortable for me. I'm more of a "blend into the wood work" kinda gal. Ms. So-in-so and Mr. What's his name made sure they touched, talked, and spent time with me… When will this end!?

"You're doing fine, Lou." Lykie whispered to me.

"How am I supposed to get use to all of this . . . to you? You could have warned me about your looks, ya know!"

"I am sorry. I didn't know that my appearance would offend you." I heard the snapping and turned to see Lykie in the familiar form of my dog once again.

"NO! It didn't offend me. It's just that you could have told me you looked like some super model or some Adonis. You know, something like that." I mumbled

"You find my appearance appealing?" I could hear laughter in his tone.

"Well, you're ok; for a two thousand year old dog, that is." I tried to sound mild and not let him know I thought his human form was **H.O.T.**

Lykie stayed in the form of my lifelong friend, my dog, the rest of the night. He sat at my feet and kept his eyes on anyone who walked up to speak to me. He had always made me feel safe and now I felt even more so; laughing to myself that I was now protected by a "HOT DOG".

"You think the funniest things Louanna."

I simply rubbed his head as I had for so many years for comfort; ignoring the fact that he had read my thoughts.

I was so grateful when the "Good byes" or "Good nights" started and people started leaving. I felt like I had aged a thousand years since this had started. I was in desperate need of a hot shower and a long restful sleep before my party with my buds.

"We need to return home, Tru . . . Louanna." Leafkin said, pushing up his tiny little glasses on his nose.

"Umm, ok, Leafkin. Bye then." I smiled at him.

"My Lady, we need a portal in which to travel." He said it quietly, as if he were ashamed to be asking.

"I don't know how to do that Leafkin." I whispered.

Leafkin walked over to the pond and looked down at his reflection, smiled and looked at me again. "Yes . . . Yes you do Louanna."

I walked to the water's edge and looked at our reflection. Suddenly the water shimmered looking like Jell-O wiggling in it. The two Speritalz smiled happily, bowed low and jumped in the water. There was no splash or wave. Not even a ripple in the surface to show they'd touched it.

"Thank you True Weaver. We will return when you have need of us." I looked at Leafkin's reflection, laughing that Leafkon was behind him bouncing and waving at me. I waved at them and then they were gone.

"This day just gets weirder by the minute" I said to myself.

Mom, Lucy, and I cleaned up the back yard and put everything away. Mom was smiling and humming but Lucy was quiet and kept glaring at me; mumbling under her breath. I simply ignored her and did what Mom instructed me to do.

"I'll finish this up, girls." Mom said "You should go on up and get some sleep."

"Are you sure, Mom? There is still a lot that needs to be done. I don't want you to have to do this alone" I said

"She won't be alone Lemoya. I will assist her with this." Lykie said.

"You go on up, your friends will be here before you know it, Louanna" She handed me my Jequota.

"Ok. I am kinda tired." I kissed her on the cheek and headed to the house. Hearing the now familiar crackling, I knew that Lykie had shifted and was helping her, I smiled to myself.

I made my way up to my room and placed Jequota back on the window box. The moon light caressed it and I felt better with it back where it belonged. I took off the beautiful dress and slipped on some comfortable jeans and a button up shirt.

"I hope you don't think I'm going to be bowing and worshiping you, Lou**anna**." Lucy said from my doorway, her voice dry and harsh.

"I never asked anyone to bow to me, Lucy!" I snapped

"Yea, I could tell how much it bothered you; "Everyone bow to the True Weaver." You were eating up all of that attention. You're such a hypocrite Lou**anna**!" She spat the words at me.

"What is your problem Lucy? I never asked for any of that!" I was furious! "I didn't want this . . . **ANY** of it! I was happy being "just me" then all this magic, Weaver crap, got thrown at me. I didn't ask for it and you darn well know it!" I screamed in her face. She had seriously ticked me off.

Looking down I found myself in the air . . . floating, about a foot off the floor. Wind was whipping around the room in a fury of gusts.

"Showing off your power doesn't impress me, **True Weaver**!" She said and left my room.

Lykie came charging in; his presence filling my room. His sides were heaving and his fists were clinched at his sides. He stood there looking over every inch of my room, taking in every detail.

"I sensed your stress, Louanna. Are you ok?" his voice was a caress on my skin.

"I'm fine; I just got a little angry at something Lucy said. I'm sorry boy . . . I mean . . . what am I supposed to call you? Lykie is my dog's name and you are **soo** not a dog." Anyone looking at this Greek God in front of me would agree... NOT-A-DOG!

He took my chin in his fingers, raising my face to look me in the eyes. "Call me whatever you wish, Lemoya." He whispered. I could feel my heart beating in my throat. His thumb feathered back and forth trailing fire in its wake. "I will always come to you regardless of what you call Me." his voice was almost inaudible.

"What happened!?" Mom asked as she ran into my room. "The pull of energy to this room was too strong to have not been noticed."

"Lucy made me mad, that's all, Mom." I said

"NO, that's not all, Louanna! Every light down stairs is blown and all the tiki torches blew out. She looked at me then Lykie "Was there anyone in the room when you came in? Were there any open portals?"

"She was alone when I entered the room, M' Lady. I found no open portals." Human Lykie stepped around me and began going over the entire room.

"Did I do something wrong?" I asked, feeling anxious.

"No, Baby, but you have to watch your emotions. Anger is a very strong emotion and if not kept in check; it can escalate to a dangerous status." She said.

"This is all too much, Mom! Even having a spat with my sister is Dangerous!? Can't I pass this to someone else, someone like Lucy; who obviously wants all this crap?" I snapped, exasperated and tired.

"Lemoya, you cannot pass this." Lykie said sweetly. "This is your destiny, it can seem overwhelming and too much to comprehend; but Adnama choose you. Adnama does not make mistakes. It is you, Louanna, who are the True Weaver."

"I. DO. NOT. WANT. TO. BE. THE. STINKING. TRUE. ANYTHING!!!" I screamed into my pillow; making sure to enunciate each word.

Mom came to the side of my bed and stroked my hair.

"Lemoya, you are stronger than you think you are. Logton will be expecting you to be "Consoyta" new, or beginning magic." Lykie said

"I can't **do** magic . . . I *can't*!" I looked at their faces; faith was evident in both. (Wasted faith)

"You found the Nivlem, the book of knowledge. No one, not even a True Weaver should be able to break through the safe guards concealing it." Lykie leaned one hip on the door frame, crossed his arms over his bare chest and, (Did I mention that he was shirtless?) bit his lower lip. (Hubba Hubba!)

"Much to do about, He should be labeled lethal!"

He raised his eyebrow "Glad you think so, Lemoya." A grin fell across his face.

Desperate to change the subject of Mr. Shirtless I said, "I don't even know how I did that though! All I did was wave my arms around." I moved my hands and the rainbow spider webs started gathering. I slammed my hands in my front pockets.

"Do you see, Louanna? You didn't even have the Weaving Wands and you were drawing energy to you. Mom said.

"How can I do something I don't know I'm doing?" I was getting more frustrated.

"You will learn with the passing of time, Lemoya. You have only had your powers for," he looked at the sky, "A little more than four hours. Control of your powers is no less than any lesson you have had to learn; it will take time and practice."

"I hope you are right. I just turned sixteen and teens are not exactly known for being able to control their emotions." I said with a bit of snip in my tone. (Loose the look… it's been rough and I'm dealing as best I can!)

"No one expects you to be anything other than what and who you are. Believe me when I tell you that you are so much more than just a sixteen year old teen girl. You're special, Louanna; you've always been special. "Everything in life happens for a reason" as dad always said; just give it some time baby." Mom's voice was calming and filled with love as she spoke.

"Okay, I'll try to not freak out about . . . all of this True Weaver stuff. I think I'm going to go take me a hot shower and hit the hay; maybe things will be better in the light of day."

Mom hugged me and Lykie winked mischievously and they both left the room.

I entered the bathroom and tossed my "Jammies" on the sink. I took off my pants and unbuttoned my shirt and froze. (Do you ever just *know* when someone is looking at you?) I had that very feeling... I pulled the shirt sides together and slowly turned around. Two smiling faces were looking at me from the mirror.

"M' Lady, sorry to come unannounced to your washing chamber; the portal in your room has been placed under a binding spell and this is the closest glass portal. We are bound to your service and had to come to your aide." Leafkin bowed as he spoke.

"Hello again, Lou!" Leafkon said from behind Leafkin; he was waving his hand like an eager child at a celebrity; I couldn't help but think how cute they were.

"Guys, you cannot come to this . . . umm, "Glass portal" this room is private; unless I call you here, Ok?" I felt I needed to add the last part in; just in case.

"Much to do about, ya just never know!"

"M' Lady, we mean you no disrespect. Your powers called us to you, True . . . I mean, Louanna." Leafkin pushed his little glasses up and looked at me with hurt in his eyes.

"Don't take it that way, lil man. It's just that I get undressed in here; I do . . . "Private" things in here that I'd rather not have an audience for." I smiled and looked at the commode.

"This is the salle de bain?" he asked,

"The salldee . . . what?" I asked and looked around.

"Salle de bain is what the French humans call the place to relieve themselves it is also what we call our relieving room." He said and turned a bright shade of red as he realized where we were.

"Yea, this is that "Salldee" thing. I kind of like to be in here alone Le . . . Kin." I winked at Leafkin causing his red to deepen.

"I tell ya what, my handsome little friends, when I'm done in the "Salldee" I'll give you a shout, ok? What do I do when I want to tell you the coast is clear?"

"The coast, M' Lady, you wish to transport to the ocean?" Leafkin snapped his fingers and a sunny beach with the bluest water I had ever seen shimmered into view behind the two little Speritalz.

"Whoa! How'd you do that?" I asked.

"Was not I, M' Lady." Leafkin said

"It was you who did that, Lou. Your power is very strong; as the True Weaver it will only get stronger. We are just here to help you . . . Lou." he smiled sheepishly at the informal way of talking to me.

"So if I said . . . Vegas?"

Once again the reflection shimmered and then the Vegas strip came into view.

"Much to do about, Vacation anyone?"

"That is totally cool!" I said and yawned. "I'm feeling really tired, and no; I didn't mean cool like a snowy mountain top." I laughed looking at the snow covered ground behind them now.

"All you have to do is call to us and move your hands like this." He wiggled his hands around "And we will be able to come to you; we await your summons." Poof, they were gone, Leafkon waving in the background like crazy.

"Well, getting to school will be quicker." I mumbled.

I returned to undressing then stopped and put a long towel over the mirror; then looked for other reflective surfaces and covered them all. (No beady little eyes are gonna watch me take a shower!)

It was dark. Only whispered voices could be heard.

"You did well!" A male voice spoke.

"I'm sick of everyone falling all over her!" A female voice spat out. "It's been that way her whole life. There were people bowing . . . **BOWING** to her at that ceremony! I couldn't even look at that circus show."

"Your power is strong; but now is the time for patience." The male voice held contempt. "Do as I say and the True Weaver shall not gain full power. She will "Fall on her face" as you have decreed. We have to be careful to not allow her to know our plans."

"I can't wait for that!"

Lykie froze; he lifted his head and listened. All Lydian Guardians had excellent hearing; evil was near. It left before he could pin point its location. He turned his head and sniffed the air . . . LOUANNA!

"Two hot showers in one week!" I giggled like a silly child at the zoo.

"Much to do about, a girl could get use to this."

I lit the aroma therapy candles and put on one of Mom's "Put ya to sleep" CD's then stepped into the shower. (I dropped the towel *after* I got in . . . just in case!)

The hot water felt divine! My whole body was sore and achy. Leaning my head back, I let the hot spray wash away my troubles; washing my hair had never felt so good. I used some of Mom's flowery body wash and my favorite loofa. Sitting on the bench in the shower, I leaned back and closed my eyes and enjoyed this "ME" time before I had to shave my *caveman* legs. If there was a more relaxing place in the world, I couldn't imagine where, it was warm and relaxing. I sighed and . . .

I was somewhere dark. There was a closed door before me; a reddish-orange glow peeked from the gap at the bottom. I took a step closer to the door and my "Henky feeling" came from nowhere and slammed hard into my senses. I always listen to my henky feeling so I froze where I was.

"You did well." I heard a male voice say.

"I'm sick of everyone falling all over her!" A female said voice full of rage. "It's been that way her whole life. There were people bowing . . . BOWING to her at that ceremony! I couldn't even look at that circus show!" The bitterness rolling off the voice was nearly tangible.

"Your power is strong, but now is the time for patience. Do as I say and the True Weaver shall not gain full power. She will "Fall on her face" as you have decreed." The male spoke with utter contempt (Even for the female he spoke to.)

"I can't wait for that!"

"Wake up Louanna! Open your eyes! You must wake up!" a voice was screaming at me, it seemed so far away. I tried to speak but wasn't able to.

It was cold. I was lying on the bathroom floor, coughing and spitting water out of my lungs. I could hear the shower still running but I was no longer under its enticing spray.

"Please open your eyes, Lemoya. I beg you, look at me!"

I opened my eyes and looked at the tear laden face of Lykie, the human not-a-dog. He held me tight and rocked me back and forth gently. His body shook with either fear or relief.

"Are you ok, Lemoya? Can you speak?" He asked, looking me in the eye.

"What happened? I was taking a shower and . . . **HOLY CRAP! GET ME A TOWEL! I'M FLIPPIN' NAKID!!!!!!!** (I could have died then and there of utter embarrassment!)

Note to self: Bathe in a swimsuit from now on!

"You think the silliest things, Lou. I have seen you undressed thousands of times." He handed me my robe. His gaze lingering on my bare legs and exposed bottom just a tad too long. (Ok, he made me blush! See a dictionary under sixteen year old girls actions around a hot guy!) (GEESH!)

"Yes, well, **Lykie**; my **DOG** has seen me thousands of times. You are far from being a dog!" I said. . . AGAIN! "I can't call someone that looks like you, my dog, or even his name. You're not-a-dog."

"Would it be easier to think of me as a Lydian when I am in this form?" he asked

"Well, maybe . . . yea, it would be easier. It would help me be less confused and tongue tied" I mumbled.

"Then so be it. In this form, I am Lydian. And believe me; you have no reason to be bashful, I am your guardian, remember?" He smiled.

"Lykie the dog; Lydian the hot guy, like you are two people . . . things . . . whatever, you know what I mean." I stuttered.

"If it helps you Lemoya." He shut off the shower and the radio. We both turned and blew out the candle. Our heads were very close; I could smell the fresh air and night dew on him.

He took a deep breath and smiled. "You smell like a spring meadow, Lemoya." He brushed a stray band of hair behind my ear.

"Unless you are going to give that dog a flea bath, I need the shower, True Weavers (losers) aren't the only ones who need to shower around here, ya know." Lucy stood in the doorway, looking down her nose at us. "Somehow I doubt that Mom will let a two thousand year old "Horn-dog" sleep in her sixteen year old daughter's room anymore." She laughed.

"Come on Lydian, let's go to "our" room!" I snapped and walked past Lucy into the hall. Lydian started past her and took a deep breath; he stopped and turned to look her in the eyes.

"I serve the True Weaver; I will eliminate any threat to her. You are Weaver and hold my allegiance, but my first priority is to the True Weaver." He walked past her and she slammed the door, fussing about ticks and fleas.

Shopping Trip

"What was that about?" I asked and turned as the crackling announced Lydian had shifted.

"I just needed to remind her that I am here to protect you. And I will do so with my dying breath!"

"You didn't have to change, Lykie. Mom knows who and what you are. You could have stayed as Lydian." I said, trying to hide the fact that I missed looking at his face.

"This is for the best. You are still getting use to this "*stuff*" remember?" He laughed. "May I?" he asked putting his paws on the bed.

"Don't be silly, boy . . . I mean Lykie. It's your room too, it always has been."

"You may call Lykie, boy. It has been several millennia since anyone called me that. I like being your boy."

"I have to call Kin and Kon; they "Poofed" in on me in the bathroom before my shower." I laughed

Lykie growled deep in his throat. "It is not proper for them to be in your washroom, they know this! I shall speak to them about proper educate."

"Says the dog who shifted into man and came into the shower and saw me naked." I laughed and kissed his head.

"Much to do about, wishing I was Lydian again."

I pretended not to hear him and went to retrieve the mirror from the hall closet.

"So what do I do? How do I get them here?" I asked

"You call them."

"Gee, I don't think they're in my contacts; do ya think they text?" I joked.

"Do they . . . what contacts?" He looked at me puzzled.

"My conta . . . never mind." I sighed.

Looking at the mirror; I saw me, Lykie, and my room. "What am I supposed to do" I thought. I took a deep breath and blew on the glass and crossed my hands over each other then back. "Coast's clear guys." I whispered.

"Who put a binding spell on the glass?"

"I didn't know it had a spell on it." I said, looking at the glass for a trace of a spell; like goo or ick of some kind.

"How did you know how to remove it?" He moved closer to the glass and sniffed.

"Did I? I don't know how I did it; I just felt like I had to blow on it, my hands moved on their own." (Seems to be the going thing with them lately.) I started feeling apprehensive.

"It is advanced magic, Lemoya. You say you just felt that was what you needed to do?" He sat up and looked me in the eye.

"Yea, it just felt like it was what I needed to do; like I had done it before." I mumbled out the last part without conscious thought.

"Hello Lou!" Leafkon said, waving his hand and smiling brightly.

"Hey there Kon, did you do something to your hair lil man?"

"Kon!? . . . How great, a special name from the True Weaver!" His smile widened. "My hair; I got my new tips. Thank you for noticing them. Red is the Senior color and blue," He stroked the new blue tips in his hair. "Is the color of a Junior Speritalz; I moved up in rank." He beamed at the news.

"Oh for Adnama's sake, Leafkon; the True Weaver does not wish to hear about such trivial dribble as our hair ranks." Kin snipped and pushed up his glasses.

"She calls me Kon, you can too." He said happily

"I call you Kin; it's just easier for me." I looked at the shocked expression on his little face and squelched a laugh.

"I prefer Leafkin, but if the True Weaver wishes to address me as such, *you* may of course do so." He looked at Kon in a knowing stare over the top of his glasses.

"Kin and Kon it is then." Kon's smile could not get brighter. I had to turn and disguise a laugh with a fake cough at the disgruntled look on Kin's face however.

"We had a disturbance here earlier; our True Weaver was just about to tell the details of the incident." Lykie interjected.

I retold the story of the bathroom "visit" and the relaxing shower, noting the low growl emanating from Lykie and the embarrassed looks on Kin and Kon's faces. I went on quickly to get their minds on the story again, how I'd gotten sleepy and sat down on the bench in the shower and apparently fallen asleep or something like it. Then there was darkness, red-orange light, henky feeling, and then voices. (I conveniently left out the "waking up naked in Lydian's arms" bit.) I felt his laughter in my head.

"You could sense the evil presence, Guardian?" Kin took out a small pad and scratched notes on it, pushing up his glasses; yet again.

"Yes, I knew it was near but was unable to pinpoint its location." Lykie sounded angry.

"We will need to tighten up the security around her, if you will allow us, M' Lady?" Kin said and bowed.

I looked at him then Lykie. If I'd allow what, I wondered.
"They need an entrance; you have to ask them into this realm Lemoya." Lykie said and backed away from the mirror.
I thought about what he had said and retrieved the Weaving Wands. I closed my eyes and let my hands move as they wanted. Reopening my eyes I saw the rainbow webs had started to gather. I started to speak, a strange wispy voice that was not my own came from my mouth.

"You seek a door, into this place, far beyond time and space.

I grant this wish, but just to thee, a door that no one else can see.

Should you have need, it will be there, but only for the chosen pair.

No one else may use this gift, but should they try . . . True pain comes swift."

When I finished speaking, (With someone else's voice) I floated back down to the floor and saw a clear spot in the "Jell-O" mirror. Kin and Kon stood gaping at me from the other side.

"Well? How was that for my first "True" try?" I laughed

"M' Lady, who were all those voices you spoke with?" he asked as he stepped through the open portal.

The crackle behind me announced Lydian had returned. "They were the Past True Weavers; Life, Water, Wind, and Fire, from the four realms." Lydian said. "How did you summons them Lemoya?" he took my hand and lead me to my bed and sat me down. I didn't realize I was swaying and light headed.

He brushed my hair from my face and paused. "Your neck!" he continued to move my hair to the side. "You bear the mark of Adnama, the sign of reincarnation of Goddess to flesh!" Lydian ran his finger down my neck to the center of my back. It felt like he had electrocuted me.

I turned to the mirror and saw a silver-blue "tattoo" of a detailed tree on my neck with vines stemming from the tree down the center of my back. Entwined in the vines were the symbols from my Jequota.

"What does this mean?" I asked timidly.

Three shocked faces looked back at me. They stared at me then each other, not speaking and making me feel self-conscious.

"I do not knot Lemoya. This has never happened before that I am aware of, have you heard of such a thing Speritalz?" They simply shook their heads but didn't speak. Kin was scratching away in his little note pad.

Lydian replaced my hair, covering the "tattoo" and said, "Maybe we should keep this quiet until we know more about its significance."

Kin scratched something else in his little pad then replaced it to his pocket. "Who do we ask about this; do you have any suggestions, Guardian? Do we know anyone with the knowledge we seek?" Kin looked at each of us then retrieved his note pad, pushing up his glasses, and tapping his finger with thought visible on his face.

"I do not know, but as Louanna has fallen asleep . . . it can wait." Lydian said quietly.

I woke feeling well rested and ready to take on the day. Lykie lay on the bed beside me and wagged his tail happily as I sat up on my bed.

"Good morning Boy." I said as I got to my feet and stretched. "I had a really Bonkers Gazoo dream about you last night."

Lykie stood, stretched and did the all over shake. He turned to look at me and cocked his head to the side, tongue lolling out and looked as adorable as ever.

"In the dream, you were a dog half of the time," I said slipping my pj bottoms off. "And the other half you were this totally hot guy. I had to have eaten something bad 'cause there were some weird things in this dream."

"Did I look something like this Lemoya?" A deep voice came from behind me.

I froze and turned around, looking into the sparkling eyes of Lydian. "Crap!" I said

"You still do not approve of this form, Lemoya?" he asked quietly.

"I'd have to be *Bonkers Gazoo* for **real** to not like *that* form." I sighed

"So why the "crap" when you saw me?"

"I was hoping it was all just a crazy dream . . . no such luck it would seem." I laughed.

"Good morning M' Lady; what interesting attire you have donned to wear this hot day, very fitting I'd say." Kin smiled happily at me.

I looked down and to my horror found myself in my high belly pj top and a hot pink thong!

"Much to do about, I need to buy granny panties!"

I snatched up the nearest pair of joggers and slipped them on. "You could have said something, Lydian!" I complained.

"Hey, you have your dreams . . . I have mine." He smiled and winked then left the room.

I watched him leave and smiled to myself. "Which is his true form guys, dog or man?" I looked at Kin and Kon in questioning.

"He is neither M' Lady, He is Lydian therefore he is both and not one or the other." Kon smiled.

"What do you mean?" I asked and looked over at Kin.

"He is both a man and the crude description you insist on calling him, dog." Kin replied. Though he didn't say it, I assumed I had insulted Lydian.

"I am insulting him!? I didn't mean to." I looked at the door where he had just left. "Why hasn't he said something to me about it?"

"You are the one who he has looked for since the passing of Lisdom, the last True Weaver. Your Tresstel, and the conformation of you as the True Weaver, released him for the form he was bound in. All Lydian warriors were trapped in whichever form they possessed at the time of her death. It is why Lyden chose death rather than live as a man and seeking the next True Weaver." He finished sadly.

"And he could not live in a world without her." Mom said as she came into my room to check on me.

"Couldn't live without her, he was in love with her then?" I asked

"Very much so; as legend tells it. After years of laughter, devotion, friendship, and togetherness it was bound to happen." She kissed my head "So what are you having for breakfast, birthday girl?" she smiled and escorted me down stairs.

Mom, Lucy and I went to breakfast then shopping. I almost felt normal until I started noticing little gnomes in nearly every store, all of which had on different shades of green clothing. I almost peed my pants when a lady picked up Kin turned him over a few times, took off his little glasses and asked for a price check. The look on his face as he tried to maintain his "statue" pose was PRICELESS!

"You didn't think I'd let you go shopping without me did you Lemoya?" Lydian's voice laughed in my head.

My head snapped up and I looked for him. I scanned the crowd and my eyes landed on a group of girls standing outside a men's clothing store; all giggling and batting their eyes. Then I saw him inside the store buying a shirt.

"It looks like you have your pick of girls to bring to my party." I said. I turned and started walking away.

"Louanna! There you are, Happy Birthday!" I was snatched up from the floor and whirled around. "I have looked everywhere for you." Lydian held me in his arms, laughing.

"You're losing your fan club, Bright Guy. Put me down." I sighed.

"They mean nothing to me, Lemoya. I belong to you; I'm *your* pet to play with, Luv." He laughed, looked at the girls and winked at them. "What can I say? She keeps me on a short leash." He smiled at me and to spite myself I giggled.

"Looks like the pound is missing a flea circus." Lucy said as she and Mom joined us.

"That will be enough of that, Lucyenda. I asked him to come with us today." Mom said. "There was a disturbance last night and felt I needed the extra security . . . for us all." She looked around and said quietly, "Grundals would love to get their hands on any one of us."

"Somehow I don't think "Grundal" hands are what you should be concerned with as long as "Rover" over there has eyes for Lou**anna**." Lucy sneered.

I could feel energy gathering all around me but had no idea how to stop it; some True Weaver I am, Hugh?

"I said that is enough Lucyenda Nicole! Lykie, would you be so kind as to escort our birthday girl to the food court, some of her friends are waiting for her there." Mom had apparently had enough of Lucy's snippy attitude.

"Yes M' Lady and I would ask that you call me Lydian when I look umm, like this." He gestured to himself.

"Very smart, it could have gotten a tad confusing otherwise." She whispered.

"Thank you M' Lady." He said quietly

"Leona, just plain ole Leona." She said smiling at him.

He took her hand and kissed the back of it. "As you wish, Leona."

I cannot tell you the number of female shoppers who; after passing us, suddenly *had* to shop in the direction of the food court.

"Much to do about, Back off!!!"

"You think the cutest things, Lemoya. We've been through this before, I'm your-'

"**FRIEND!**" I blurted "We are in public, here on good ole planet earth and yes, we are *friends*"

"As you wish . . . friend." Was all he said.

I could have been wrong; I am quite often here lately, but Lydian looked hurt at being called a friend.

"Buds then?" I asked and jammed my shoulder into him in a playful gesture.

"Whatever pleases you, Louanna? I am yours to command." He smiled.

I melted at the smile on his face. His smile widened and he turned his head. This Vulcan mind thingy has more downs than ups. (And even the downs are pretty darn good)

As we came around the corner my heart lightened; I saw the Farmers "tag team arm wrestling" DJ. They were both yanking and pulling on one of DJ's arms with all their might. With his free hand DJ was eating a huge slice of pizza.

Several passersby stopped and cheered while others looked at them with distaste and moved on. Pixie sat across from DJ pretending to be unimpressed. Squeaks sat with her nose deep in a book but was still peeking around and giggling at their shenanigans.

Leah sat looking in a compact at the new shiner she was sporting. No doubt, her step dad Larry had come in drunk or wasted and decided that she had done something wrong. It wasn't the first time she'd come around us with a new "trophy" as she called them. It was an unspoken rule among us that I was the only one who could ask about what had happened when Leah had been hurt.

As we walked closer I could see the look of anger and humiliation as she mumbled her silent disgrace to her reflection in the tiny compact. That's just how Leah has always handled things. She never really lashed out at Larry but would tell her reflection what she "should" have said to him.

When she saw me her expression instantly changed. She put the compact away and smiled. I whistled low. "Shoulda seen the other guy?" I joked.

"Shoot, you better know it girlie head." She laughed.

"What happened this time Leah?" I walked over and we sat down just out of ear shot from the others.

"Same ole, same ole; one of Larry's friends thought that "Get out of my room" meant "Come on in and let's get to know each other better.". When I told "Dear ole Dad" he called me a dirty tease and belted me in the eye. I slept in the park, it was warm though. Did you see how full the moon was last night?" she asked, smiling.

"Why didn't you come by the house and sleep there? You know the guest room is always open to you. Or stay in my room if you don't mind my "sty." I sounded worried and she hates it when people sound like that about her.

"I came by, Chickadee. Ya had quite a big ordeal going on in your back yard. I just figured I'd chill at the park 'til it was over and I wound up falling asleep." She looked at me then at Lydian; raised here eyebrow and said "And just who is Mr. Hunky there?" she stepped around me and held out her hand. "Leah Armstrong and you are . . . ?"

I laughed as the rest of my buds all gathered around to "Inspect" the newcomer.

"Guys," I giggled "This is Lykie, only I call him Lydian when he's all . . . dressed up like this."

They just stared at us, mouths agape. I'm sure that I had the same look on my face when I first saw "Mr. Hunky."

"You think the most adorable thoughts, Louanna." He said cheerfully then kissed the back of Leah's hand. "Lou disapproves of this form, she gripes at me endlessly that I have no shirt on." His smile was bright and when he moved his head quickly to flick the hair out of his dreamy eyes, Leah, Squeaks, Pixie, me, and about a dozen females who were standing around all did the nervous girly giggle. Lydian simply smiled and introduced himself to the rest of my buds.

"I'd gripe if he had a shirt on! All though that polo he's wearing looks just fine if ya ask me." Leah whispered to me and we broke into a fit of giggles.

"So," DJ began, "How'd it feel to sleep outside last night? I'm sure Ms. Leona didn't allow… *you*, to sleep in Lou's room with her." He grinned at me like a baboon.

"I am her guardian, Leona has no reason to keep me from Louanna, and I would give my life protecting her so that no harm can ever befall her. We are . . . buds."

I could tell that the statement hurt his pride. Guardians held a certain degree of prestige; being downgraded to the rank of "Buds" had to be a humiliation on some level. I felt bad and didn't know how to make it better. He deserved honor; It seemed like I was ashamed and **I'm not**. He isn't from here; this time and place, and people here just wouldn't understand.

"Lemoya, I know your heart; it has been open to me and is filled with love, honor, and devotion. I know what we are."

Vulcan mind thingy = BLUSH

"So . . ." Pixie grinned as she spoke "Do all the T-Weaves get a . . ."bud" like you or is it only the head T-Weave that has that honor?"

"M' Lady, as much as it would please me to say yes, I'm afraid that it is only the head "T-Weave" that has my particular kind of "bud" but as her comrades I will be at your disposal should there be a need." He smiled and kissed the back of her hand in his old worldly manner.

These are my buds, friends, companions and my own band of T-Weaves, I love each and every one of them, I'd fight to the death for any one of them; So why does it set my teeth on edge to see him kissing the back of their hands? (I'm so petty!) I felt the familiar popping in the air and the kiss of a breeze that shouldn't be indoors.

Everyone stopped joking and turned to look at me, how humiliating!!!!!

"Did you get your hair done for your birthday Lou?" Squeaks asked, taking my hand and bringing me back to reality.

I took a deep calming breath and smiled. "You could say that, Squeaks. When I had the other *"party"* and got my birthday **gifts** and Lydian," I winked "My hair sorta got zapped to look like my Jequota, cool Hugh?" I flipped my hair and laughed.

"Not as cool as the new tattoo you're sporting," Andee whistled low and brushed my hair away from my neck. (I could swear that Lydian growled)

"Oh, that . . ." I stepped away, replacing my hair. "We'll talk about that at another place and time." Nothing more had to be said my Buds accepted what the unspoken part meant.

We walked over the entire mall; going in and out of stores, laughing and having a good time. (It felt good to be normal again.)

"I have to ask, what is the gnome fetish all the stores seem to have?" DJ said picking Kon up and flipping him over to inspect the workmanship. "My Grammy loves these ugly lil buggers."

I burst out laughing. "They are not ugly, DJ!" I said between gasps for air. "You could hurt their feelings saying things like that about them, ya know."

"The fact that they are ugly is probably not a surprise to them. I'm sure they know they could all belong to the lollipop guild and are uug-ly!" he laughed and replaced Kon on the shelf.

I looked over my shoulder as we left the store as Kon made a universal rude sign to DJ; and I laughed.

Lydian was very polite to everyone, speaking and laughing, but he was keeping a distance between himself and the girls. I should feel guilty, maybe . . . do I? _{No.}

"Feel no guilt, Lemoya the path I chose is of my own volition. Your happiness; as well as your safety and wellbeing, are important to me. I serve you." He gave that cocked half grin that, (darn his hide) he knew melted my heart.

"Your heart, Lemoya?"

"Vulcan mind thingy isn't fair ya know." I rammed my shoulder into his side again

We continued to shop and enjoy the day, the girls eventually banned me from going into a store and I was placed under "Bud arrest" so they could shop for birthday gifts.

"So, I take it you have a thing for our Lou here." DJ said, drawing Lydian's immediate attention.

"I am her protector; I am hers to command. Why do you ask?" Lydian asked, looking around the store; scanning for danger, always on alert.

"Well ya have to know that the rest of the roosters would get nervous when a new cock came strutting around the hen house." He wiggled his eyebrows at his crude description.

"Your meaning eludes me, Devaine; are you threatened by a rooster or some other form of poultry you need my assistance with?" Lydian's voice held humor and mischief.

"Naaaw, Man!" DJ said and slapped Lydian on the back. "A guy just needs to know where he stands in a pack; you're a good looking guy, or so I've heard, I just don't want any competition. My girl, Dixie," He leaned in and in a *conspiracy* tone whispered. "She's in denial about her feelings for me; I don't need the complication."

"I see, but you have no reason to fear; this *"rooster"* has eyes for one hen." Lydian didn't look my way and I was grateful because I could feel the heat in my cheeks.

DJ smiled mischievously and gave Lydian a high five. (Guys are so predictable!)

SPLAT!!!

DJ was hit in the right temple with a very juicy spit wad. Pixie had apparently caught some or all of their, "Dixie is mine" conversation. She had wadded up her straw wrapper and delivered the tiny missile with deadly accuracy.

"AWWW! Come on, Dix, you said you'd stop doing that crap!" DJ whined as he wiped off the moist debris.

"I'm not sure what all "that" was about or what exactly was said just now, but I'm sure you deserve more than a spit wad." She laughed and punched him in the chest.

He couldn't feel it but acted very dramatic like she'd wounded him. (They are so cute together) He picked her up and twirled her around and called her a "mean ole brute"

"Ahh, youth." Came Lucy's cold voice.

"Ahh, high and mighty." Leah's retort was quick in coming. "How's it feel to just be the older sister to someone as extraordinary as our Lou here?"

Lucy's jaw twitched in a show of agitation but she did not comment. My buds had all gone on instant alert and were standing around us; if Leah needed back up . . . it was near.

She looked at Leah then sneered, "What happened? Run your smart little trap to the wrong person and they give you a much needed lesson in manners? Lucy's voice dripped with venom as she spoke.

The air around us grew cold . . . It seemed Lucy had some skills of her own.

"Back off Lucy **enda** or you'll get firsthand knowledge of what it would be like to try to teach me a lesson in manners!" Leah's voice was low and lethal.

Lydian stepped between them and placed a calming hand on Leah. He turned to Lucy in question and asked, "What is the reason for your visit, Ms. Lucy?" He spoke politely but there was a snap to his words.

"Down Boy!" Lucy stepped back from us. "I *assure* you, I do not enjoy being seen around Lou**anna**'s "flea infested" primates; no pun intended." She smiled and batted her eyes in an attempt to look innocent. "Mom sent me to umm, *fetch*, her and her *pet*."

"Stop it Luc! Why do you have to be so . . . so . . . so **mean**?" I yelled in her face.

"Tut . . . Tut . . . Louanna, you can't show your special "*gifts*" here. What would all these people think?" Lucy sneered.

Oh how I wanted to slap that smirk right off of her smug little face! No sooner had the thought formed in my head than I heard the audible sound of skin being struck. I saw Lucy's head jerk sideways from the invisible blow.

She slowly turned her face around to glare at me; an imprint of a hand was already visible.

"Nice" Was all she said, and then she turned and stormed off.

"HOLY CRAP, LOU!" The Farmers said in unison, mimicking slapping each other.

"How did you do that? I'd love to have that skill." Leah laughed.

"I don't know how that happened. I don't know what it was." I mumbled with confusion.

Through The Looking Glass

Ok . . . so the ride home was interesting; to say the least. Mom gave lecture after lecture one following the other; I have got to get control . . . Keep my emotions in check . . . watch out for things that cause strong feelings . . . Yada . . . Yada . . . Yada . . . like anything she could possibly say would or could make me feel any worse than I already did.

"Are you even listening to me, Louanna Marie Teelf?"

***CRAP**!! My full name plus Mom being upset = I'm waaaaay deep down the 'trouble' hole!

"Yes ma'am I am. I told you, I don't know what happened." It was the truth; I had absolutely no earthly idea what I had just done or how I'd done it.

Lucy gave a disgruntled sniff and rubbed her jaw. Normally I'd have something snotty to say about her being overdramatic but I could still see the outline of a hand print so I kept my snide comment to myself.

"I'm sorry Luc; I swear I didn't mean to do anything to you. I don't know how I did that!" I felt just awful. I hated what she was saying and how she was acting but I'd never really strike anyone; least of all my only sister!

I spent the entire ride dishing out; "I'm sorry" . . . "yes, Ma'am" . . . and several other forms of groveling. It would not be so confusing if I knew what had happened but the mystery of the slap to Lucy's face just made it worst. If it happened once and I couldn't control it; what's to say I wouldn't do it again to someone outside my family!!

I sat on my bed . . . thinking. How can the plain life of a plain girl get so plain out of control in such a short time; and to me of all people! I am not the True Weaver; this has to be a nightmare of some kind. Maybe this is a prank! Yeah! That has to be it. All of my friends and family had gotten together and were playing a (really sick) birthday prank on me. I laid back and closed my eyes; I just needed to get away from the mess that my life had become and a nap seemed as good of a way as any at the moment.

I heard birds singing and felt the sun's warm kiss on my skin. Opening my eyes I found myself once again in Xela. I closed my eyes and breathed in deeply, savoring that I was, even for a moment, away from my crazy life and all the True Weaver madness.

"You cannot get away from what you are my luv." Papa's voice brushed across me like a summer breeze.

"Papa, I don't even know what's real anymore." I whined, sounding much like a small child even to myself.

Papa's handsome face appeared in front of me. He sat down in the soft grass beside me and began to mindlessly pluck at the blades growing there.

"What am I supposed to do Papa?"

"You are to be Louanna Marie Teelf. There is no other answer to that, Lemoya." He smiled at me.

"Everyone wants me to be this magical "True Weaver" thing and I can't even get being Lou right let alone all the other." I plucked at the grass "I have all this magic junk falling on me and then there's me and Lucy; we can't even talk without it ending up in a huge argument anymore. I slapped her today." I said the last part quietly. He stopped and looked at me. "Not "slap" slapped her; I just kind of thought I'd like to slap her and an invisible hand did!! It even left a hand print."

"What made you believe you did it Lemoya?"

"Who else would have? I had just barely gotten the thought in my head when it happened. I heard the slap and saw her head turn just like it would have if a real hand had slapped her." I felt like crying.

The sky began to cloud up and tiny drops of rain started to fall.

"Your sadness has brought us rain Mia noja. Rain is good; it brings us life and helps things grow." He smiled and got to his feet. "Walk with me." he leaned down and took my hand and pulled me into a grizzle hug. "That was overdue." He laughed and we began to walk.

"What do you know about Adnama, Papa?"

"The more pressing question is what do you know of her?"

I thought about it, I didn't know much of anything anymore. "Why would Adnama choose someone like me for this; someone who . . . does not want to be a True Weaver?" I felt like such a coward.

"Adnama sees in you the flower that will someday bloom. A tiny seed does not believe that one day it will stand as a mighty oak; it only sees the tiny shell to which it is born." He stopped and picked a daisy and placed it behind my ear.

"You make everything sound so . . . right Papa. Why can't you be the True Weaver? You have all the answers."

He laughed, "No, Little one, I do not have all the answers; only answers to things I know. I cannot be the True Weaver;

that is your job. I sense unspoken worries; what troubles you Mia Noja?"

"Well, for one, look at my hair, it changed when I got zapped with power; and then there's this." I moved my hair, reviling the tattoo. I heard Papa's intake of breath. He took several minutes to look at all the incurrent details.

"When did you discover this gift, Louanna?"

"At my Tresstel; when I wove a doorway or hole and found the Nivlem."

"I think I need to hear the whole story, Lemoya." He said "It sounds as if this Tresstel was quite an event."

For what seemed like hours we walked around the field in Xela and I told him everything. (Well, not the naked, shower, Lydian, and pink thong everything, but everything else)

"Much to do about, not going there with my Papa!"

At the end of the story we came up on a huge tree with a picnic table beneath it and we sat down. I waited for him to respond and hoped he could help me or just fix everything I had most defiantly messed up.

"It's obvious that Adnama has great plans for you Louanna. I am sorry to say that my help here will be quite limited. I do think I know of someone that will know the origins of the brand or tattoo you have. Your Lydian should appoint a trusted pawn to go to the white sorceress: Kaeli VonLunar." He scratched his head thoughtfully "She is the oldest and wisest ally we have.

The rain had stopped falling and a dazzling rainbow replaced it.

"Will Lydian know how to find this sorceress?"

He beamed a knowing smile at me and said, "I'm more than sure that your guardian will know of whom I speak and where to find her, mia noja. Speaking of your guardian, he is about to wake you. Go and believe in who you are as I most certainly do, I love you Lemoya."

"Louanna?" Lydian's strong voice sank deep into my dream state and brought me away from Xela, and Papa.

"Louanna, tis time to wake; your party is in under an hour's time. Is it your wish to sleep it away?" there was humor in his tone.

I opened my eyes and smiled at him. "We really have to work on the way you talk."

"My appearance . . . my dress . . . and now my speech; is there nothing about me that has met with thy approval, M' Lady?"

"Well, I do kinda like the way you laugh." I lied. I liked almost everything there was about him, I had loved Lykie for so long and seeing him as Lydian wasn't so hard to realize the same loving being stood there in either form.

"Much to do about, not telling him that!"

"My laugh?" he did that half grin-eyebrow raised thingy that he knew I adored then a full smile spread across his lips and he left my room.

"I'm never gonna live through all of this!" I mumbled to myself and got up to get ready for the party, my real sweet sixteen.

The backyard looked nothing like it had last night. Rows of colored lights, streamers, balloons, a DJ (Not the T-Weave DJ) tables, chairs, a stage for dancing, and a huge silver wall with water flowing down what looked like a twelve foot wide rainbow; colored spotlights aimed at it so the water changed colors every few minutes. It looked like the inside of a club! Well, what I've always thought a club would look like anyway.

The only thing that remained from last night was a few tiki torches placed around the food tables and the dance floor. Mom had gone all out it seemed. Lucy's sweet 16 was all princess stuff, like Lucy. This party just seemed to scream . . . ME!

My buds were the first to arrive. Mom put them on last minute work detail. The Farmers kept trying to wrestle around and Mom threatened to put them in "time out". The night was off to a great start.

The music was thumping and everyone was dancing when I left the dance floor to retrieve a cold soda from the cooler and catch my breath.

"Happy Birthday, Lou."

"Thanks." I said without knowledge of who had said it. I turned to see the face of my "well-wisher" and nearly dropped my drink. DeLainey Landon stood just behind me. "DeLainey, when did you get here?" I stammered.

"De" he mumbled "I just got here. Your mom is friends with my Aunt, she invited Me." he sounded so unsure of himself "If you don't want me here, I understand. I mean it's a party with your friends and we hardly know each other."

I just stared at him, at that stray clump of hair and those ice blue eyes. "No, I mean of course your welcome to stay. I would have invited you but I wasn't sure that this---"I gestured to the birthday sign, "would be your thing." I laughed

He smiled in return "I don't know many people; it's good to have a few I can hang with." He toed the ground nervously with his foot and looked around at the back yard. "I have a gift for you. I don't know if you'll like it though; it's something I made." He sounded shy and bashful about the gift.

"My Papa once said that a gift made by hand is a gift made with . . . thought, I'm sure I'll like it DeLainey." I didn't say "made with love" like Papa had actually said.

"Much to do about, not going there with Mr. Blue eyes!"

"De" he corrected . . . again. "I have it over there, if you're sure that you want it." He motioned to a secluded spot by the edge of the tree line; off in the shadows.

* . . . . . . No henky feeling . . . . . .*

"Ok, let's see this gift." I said and followed him to the spot he'd indicated.

He reached behind a bush and pulled out a large 10 X 13 sized neatly wrapped box. Sheepishly he looked down at the gift then handed it to me.

I took the package and looked at DeLainey. He tilted his head and chewed nervously on his lower lip. Slowly I tore away the wrapping and stared in awe as I stared back at myself. My face in immaculate detail on a sunny day with the wind blowing my hair was painted on a framed canvas. It was so realistic that I could almost feel the sun and breeze just by looking at the painting.

"It's... beautiful, De. You have such talented hands. You can actually see wind in the brush strokes, like you froze a moment in time and put it on the painting. "I meant it as a compliment but I think it startled him.

"I didn't stop time, I just stand in front of you in art; I see you in the sun. But if you don't want it . . ." he reached for the frame and grabbed my hand instead. We stood there; semi holding hands while some sappy romantic song played in the background. What does timing have against me!?

"NO! I want it--" I started but was quieted as his mouth settled over mine in a kiss. Yes, you read that right, smack on my lips, DeLainey Landon kissed me. It was my first boy/

girl not family or relation kiss and it happened on a magical night. All except for the low growling I heard coming from just beyond the trees. I jumped back from DeLainey so fast that he nearly fell over.

"What was that?" he asked

"The wind, I think." I lied "I need to get back to the party and the rest of my guest." I walked away so fast I felt like the road runner with a rocket on my rump. (Say that three times fast)

I got back to the food table and stood there, like the True Chicken I am. I mean, what's wrong with me!? DeLainey Landon . . . The **DeLainey Landon** had just given me a beautiful gift; he had put a lot of time and effort into it too. Then . . . THEN, he kissed me . . . at my sweet 16 birthday party . . . in the shadows . . . with a very slow love song playing in the background, how romantic is that? I should be somewhere giggling with my buds telling them about it or standing around holding his hand. (Give me a break; I'm new at this whole girl/boy thing.) Am I doing any of those things? . . . NO! Not Louanna Marie Teelf, I ran like a scalded chicken on "grill out" day. It's official; I just surpassed myself in spazizum. And that's saying something even for me!

"Did I offend you Lou?"

Great. . . . Hot lips must have followed me. I can't think straight when he's looking at me and I'm thinking about that kiss. His eyes gleamed and a half grin fell across his lips.

Why is it that a half grin on a hot guy only seems to make him even HOTTER??

He bit at his lower lip, trying to suppress a full smile. "No, De, it wasn't you," I said trying to sound casual "I was just trying to quiet my growling tummy." I picked up a slice of pineapple and bit into it. "Mmmmm, much better" I lied.

"Would you like to dance?" he held out his hand and took mine, leading me to the dance floor. I fell into those "ice blues" and just followed him like a hypnotized drone. All I could think was 'Sweet Adnama, please don't let me drool.'

The song was a slow ballad; he put one arm around me and drew me in close to him. The other hand held mine close to his chest. I could feel the beat of his heart and it was steady and strong. Mine seemed to be racing and erratic in its rhythm, like it was trying to send Morris-code to my brain. It was like time had stopped and all of the sudden I felt weightless. I looked down and was relieved to see both feet on the ground and not floating a foot in the air.

"I feel really comfortable around you Louanna. I don't usually feel that way around people; I always feel so out of place, especially in a crowd." He confessed.

I laughed "Why do I think you'd fit in anywhere?"

"Hardly, I don't really feel like I fit in anywhere or with anyone. You'd never understand that." He sighed.

"Don't bet on that, De. I think turning 16 made it even worst." I looked around the crowd and spotted Leah. She gave two thumbs up and winked at me. I simply went scarlet and finished the dance.

After the dance ended, I excused myself to the restroom to try to gather myself and see if I remembered how to breathe properly. My life was spiraling out of control way too fast for me.

I wanted to like De, I do like De. A girl'd have to be Bonkers Gazoo not to like that guy! I should be happy; he said he feels comfortable around me. . . . Dag-gum it!! Why am I not happy? (Because of my magical talent of True spazizum?) I splashed cool water on my face, thinking that I do that a lot here lately. (Good thing I don't wear makeup.)

I sat on the side of the tub with my head in my hands, like the coward I found myself to be, listening to my party going on outside. I closed my eyes and sighed, everyone seemed to be having a good time. Mom had danced with some of my friends. Even Lucy hadn't made any snide or degrading remarks . . . So why did I have this chewing feeling at the edge of my senses? Like there was something, right out in the open that I just can't see.

I concentrated and called on Adnama for help.

Instantly I was drawn down into a dark room, the orange-red glow seemed brighter, more sinister; causing a feeling of foreboding to choke me. "I am the True Weaver," I thought "I can . . . No! I will do this!"

"Everything is going as planned." The male voice was eager.

"It's taking too long!" the female said in a whinny tone "I've had to sit back and watch her for far too long now! With her out of the way, and my powers growing stronger each day, we will have the active Jequota. It's my time to shine, I have waited long enough!"

"You know nothing of time." The male spat "Lisdom's Jequota was within my grasp, for not the interference of her guardian." His voice lowered and seemed oily and colder. "He took it from me, sealing it somewhere in the folds of time. There will be a penance paid for his actions. She chose her fate."

The voices faded. Once again I felt light headed. This carnival ride didn't even allow the thrills and chills, just the woozy feeling when I step off the ride. I tried to gain my bearings. I sighed and opened my eyes. The, now familiar, rainbow webs were fading and the wind was dying down. A gentle tap on the door was followed by Lydian's voice

"Lemoya?" he sounded concerned. "Are you ok? You are broadcasting stress little one."

"Come in, it's not locked. I'm afraid to lock doors anymore." I mumbled.

The door cracked open and he peeked in. "Are you . . . dressed?"

Despite the woozy feeling, I laughed. "It wouldn't matter, you've already seen me, all-nat-tural." I joked.

He looked around the bathroom then came in and shut the door.

"I, as well as others, felt the pull of energy." He sat down beside me, causing the room to seem smaller, (With less air) "I came straight to you. I feel an uneasiness in you Lemoya, would you like to talk with your . . . umm bud about it?" he asked.

"You're more than that to me."

"Yes, I am also your guardian . . . and your K9."

"Please don't say it like that; it's not what I meant. You know this is all new to me; you've had a lot of time to come to terms with this, me? . . . Not so much. But I know you're not a pet." I wasn't sure how I felt about Lydian, but I knew he was more than just my faithful dog Lykie.

He smiled at me and took a runaway band of hair and placed it behind my right ear. I wanted him to kiss me, how sick am I?

News flash: Girl turns 16 and becomes a girlie girl, film at 11:00

I had just been outside, dancing with DeLainey, talking with him, kissing him; and here I sit not ten minutes later hoping another guy will kiss me.

"You are broadcasting your thoughts, Lemoya. It makes it hard for me to be honorable."

Oh yeah . . . Vulcan mind thingy, CRAP!!!! "I'm sorry; I guess I need to censor my thoughts." It was all I could think of to say.

"You have no reason to feel anguish, I'd love to oblige you and grant a kiss. However I feel that you may wish to be elsewhere, perhaps with another."

"What!? No! I! What!?" I had suddenly adopted a very dysfunctional way of speech.

"Did I speak out of line? I am sorry. I saw you receive your gift and then your kiss from that young suitor."

Was I wrong or did I detect a hint of jealousy in his tone? . . . Naa!! He is a Lydian guardian, he doesn't want . . . Me! Look at him for Adnama's sake he's a 'Dream boat'

"You always have the silliest thoughts running around in that little cranium of yours Lemoya. Any guardian would leap at the chance to be yours." He stood up and ran his hand through his hair in frustration. "For twelve years I have watched you grow, seen the light inside you brighten and strengthen as you did so." He began pacing back and forth. "Each day I prayed to Adnama that you be the True Weaver so I did not have to return to the search for her. I knew in my soul that you were the one." He stopped pacing and turned to face me.

"I'm not special Lydian. The fact that I have these 'powers' does not change who and what I was before, just Louanna." I stood and walked over to his side "Look beyond the True Weaver stuff, all you'll see is a 16 year old girl, nothing special."

"We will have to agree to disagree on this subject." He smiled at me. "What happened before, what caused the pull of energy to you?" he changed the subject, (Glad I'm not the only chicken)

I told him about the voices and the feeling I got when I heard them.

"The folds of time?" he mumbled "There were two voices; could you tell if they were the same ones as before?"

"I think it was, they sounded the same but then again I can't swear to it."

"Well, that gives me more to think about." He laughed "I need to get you back out to your party, come, and let's not keep your friends waiting." He took my hand and led me out to the party; still in full swing. Everyone was still dancing and having a good time I was grateful it seemed no one had even noticed me gone.

De came walking over to me, I felt Lydian stiffen but he released my hand and walked into the crowd, leaving me alone with De. I didn't know if I wanted to be left alone.

"You are never alone, Lemoya. I am always with you"

"Thank you" was all I could think of to say.

"I was starting to think I'd run you off from your own birthday party." De joked

"Not at all, didn't you know that girls always linger in the Salle de Baines?" I tried to sound casual

"Well, I'm not sure what that is but I'll take that as a good thing and be glad I didn't run you off."

We stood and talked for several more minutes. I was glad the music was fast and De hadn't asked me to dance again. I looked around the crowd and saw Lydian talking to Squeaks. He looked at me over her head. De was rambling on about different things associated with school.

Leah raised her eye brow at me and beamed a telling smile. I couldn't help the flood of heat that crawled across my face; settling in my cheeks. She went into the house with a" thumbs up" sign in my direction.

Life Weaver

De and I walked over to the rainbow water wall to look at the pretty colors and to toss in a coin. (Mom had made it a wishing well) I grabbed a coin and tossed it in; wishing I knew what I had to do as a True Weaver. DeLainey took his coin and looked at it but put it in his pocket. "I got my wish already." He smiled

I knew he was about to kiss me again but several things happened at that exact moment. My henky feeling hit me a millisecond before the silver behind the water wall took on a Jell-O quiver. A little man with red hair and eyes looked me in the eye and shot a dart from a wooden rod into my neck.

I felt the dart inter my skin just as the red eyed man smiled and disappeared.

Time froze.

Movement stopped.

Pain shot down through my body and I went to the ground. My vision grew blurry but I could hear sounds.

"What's going on?" DJ asked

"Why has everything froze but us?" Pixie's voice followed DJ's

"Who among you is the time bender?" Lydian's voice boomed. He had gotten to my side in a blur of speed. He wrapped his arms around me, holding me tight. "WHO?" He demanded, his body shaking. (Fear or anger?)

"I am." DeLainey's voice spoke quietly "I saw the dart at the last second and froze time to try and save her . . . I failed." He sounded sad.

"You're a freak like us." Andee laughed "So why are we not all . . ." he made a bad statue pose.

"I'm bending time around Louanna . . . and her friends." DeLainey said. He sounded bashful and ashamed of his power.

I heard gasps and then Kin and Kon as they came through their personal portal. I couldn't help but think I was glad I'd made that door for them. Now they could travel here without me having to open a door each time.

"My Lady, what has happened!?" Kin asked, sounding beyond concerned.

I tried to respond to him but found I had lost the ability to speak. Where there had been pain before, I found a dull numbness settling in.

"She must be taken into the Mystic Realm; the poison inside isn't from your time and place therefore it cannot be treated here." Kin gave a large sniff "I smell the stench of Grundal evil in the air" he whispered.

"I cannot open a door to which I can travel, Speritalz." There was a sharp sound in Lydian's voice. "I shall have to take her through the portal you arrived in."

"But Sire, the Lady Louanna spun a warning spell on the portal. Only we may travel by it." Kon sounded alarmed that Lydian had even suggested the portal.

"There will be danger to any who tries to access the door, Sire." Kin finished.

"Regardless of the danger, if Louanna isn't taken to Mystic Realm then we have most certainly lost her. The poison is working quickly in this time and place so we must do this with much haste." Lydian tightened his grip on me "Neither of you can lift her to carry her nor can you use magic in the portal. My taking her is the only answer; I am her guardian." Lydian's voice was like a whip.

My body began to convulse and jerk. Hands fell on my arms, legs, chest, and stomach. I felt my body fighting gravity as it tried to float up. The restraining hands were all that held me in place. My skin felt hot and it felt like I was going to explode into a million pieces.

"The poison is advancing. We have to move her now." Lydian barked out the order. He grabbed me tightly in his arms and headed for the rainbow waterfall.

Reunited

I could feel Lydian's heart pounding, he held me so tight. I thought that it was funny that I was going numb yet could feel his heartbeat, its rhythm matching that of mine. I knew I was slipping in and out of consciousness but was helpless to do anything about it.

"Wait!" Squeaks yelled "Where are you taking Louanna?" her voice was filled with fear and I wanted to comfort her.

I felt Lydian stop and turn in her direction. "Little one, Louanna has been poisoned" he spoke softly yet it was strained, clearly having trouble controlling the urge to just take off without explaining to her. "The poison is not from this world, not even from the realm to which we are in; if I do not take her through the portal to someone who can remove it we will have lost her. I would never take her from you. But she must go."

"But how will I know she is alright? I'm coming with you." She demanded.

I could feel the shift of my weight as he leaned down and kissed her on the top of her head. Straining my eyes I could see the crimson color of her hair and wished I could just hold her so she wasn't scared.

"I cannot allow you to do that, little one. It is dangerous to go through this portal; there has been a restriction on it." Lydian spoke gently.

"I can't live without her." Squeaks spoke so timidly that she sounded like a small child; lost and lonely. It broke my heart.

"I will not allow her to leave us, but I must take her where help can be given," he sighed, sounding unsure of the words he said.

"Can you still talk to us . . . like you do Lou?" DJ asked

"Telepathically" Squeaks interjected

"Yeah, telaphoneyly." DJ said trying to joke and lighten the mood.

"I will do my best to see to it that you all are kept informed, but I must leave now or risk losing her for good." He sent the message to all of my buds (our buds) then turned to enter the portal. Entering the portal felt like sticking my arm down into a nylon stocking; it was tight but still comfortable. As we entered the realm all of the pain and numbness seemed to ease. I heard someone screaming in pain; there was a snapping sound and then I was struck hard down the right side of my body then something slammed into my head. I tried to open my eyes but was unable to pry them open.

To my left I could hear something or someone whimpering very close to me. Trying to turn in the direction of the sound I realized I was on the ground, nothing had hit me . . . I had fallen, or was dropped.

"Lydian?" pain shot through my skull when I tried to use the Vulcan mind thingy. "**LYDIAN!**" I screamed. It felt like my brain had bolts of lightning striking it from every angle. Something trickled down from my nose and I could taste the coppery tinge of blood.

Gathering all the energy I had, I forced my eyes open. The pain was beyond words. The trickle of blood was now coming from my nose and ears as well.

My vision began to clear and I saw light. I squinted my eyes and saw the light was torches hanging on the wall. It looked like I was inside a large cave. My heart drummed loudly in my ears causing my vision to go fuzzy. I could make out the shape of Lykie, not Lydian, lying inches from me; blood was seeping from his muzzle making a puddle on the ground.

I needed to get to him, to make sure he was ok. The pain was still far too strong for me to move. I gathered my strength and tried to get up and the blackness closed in and took me under.

I knew I was in Xela but a thick fog seemed to have fallen over everything. I looked around but could only see a few feet away from me in any direction. I could no longer see the peaceful meadow that had been here before.

Wondering why I suddenly found myself in the spirit plane when I had just been at my birthday party with all of my friends.

"Back so soon, Mia noja?" Papa laughed; however, he looked worried.

"Papa," my voice sounded hoarse and scratchy. "Why is it so foggy and colorless here now?"

He hugged me tightly. "Louanna, you determine the stage of Xela. This is your own personal spirit plane, it is your doing angel."

"What's going on? I don't understand any of this Papa. I was just at my birthday party and then the next thing I knew I was here." My heart was pounding in my chest.

He looked at me with an intense stare, put his hands on both sides of my face, and looked deep in my eyes.

"Wonkot deeni tahwl aever eyesd nimym hguorht." His eyes seemed to glow as he spoke, words I didn't understand. He said them three times as he stared deeper into my eyes. I had the feeling of being sucked through a straw backwards.

Finally he blinked and the feeling stopped. "Louanna, you are not here by choice. Your spirit languishes in the other realm." He turned and looked around the field.

"I must have fallen asleep, Papa. My party must have been a real snooze fest if I fell asleep." I laughed. "I must be asleep on the john, I do that a lot."

"No Lemoya, you are not asleep." He looked at the tattoo on my back. "It is only your connection to Adnama that holds you to life." His voice sounded so grave it made me shiver.

"What are you talking about Papa? I'm asleep in the bathroom at my party. I guess I just wanted to see you on my special day, so I came to see you." I was feeling irrational and out of sorts, any excuse for being here had to be a good one.

"The words I spoke were simple but powerful. *Through my mind's eye reveal what I need to know.* Those simple words said backwards whilst I looked into your eyes, I saw what brought you here. I saw you being poisoned and falling unconscious then coming here." His words made me feel like a frightened child. "You must return to your body Louanna, you must fight to live." He started backing away into the fog; my heart ached to see him leave. "Go my angel; you must not give in. . . . GO!"

I didn't want to leave Papa. He was always the one thing to make me feel safe and strong. I missed him more than I could begin to explain. I wanted to do what he had told me to do. Closing my eyes to the pain, I whispered, "Good bye, Papa."

Sounds and smells became clear. I was somewhere warm. My body felt sore and battered. I moved my arm and moaned as the pain ran in every direction.

"My Lady" A soft voice spoke, "Bye the gifts of Adnama, you are at last awake."

I felt a cool cloth on my forehead and was instantly grateful to my unknown companion. Small hands stroked my hair and cooled my skin with the damp cloth.

Opening my eyes caused a wave of nausea to wash over me, rolling to my side I began to retch and heave. Every movement caused pain. Tears ran unattended down my face as I tried to fight off the relentless ache.

"There now, My Lady. You have been gone from us for many risings. I was feared you would not return to us." My blurry vision reviled a Speritalz, holding a goblet of water to my lips. I drank it greedily.

"Where am I?" I wasn't sure that it was me that had spoken. The voice I heard was dry and raspy. The only indication that it was me was the fact that when I spoke it felt like I'd swallowed a pack of razors.

"Many pardons, My Lady. You are in my Idnar, my home. We are in the Mystic planes of Voleer. I am ArDonna, a humble Speritalz.

I could see she wore a little green dress, dark green apron, and brown moccasins. Her green hat was flat and ruffled around the edge. Unlike Kin and Kon's hair which spiked up and out from under their pointed little hats; ArDonna's was long, straight and hung around her face and down her back, showing off her adorable face. The glow of her eyes was far less than the bright yellow of Kin and Kon's.

Feeling the water hydrate my mouth and throat I tested my voice again "Are you related to Kin and Kon?" I asked

ArDonna took the goblet to refill it. "I am not sure of your meaning My Lady." She handed me a full goblet of water. "Your manor of speech is unfamiliar to me." she said as she fluffed the pillow and gently pushed me back on it.

"Kin and Kon are two Speritalz that have helped me, I just wondered if you knew them." I smiled at her and drank more water. I could see confusion on her adorable little face and realized what I had done wrong.

"Much to do about, not using my head."

"I am sorry ArDonna, I believe their names are Leaf**kin** and Leaf**kon**, I gave them both nicknames." I laughed

"You are acquainted with Leafkin and Leafkon?" she smiled brightly "They are my elder twine."

"Elder twine?"

"Indeed. They entered life and were in the service of Adnama upon my conception and birth." She brought over a steaming bowl of something that smelled de-lich-ous! "You are no doubt famished . . . What is thy name, My Lady?"

Finding my manors had been shoved out the back door I regained them and reached to shake her hand. "I'm sorry, that's very rude of me. My name is Louanna, Louanna Marie Teelf, but please calls me Lou." I smiled

The bowl of food shattered on the floor as ArDonna bowed low and began mumbling apologies to me.

"Whoa, please don't bow to me." I began and tried to get up to help clean up the wasted food.

"True Weaver, I am most sorry. I did not know it was thee in my Idnar." She began to fiddle with her hair and dress "I must look affright" she continued to fuss over her appearance "I will put Zwingles in their dressings at cleaning day for this." She mumbled. She looked at the shattered bowl on the floor and I could see her hands began to shake. "Oh, True Weaver, your meal has been destroyed due to my carelessness. I have spoiled thy eating, please forgive me."

Reaching for the bowl fragments I was forced to squint as I saw the pieces vanish.

"No My Lady! The True Weaver must not clean a mess made by a fawn such as I."

I laughed and put my hand on her shoulder. "You're just as important as I am. I'm not any more important than you are. It was my fault that the food spilled; it's only fair that I help to clean it up."

She raised her head and looked at me, tears glistened in her eyes.

"True Weaver, you honor me."

"Please call me Lou, or Louanna, all of my friends do and I'd love to call you my friend."

"I could never speak so freely in your presence." Under her breath she mumbled "They will receive Zwingles this rising."

Laughing I asked, "What on earth are Zwingles?"

"I would never put them near you, True . . . Louanna" she corrected, as I raised my eyebrow to the 'True Weaver' reference. "Zwingles are small parasitic creatures that bite and suck blood from a host leaving large whelps of oozing soreness." She looked mischievous "Elder twine should have told me who they had brought. I may be but a wee fawn but I have the right to the knowledge of who I am attending."

"I'm no one special, believe me." The light headedness again swarmed over me. I leaned back and closed my eyes.

"Here, My Lady. Try to eat something." I opened my eyes to ArDonna's smiling face and another steaming bowl of food. "Please, eat. You have been under for many risings, Louanna." She smiled at saying my name

"I will eat if you will join me." I said and sat back up to take the bowl. "I'd enjoy my meal much better if I could eat it with my new friend."

"Of course, I'd be honored to sup with the True Weaver." She beamed and retrieved another bowl.

I enjoyed the stew. ArDonna said it was called 'Gnargle' after the cow-like animals it came from. It taste just like beef stew. Eating and moving around a bit made me feel ten times better.

Talking with ArDonna was surprisingly easy. Basically they live the same way we do, they just have different names for things and use magic or 'power' to do the things we do by hand. Ex: chores, cleaning, appearance, things like that. I didn't comment on the fact that slowly her hair, house, and clothes all became cleaner and more tidy when she 'casually' waved her hand in its direction. (Insert smiley face here.)

I really enjoyed my time with ArDonna but I felt like there was something missing; something I should remember . . .

"Much to do about, **Think Louanna!**"

I had been here for several 'risings' which I interpreted as days which would explain why I was so hungry and thirsty. With her help I managed to get up and move around in the cave. FYI: my body was not a fan of all that movement . . . no sir, not one little bit.

After a while, ArDonna left and I sat alone on the little bed, trying to sort out everything. My body wanted to curl up and sleep but my brain said this puzzle needed to be sorted out and put together. The pieces were there, all in plain sight, all I have to do is put them together. What would I be doing if I was at home in my room on my bed . . . ?

LYKIE!!!!!!!!!

"Lykie?" my head felt funny, and not the "ha ha" kind of funny that people enjoy.

"Lykie, *please* answer me. Where are you?"

There was still no answer. His silence sent a cold chill down my spine.

"Please Lykie, I **need** you boy! I'm scared . . ." again I was met with silence.

"Lydian!?" I screamed it. My head was pounding. He wouldn't just leave me; he had said it a hundred times, he was my guardian. What could have made him . . .?

Blood.

My vision blurred and my ears began to ring.

Pain . . . Blood . . . Cold . . . Alone.

I remembered.

My party, the kiss from DeLainey, The voices in my head, Lydian, the dart. It all came rushing back in a hurricane of emotions. Flashes of everything like a reel to reel movie that was skipping. I saw it all, ending with Lykie laying inches from me with blood coming out of his muzzle.

"Lykie, you said you'd never leave me!"

I gave in to the grief that was choking me, closed my eyes and cried for my lost friend. I don't know how long I lay there crying. My concept of time has been altered here lately. The pain was less than it was before in my body and knowing my friend was gone was hard to comprehend.

Movement brought me out of my stupor. I reached out for my 'spidey sense' but I felt no danger.

Opening my swollen eyes proved to be painful. My vision was still blurred from the tears. Looking around me I saw three sullen little faces staring at me. Kin Kon and ArDonna stood just inside the doorway, each pair of eyes looking as sad as I felt.

"Louanna . . . My Lady, your sadness can be felt for miles. What has you so distressed?" Kin spoke softly as he walked into the room.

I like these little people . . . things . . . you know what I mean. I'd never hurt them on *purpose* but my grief; compounded with the pain raking through my head, I snapped!

"Oh, I don't know. Let's see, shall we?" my voice was shaky and with my emotions, I felt so raw making me feel venerable. "1, where am I?... 2, How did I get here?... 3, How long have I been here?... 4, Where are all of my friends and family?... 5, Where is my guardian? Do I really need to go on?"

Yep! I'd done it again. My hair was all 'floaty' around my head from the wind blowing; I was floating in the air about a foot from the ground and the little rainbow webs were gathering around me. There was a warm-tingling sensation in my neck and back that made me calm down.

"My Lady," ArDonna gasped "Your markings, they are changing."

I craned my head around and looked down my back. There was a bluish glow emanating from the vine tattoo as it grew and spread.

Great, as if I didn't have enough to worry about, now I look like a human disco ball in a biker bar.

"Much to do about, when will this end?"

"Lou," Kon said with his usual smile and twinkling eyes. "You are in the Mystic realm, where we," he gestured to the three of them "are from. You got here through the portal you wove for us. . You have been here for, I believe you call them days, and there have been four. You were brought here because a Grundal poisoned you at your aging celebration. And lastly, your guardian is in the next cell." He beamed at me.

"Cell? He is a prisoner? Are we being held captive here?" I could hardly breathe.

"No Lady Louanna, his cell tis as yours. He is well kept and cared for. We honor all Lydians, he is no prisoner." ArDonna smiled weakly.

"Show me where he is." I stood and walked to the door. I could feel the bile in my throat. "I need to see him. . . . Please!?"

"As you wish, My Lady."

Kin led the way out the door and down a narrow hallway. Torches hung along walls throwing a soft glow over the area. We had only moved down the wall a short way when Kin stopped, bowed and pointed to a closed door. My heart pounded so hard I was sure that everyone could hear it.

The room was dark, a lone candle burned across the room throwing an eerie feel in its wake. The bed remained made, a plate of uneaten food sat on a small table, seemingly forgotten.

"Lykie?" I whispered.

I looked around for any sign of him. I closed the door and waited for him.

"Lykie, come on boy. I know you're here; why won't you talk to me?"

There was a feeling that suddenly crept into the room. A sorrow or . . . a sadness. It wasn't mine but it was just as real. I followed the ebb of energy coming from the sadness and I found Lykie. He lay in the corner, curled up on the cold floor. He didn't look up when I got close to him but I could tell by his breathing that he knew I was there.

"Lykie, I know you can hear me." I wanted to snatch him up and hold him . . . or shake him; I'm not sure which one. "Why won't you even look at me?"

He only lay there, dead still, refusing to even acknowledge I was there.

Now he's just ticking me off!

"What!?" I snapped "Everything you said . . . all that . . . that . . . bull hockey you said about honor, loyalty and . . . and . . . and . . . all that other stuff I can't remember now, was all just lies? You said you waited over two thousand years to meet me and now you won't even speak to me; or look at me for that matter." I felt furious. (Insert mad face here.)

Lykie moved, just his head. He turned and looked at me, he looked tired and worn. The fur beneath his eyes was wet and soaked with tears.

"I do not deserve to gaze upon you, True Weaver." He sounded frail.

"We're back to this *'True Weaver'* crap again I see. I thought we were beyond that, Lykie."

"You *are* the True Weaver. Had I not been lax in my duties to you, perhaps the danger that befell you would not have occurred and nearly taken you from us." He sighed "I am not worthy to call myself the guardian to you. I acted like a pup, a whelp. Not like the alpha I need to be as guardian to the True Weaver. It is my duty to you and I did not uphold the honor of that title."

"Big Deal!" I snapped "So you made a mistake. Gee, does that mean you are NORMAL!? Everything in nature is capable of making a mistake, Lykie. You are **no** exception!! And while I'm ranting, how are you talking to me and not pulling the Vulcan mind *zap* on me?"

"I'm from the mystic realm; I can speak in either way here. It is only in the Earth realm that speech is prohibited in ***dog*** form."

"You. Are. Not. A. D O G!!! I hissed it through my gritted teeth.

"I'm not a proper guardian!" he threw it back at me.

"You *are* a guardian, you are **my** guardian!"

"The True Weaver deserves an alpha . . . The Alpha guardian! You had your powers less than one full human day and I let you get attacked by a Grundal!!" He turned his head away.

"Somehow I doubt that you 'let' me get attacked. Nor do I think you didn't do everything in your power to help me after it happened. They caught us with our pants down, that's all. We know now that they are on to us and we will be better prepared."

"Had I been doing my job and not acting like a pup because a male had gotten near you, rubbed his scent all over you; I could have prevented this." He stood up, obviously not having done so in days, he winced at the motion. "They almost took you, Louanna. I just found you and nearly lost you the day of your Tresstel."

A male getting near me . . . rubbing his scent on me . . . Lykie was jealous of De!? OMG! That's the problem? He's mad at himself for feeling jealous!

"You have been in my life for a long time; we have been through a lot of stuff together. You've been my one true friend for as long as I can remember."

He turned and looked at me, "Yes, we are buds."

'Yes, you and I are buds . . . but I feel differently for Lydian. I know that you are the same person . . . being . . . you know what I mean, but he is just . . . different. I am human, Lykie. My brain thinks in human terms. I see you as my life long pet, my pal! I see Lydian as an eighteen or nineteen year old hottie. What can I say, I'm a sixteen year old girl." I joked.

I saw the tip of his tail move as he wagged it. "I assure you Louanna; Lydian is nowhere near an eight-nineteen year old. And he knew to do the job he was honor bound to do."

"I'd like to see him though, I miss his smiling face; just don't tell him though. He'd get a big head and we don't need that." I joked.

"Alas, you ask of me the one thing I can no longer give to you Mia noja."(Now he's gonna call me my love!?)

"And just what might that be?" I asked and scratched his head for comfort.

"That you wish to see Lydian." He sighed and looked at the floor "I can no longer shift."

A Quest Begins

How many times can a person's heart stop, skip, or stutter before you die? With the way my stinking heart keeps sulking up I believe I may be nearing my quota. Here's hoping a heart's beats aren't like the lives of a cat, I'm *waaaaay* past **9** lives on this ticker.

"You can shift, Silly. I've seen you do it; so make with the breaking twigs sound and do what you do to be tall dark and aggravating." I laughed. I reached for the abandoned plate but Lykie stopped me by putting his paw on my arm.

"No Lou, I can no longer shift. It was the sacrifice for entering a portal not meant to be used by me. My 'True Pain' was to have my shifting ability taken from me and to be locked in this form once more."

I felt numb . . .

I had done this. . .

I am the one who opened that door. . .

I am the one who cast that spell. . .

I am the reason Lydian had to go through that door . . .

I had done **all** of this!!!!!!

"Do not think such things, Lemoya. I would give my life for you. It is not you doing that that has brought me here. I am responsible for the deeds I have done and my choices are my own to have made. Never take the blame for someone else's choices."

A soft knock on the door reminded me that we were not alone. "My Lady, are you in need of anything?" ArDonna's soft voice came through the closed door. She opened it and peeked in. three sets of eyes gazed in at us.

"I'm fine ArDonna. Thank you." I looked back at Lykie, hating the sadness I found in his eyes. "Is there any way to fix this, a spell or potion; maybe a magic frog you have to dance with?" I joked.

"I do not know of a spell or potion; however, it would do me no good to find a frog, for I do not know how to dance." For the first time since we had begun to talk, it felt like the tension had eased in the room.

"Well, all jokes aside; there has to be something to fix it. A spell did this, maybe a spell can **un**-do it."

"I do not know, Lemoya. I fear that this is just how it is meant to be." He whispered the last part, as if saying it out loud somehow made it more real.

"Perhaps not, My Lady." Kin said

"What do you mean, Kin?" I motioned them on into the room.

"There is the white sorceress, Kaeli VonLunar; she is the oldest and wisest being in this realm. We were to seek her knowledge regarding the brand you wear on your back." Kin pushed up his glasses and looked at Lykie. "If there is a way to restore you to the alpha status you hold and were born to be, then she may be our best hope for answers."

"Kin, I could just kiss you." I said

He instantly turned every known shade of red there is, and even a few light purple ones then said, "My Lady, the things you say."

Everyone laughed, even Lykie. It felt good to laugh . . . it felt normal. And right now that was a feeling I welcomed with open arms. Now all we have to do is get a plan.

"Much to do about, it's about stinking time!"

We all agreed that Lykie should eat and then all meet in my cell (Umm, room.) to start strategizing. They all left Lykie to eat but I stayed behind to make sure he ate and drank plenty. ArDonna said he had done neither and I was determined that he would at least this one time get some food down.

It's so odd the things that trapes around in my little head. For instance; eating, we do it every day, often several times a day so it just struck me as strange that something like grief or sorrow can be so overwhelming that it would override the primal need to feed yourself.

Lykie had blamed himself for the chaos that my life had become. Yet none of this was his fault. I'm not even sure that it is my fault either. The way I see it is this; life is a new pair of nice shoes. And all of this Weaver 'flippity-doo' is a huge mud puddle I had just stepped in to up to my shins.

After he ate and drank we went to my room (I just can't say I went to my cell. Eww!) When the others got there we started to plan.

"Ok," I began "The way I see it, basically we need to get to this Kaeli Von What's Her Doodle. I get Kin and Kon to zap back to my room, bring Jequota and the two lil twigs; then Bippity Boppity Gazoo, I make a Jell-O door and poof . . . we're there."

There! I'd come up with a quick easy plan; flawless in design, if I do say so myself. We should have Lykie fixed, poison poofed, and tattoo riddle solved in under an hour. One clean neat little package.

"Much to do about, who's yo T-Weave?" (Smiley face)

They all four stared at me like I had broken into German or something. I had to fight off the urge to ask "Sprechen Sie Englisch?" but I didn't. Finally ArDonna spoke up. "My Lady, it may just be me, but I have Na a clue as to the meaning behind that speech." She blushed "I am a fawn; a mere thousand twelve, so please forgive my lack of knowledge."

Ok, at some point in my totally Bonkers Gazoo life people are gonna **have** to stop saying things like "I am a *mere* thousand twelve."! I think I just got my first grey hair! Geesh Lykie burst out laughing. (**Stupid Vulcan mind thingy!**) "Oh Lemoya, the thoughts that trudge around in that sweet little head of yours." He said causing the others to look at me in puzzlement "Louanna was just thinking that some of the things we say are hard for her to comprehend as well. What she said before was in the language of the youth in earth realm, simply this; Kin and Kon go through their portal to retrieve her Jequota and weaving wands. Then she would make a portal from here to," he paused and wiped his face to remove the 'ha-ha tears' from his eyes "Kaeli VonLunar's; aka Kaeli Von What's Her Doodle's" then he had another fit of laughter. Joined; much to my dismay, by the three little meanies!

"I guess I'm not getting the joke." I snipped.

"Only you would be so bold as to refer to the oldest wisest being in any known realm as 'What's Her Doodle'." Lykie jumped up on the bed beside me and licked my hand. I rolled my eyes at him, but still scratched his head.

"Well besides the 'What's her Doodle' part, I think it's a good plan. You'll be you again in no time. I said.

"Part of the plan is great, the retrieval of your things for starters. We will most defiantly need them." Lykie said.

I looked at Kin and Kon, "Ok guys, are you up to it?"

"Yes My Lady, as you wish." Kin was on his feet walking to the wall. "Leafkon, I think . . . here would be good."

The two Speritalz stood side by side and said, "Passage to the True Weaver's sleeping cell." There was movement on the wall. It looked like chocolate icing had been put on a hot cake and it was melting and running down the wall. Then; there was my room on the other side of the opening.

Note to self: I *really* do need to clean up that room.

"Maybe I should go and get what I need. I may see something I need to take that I haven't thought of." I started for the opening.

"NO!" came all four voices at once.

"Louanna, there is a spell on that portal. Only Kin and Kon can go through it." Lykie said

"Tis not safe, My Lady." Kin said, pushing up his glasses.

"Don't worry Lou; we will get the things you require. We will not fail thee." Kon said and blushed when I winked at him.

It felt strange being so close to my home and not being able to go there. All I could do was stand and watch my two little friends pop through the opening and into my room.

I walked back over to Lykie "You said 'part' of the plan was good; why just part of it?" I asked

"The White Sorceress will have many bearers in place. One can only reach the Castle of Winds by foot or air if you have a natural flying creature that doesn't require a spell. Magic will not serve you there." He said

"So I'll just open a door above her house and we'll 'drop' in on the old gal. Old folks love to have company." I laughed.

"No Lou that would still be within her boundaries and it would require magic. By foot or air is designed to take away the threat to her. She will still have her magic so any thought to harm her can be dealt with swiftly." He dropped his head. "And it is many a day's journey from here."

"**LOUANNA!!!!**" Mom's voice came like a fog horn. "Baby, I have been so worried about you." She looked like she had aged several years since I had seen her. "Come here, come home baby." She started for the opening and five voices yelled "**NO!!!!**"

We had to explain about the 'Kin and Kon only' door; what had happened to Lydian. Just thinking about it hurt and I couldn't look at Lykie when we said it; and the crusade we were about to embark on.

"Well young lady, you just take these weaving wands and open another door and get home this instant." She looked so worried and sounded out of character for herself.

"Much to do about, I'm tired of those I love hurting because of me."

Behind mom I could see rain hitting the window and in the distance behind me I could hear thunder rolling. Great, I'm making it rain in two planes now. (Sad face)

"Leona, I am afraid that for now Louanna must remain here, in the mystic planes. Though we have been able to slow the progress of the poison in her system; the herbs and roots grown here have been unable to remove the Grundal's poison. If she came back to your realm she would pass on to beyond Xela by night fall. Here . . . we have about a week." He turned and looked at me.

Have you ever said the phrase, 'Things can't get any worst"? Well, **THEY CAN!** And in my jacked up life, always seem to.

Mom gasped and looked at me. I raised my hands and shoulders in mock surrender; like I already knew this information.

"Louanna . . . baby," was all she could get out before she broke down and started to cry. Me? . . . I'm all cried out at the moment. My tear ducts were in over load and trying to recoup. I just hated seeing my mom cry when I was unable to at least console her.

I heard a small sniff behind me and turned to see ArDonna wipe away a tear. I guess it bothers everyone to see a mom so heart broken. I turned and hugged Lykie, he was the only connection to home I had. Many a night had passed since my fourth birthday when he was the comfort I needed. The nightmares seemed to lessen over the years.

I guess my silly childlike thought that Lykie was chasing away all the bad dreams wasn't so far off after all.

"We have a strong bond Lemoya. When a dream became troubled for you I could; for lack of a better phrase, 'chase' it away."

"Thanks Lykie. I always felt safe when I had you there. After Papa left us, (I never say **died** . . . hate the word!) the dreams would come at me hard. I don't know what I would have done without you there to make me feel safe."

I was glad for the Vulcan mind thingy; I didn't want everyone to hear everything. I had talked to Lykie so often before I knew he was *not-a-dog*, that it just seemed natural to do it now. Even like this.

Mom's sadness could be felt by me, even through the portal. I wondered how much damage it could do to just stick my hand through the opening and touch her. A low rumbling growl was my answer.

Kin and Kon were great with her. They patted her back, hugged her, got her tissues . . . I wanted to be the one to do that for her. This realm, spell, magic stuff stunk like last month's dirty dish water. If I'm this great and powerful 'Wizard of Weave'; I should be the one to comfort my own mom.

Mom finally pulled herself together enough to help Kin and Kon. She got my old camping backpack, put Jequota and the weaving wands in it then she flew around the room gathering clothes, shoes, socks, and even the Nivlem. I had to laugh as I watched her scurry around my room and every so often the word "sty" was mumbled.

After several minutes, mom carried the backpack to the edge of the opening. I could see the thought in her eyes, "It's just a step away." But we both knew better. There was more at stake than just stepping through that door.

"How will I know how she is? How are you going to manage to keep me updated?" she looked at Lykie

"The only sure way I have come up with is Xela. I believe there is a way that if need be, I can access your Xela and inform you. Magic will be no use to us in part of this journey; even this portal of Kin and Kon will not grant us access due to its magic but Xela isn't magic, it simply . . . is."

"I don't always remember my dreams." She confessed.

"You will know, Leona. Should there be a need, you will just feel it, you will remember if you are to know something."

"And remember the old saying Mom, "No news is good news." I joked

"Yes, I will only try to contact you if there is a need. I have to keep my focus on Louanna and the task at hand." He sounded so much like Lydian; my heart ached at his sacrifice, it was breaking my heart.

He looked at me; the knowledge in his eyes seemed endless. There was so much sadness here. Ok, maybe it wasn't 'my' fault per say, but it was partially my fault. Why did I have to put that 'loop hole' on the door? Showing off? I'm not sure why, Papa always said that "Everything happens for a reason" I'm not sure why Lydian would get his power to shift then have it taken from him so soon afterwards. It all seemed so wrong and was really stressing me out.

"I am sorry to cause you sadness, Lemoya."

"We **will** fix this Lyki . . . Lydian." I corrected myself. Lydian was still here, he wasn't gone for good. I won't let that be the case. Lykie had been a lifelong companion, he deserved to have the powers he was born with.

"I have faith Mia noja, we will reach our destination and find the cure . . . for both of us." He sighed. "I know you have the power that it will take to make this quest a success. You do not believe in your skills, but I do. You are the True Weaver and this is not an obstacle that will hinder you; to use one of your phrases, "We got this!" he laughed.

I hope so . . . . . .

It was beyond hilarious watching Kin and Kon drag that backpack through the portal. Even mom managed to laugh, the sound was refreshing. After "Doing it the earth realm way", Kin and Kon both looked at me with bright smiles at their accomplishment.

"Great job guys!" I praised their efforts then showed them how to give a high five; or in my case an 'around the middle' five.

Mom and I stood at the opening. We smiled at each other but both had silent tears flowing down our cheeks. I couldn't help but wonder if I would ever again see her beautiful face. I don't know exactly what she was thinking but flashes of me in my baby bed kept flashing in my head. I couldn't stand to see her cry any more. I didn't know what else to do and since the urge to leap through that foot of space between us was getting stronger I simply said "I love you Mom. I'll be home in a week." And waved my had to close the portal before she could respond.

I shut my eyes so the image of her would be there even when I knew she wasn't. A slight breeze blew from behind her the smell of fresh spring flowers surrounded me, I opened my eyes and stared at the blank wall in front of me.

"Much to do about, I miss my Mom." (Sad face)

It is so strange to think of the things we do every single day of our lives without thought of just how precious they truly are. A simple smile from a loved one or a visit from a friend should never go unappreciated. I made a vow to myself that once this was all over and I was back home where I belonged I would never take my life for granted. I would stop and smell the roses from time to time.

Knowing that Mom had just been there a few feet from me and that she knew I was semi-ok made my heart ache. I'm glad that she knew I was still alive but I knew she was worried and that made my heart pound inside my chest. There were so many people hurting because they were worried about me. Once this was over I would find a way to make it up to each of them.

Finding a Cure

No one spoke to me as I retrieved my backpack and mindlessly went through it. Mom's hands were just touching all of these things. This magic stuff was still hard for me to wrap my head around and times like this were making me resent having powers and magic.

I laughed to myself when I saw that Mom had packed in shampoo and other toiletries that a girl might need while off in a wilderness safari. (Even Chap Stick)

"I have a few questions." I said, addressing everyone. "One: am I a walking corpse?"

"My Lady, you are sick and like anyone sick, you need proper treatment or," ArDonna bowed her angelic little face, unable to look at me. "You will indeed pass on past Xela. Your shell is weakening from the poison and taking its toll on you. You will get weaker."

"Ok then, as for Q and A number one: **Yes**." I sighed. "Now number 2: if we can't use magic where we're going; is that going to include the Adnama stuff that I do without the weaving wands?" I felt smart asking all of these 'grown up' questions.

"That is an interesting question, Lemoya." Lykie answered. "We are not certain of the depth nor degree of your connection to Adnama therefore we cannot answer that question."

"Ok, Q and A number two: undetermined."

"Kaeli VonLunar should know, Lou." Kon said with a big grin. I winked at him and he instantly went scarlet in the face.

"Number three: can I bring my buds in on this? We are all human; or as close to human as a gang of freaks can be and we are used to doing things without magic so it may come in handy."

No one spoke, I felt a little apprehensive as they all just stared at me.

"I think that if they are willing to come along, it is a great idea. There may be things on this journey that will require their assistance." Lykie looked at me "Should you become unable to walk on your own, there would be someone to carry you."

"Well, since we are on a time table, I say we get started. The wind began to blow; I closed my eyes and felt my feet leave the ground. Knowing the rainbow webs were already gathering around me. I opened my mouth and heard the mysterious voice or voices emanating from my throat.

"Hear the words that I now speak.
My heart's true friends are who I seek.
My need is strong it cannot wait.
Open now a travel gate."

I opened my eyes and saw an opening in the space between and in the wall. I hadn't given much thought to a reflective surface when I started this; yet a portal floated in the air in front of me.

"My lady, your nose!" ArDonna came rushing over to me with a small towel. I felt the trickle and tasted the coppery tinge and knew that once again my nose was bleeding.

"LOU!!!" Dixie's voice sang out. I saw her smiling face followed by DJ, the Farmers, and my baby, Squeaks. I was swept up in a barrage of loving arms as one after the other each of my buds came through the portal.

I felt sane and whole once again. Looking at their faces I could see concern and genuine love. My life seemed complete when I had them in it.

"Much to do about, you don't know what you have until it's gone."

Squeaks clung to me. She was like a small child that had been away from its mom and was just getting to see her again. I held her close and never wanted to release her.

"I thought I'd never see you again." She said it so quietly that I almost didn't hear it. She made my heart melt.

When I was around Squeaks I could tell I had a strong maternal instinct; I'd hurt anyone that tried to harm her in any way. I leaned over and kissed the top of her little head. She moaned with delight when I squeezed her.

"I told you I'd never leave you baby." She looked so young. "You know I wouldn't just abandon you; any of you." My buds all smiled at me; they knew I would fight tooth and nail to stay with them.

"Besides," I went on, "You had Leah to fuss over you while I was gone." I looked around at my friends. "Where is she anyway?"

They all looked at each other then they turned and looked at me

"She's gone." Allen spoke up "That little guy came and got her right after you and Lydian went through the portal; he said you sent him for her. We thought she was with you."

"What do you mean, 'little guy', Allen?" Lykie asked, coming to a high degree of alertness.

"Whoa! You talk!? I thought you could only talk when you were tall dark and . . ."

"FOCUS!" Lykie snapped. "Little guy? . . . What exactly do you mean a little guy said Louanna sent him for Leah?"

"Yeah, he looked like them." He pointed at Kin and Kon. "Only his clothes were different." Allen said

"His hair and eyes were different too." Andee added.

My heart sank; instantly I knew that Leah had been taken by a Grundal.

Pixie must have picked up on my 'something's not right' vibe. "He said that Lydian knew him." She said, searching my expression. "He said to make sure that we remember his name and relay it to Lydian so he'd know that Leah was being properly taken care of. He called her by her name and when he called Lykie, Lydian, we didn't think anything of it." She took a nervous breath, looked at the Farmers then DJ "He said that he use to work with Lydian's brother and that his name was Logton. He wanted to make certain that we relayed the right name to Lydian."

At the sound of Logton's name all three Speritalz became restless and that 'jumpy alert' that people get when they are nervous. Kin and Kon both took up defensive positions beside ArDonna and the tension in the room became a tangible substance.

"He liked to smile." Squeaks said "he seemed . . .'overly' friendly, like he was really having to work at it. But Leah didn't hesitate; she just said if Lou needed her, she was there; and went through the opening he had made. None of us thought to question it; he seemed genuinely concerned and in a rush to get Leah to Lou as fast as possible."

"It didn't look like the one you make though, like this." DJ said and gestured to the open portal behind him. "The one he made was jagged and sharp looking, like a piece of ripped paper; yours are smooth and floaty, like space has just parted of its own choice." I liked the way he described mine vs. Logton's style of magic.

"When exactly did he take her?" Lykie asked.

"It was shortly after you took Lou through that other opening. It was hard to tell exactly how long though, DeLainey was still making everyone else play 'freeze tag' so time wasn't really moving." DJ made one of those body builder poses and froze, earning him a pop on the head from Pixie.

"Can you get serious muscle head?" she scolded.

"Come on Dix! Everyone looks like they needed a good laugh, even if it was a cheesy one. I'm only giving the public what they need." He flexed his muscles at her and she rolled her eyes but had a look that said she agreed with him.

"De said if we needed him all we have to do is say the word." Squeaks said "He was really worried when you left; we all were."

I could feel the weight of sadness on Lykie, he wouldn't look at me. I'm not sure he could look at me. He knew I blamed myself for this and I knew he blamed himself. Then add in the fact that my heart pounded at the mention of DeLainey and me knowing Lykie didn't care for him being close to me . . . it made a pretty interesting bowl of slime soup.

"I think having a time bender in the group would be a splendid idea." Kin said "How advanced are his skills, does anyone know?"

"He is well advanced." Lykie spoke up "It takes control and skill to bend time around things while freezing others. If he is willing; I think we should get him on board."

Excuse me? Big black not-a-dog who hates DeLainey says what?

Kin pushed up his glasses and took out his lil note pad "If you tell us where the young lad is, Leafkon and I will go and speak to him for you. If M' Lady Louanna is ok with that."

I could feel my heart taking its little jack hammer and pounding at the wall of my chest. Did I want DeLainey here? My mind jumped to the kiss at the party. (Sweaty palms enter stage left.) I wanted Lydian here too. I have Lykie but he's . . . Lykie and though he's not-a-dog Aaaaaaah, this is all too confusing!

"Much to do about, I hate being a teen age girl right now."

I didn't respond either way. DeLainey is a really nice guy. He has been nothing but nice to me so I have no reason to not want him to come to this 'journey'. Other than the attraction that I, (and any normal girl would) have to him. It was hard enough at my party when Lydian could shift now with him being trapped and unable to shift it was like kicking him when he's down to have someone around that he was not so fond of.

The image of a big foot kicking a dog was suddenly thrown in my mind. I looked at Lykie but he was in a conversation and acted like he hadn't put the image there. I sent the image of my foot kicking Lydian's shin . . . hard . . . back to him. He turned his head at me then and with his tongue hanging out, head turned sideways, and that one ear flopped down . . . he winked at me. Honestly! The male race eludes my train of thought.

After Squeaks told Kin and Kon how to get to where DeLainey was; they Bippity Boppity poofed through their portal to go and talk to him. If he agreed to come along, Kon would come back and I'd weave a door for him to come through.

"That reminds me," I started "I was so glad to see all of you then side tracked with Leah being gone, I forgot to tell you guys what's going on."

I sat down on the bed and told them the whole *long* story. "And before I finish," I went on "I want you to know that there will be 'NO' hard feelings if any or all of you decide to not join this little quest to find a cure."

"So, you're not cured?" Pixie asked

"We could still lose you?" DJ put his hand on Pixie's shoulder in comfort.

"Louanna has the necessary tonic to hold the poison at bay. But this will only last for about six more days." Lykie told them "The journey to the Castle of Winds isn't going to be easy. And unfortunately; every day that passes the poison will progress causing her health to digress, even with the tonic."

"So what I'm saying" I went on, feeling a lump in my throat "Is that, this is *my* quest. If you can't go or don't want to. . . I understand. I just wanted to give you the chance to make the choice on your own." I finished

"This crazy stuff is all really happening, isn't it Lou?" Andee asked quietly, all note of humor gone from his tone.

"Yes, I'm afraid it is." I looked at the ground, suddenly very interested in a rock that needed me to flick around with my toe.

The Farmers looked at each other. "We're in." they said together. "Just let us go back and get a few things." Allen said "I can say we're staying with DJ and he can say he's staying with us, that way there won't be a massive child hunt." He laughed

"Luckily my dad's outta town for the next couple of weeks." DJ said "No one'll be lookin' for 'yours truly'. I'd like to go and get some stuff too though."

"Ok then, everyone go back; if you can do this, be back to that spot in one hour. I will open a portal and the ones there can go with. If you are not there I'll know that for one reason or the other you are not going. I will shut the portal door then and those here will go on with us. "This is a one shot deal . . . once I close the gate, I won't open it again so be on time, ok? Make sure you want to do this 'cause once we go . . . we're all in, got it?"

"Got it." They all repeated.

After they all left I sat in thought. Time is such a fickle thing; it either crawls by and covers you in dirt. **Or** it jumps in a supped up GT Mustang, runs you over and covers you in dirt. Either way . . . ya end up covered in dirt.

"You look warn, M' Lady Louanna." ArDonna said. "Perhaps a nap before your journey would help. I have your tonic mixed in a warm drink; it will also help with the soreness." She was so cute. How anyone could resist that little face was beyond me. Her eyes looked too big for her face but were very expressional and made her just too cute for words.

"Ok, ArDonna. I do feel a bit tired, Thank You." I said and took the goblet. I inhaled the aroma, it smelled like blueberry tea. Taking a sip I savored the taste of the warm liquid as it slid down my throat, coating my churning stomach and easing my pounding temple, soothing my very essence.

"It taste like warm blueberry tea." I said taking another sip "What is it?"

"Dottle berry juice and leaves from the hopper tree, M' Lady. I heated the leaves in water, add the doddle berries and your tonic and let it set for a short time."

"Ha, it is blueberry tea; well dottle berry tea." I corrected.

I took another drink of the tea, feeling its warmth bleeding down each of my limbs. I felt relaxed and the soreness from before had slipped away. I looked down at the now empty goblet and realized I had drunk it all. Mom would be so proud of me for taking my medicine without kicking up a fuss, like I do at home. (If my meds at home taste like this . . . I'd not fuss, take it, do the all over body quiver, and say I hate it.)

"That tea is really good ArDonna Thanks. I already feel better."

She beamed at me. "I shall have plenty for you to take on your journey. Now lay back and get some rest, while you can." She was fussing over me like a little mother hen. I closed my eyes and smiled at her kindness.

Sleep was there with waiting arms. It wrapped me in a warm cocoon and I fell asleep.

The hallway was dark; there was a dampness that seemed to cling to everything.

"What if she doesn't come?" the female voice asked and for the first time sounded nervous and unsure.

"She will come. I have her friend. It will not be long until they discover that I have taken her." The male voice was clipped with anger. "If the poison doesn't kill her before she can attempt a rescue." Saying that seemed to give the voice pleasure.

"And what are your plans with her 'friend'? What are you going to do with her?" the female laughed nervously.

"It is interesting that you should ask that question, my dear." The male's voice seemed to be coated in tar, sticky and smothering. "We will need something to send to our beloved True Weaver so she knows how her 'bud' is being cared for."

Leah's screams filled the silence . . . choking me causing pain to my heart.

I sat up right in bed, gasping for air; sheen of sweat covered my skin.

"Leah" I whispered.

Lykie came bounding into the room, shackles raised and looking fierce. "Louanna, what is wrong? The pull of energy to you was suffocating." He said

"It's Leah. That voice I've been hearing . . ." I tried to center myself. "The orange light, the eerie feeling, it's been Logton all along. I just heard the two voices again. He said that I'd come for my friend. He said he would need something to send me so I'd know how 'well' she's being taken care of and the next thing I heard was Leah screaming."

I was crying again, deep hard sobs that seemed to be ripped from my very soul. My lungs burned from the lack of oxygen I couldn't seem to pull in air and my eyes seemed to be on permanent blur-vision… it was as if all of my body functions had forgotten how to properly maintain themselves.

"Leah is my best friend in the whole world. I've known her since *Kindergarten*. She has been abused and mistreated her entire life; now this happening to her because of me!"

I turned to the little bin by the bed and threw up. My heart was shattered in a million pieces. How can this be happening? I sat back on the bed and closed my eyes. Lykie put his head in my lap and licked my hand. "We will save her Lou, I promise that I will help you in every way that I can." he looked as heart broken and sad as I felt.

Leah was always the one to stick up for me, to come to my defense when there was trouble or a problem I couldn't get out of. Leah was probably the strongest person I knew. Even with all the heartache and abuse she had had to endure over the years, she always found a way to smile.

I couldn't imagine my life without her in it. Lykie was right… we were going to save her from that house of horrors she was in. She would walk through fire for me and I was going to repay her if it cost me my life!

Journey Begins

The hour had passed and it was time to get my buds; or see if any of them really did want to go on this 'thing' with me.

I closed my mind to the idea of going through this without them yet at the same time was terrified that they would go. I was putting them all in danger by even asking them to go with me. Knowing that there would be no stopping them from coming if they felt I needed them, I took a deep breath to calm myself then I began to weave the portal; feeling the wind blow around me and the rainbow webs gathering; feeling my feet touch ground, I let out the breath and opened my eyes.

Through the portal I saw the smiling faces of my buds beaming back at me. Kin and Kon stood by with DeLainey in tow as well. My heart jumped then stuttered, this was not a sleep away... this was life and death one way or the other. I took in each face; most of them were wearing camo and looked like they were going on a camping trip.

The only face I didn't see was Leah's. As happy as I am to see the rest of them; my heart was breaking for the one who was taken from me. Alone. Hurt. In pain. One way or another I will find her . . . I hope.

"Honey, I'm home!" DJ said as he entered the portal.

"Do we have to take the meathead?" Pixie asked and winked at me.

"Someone has to come along that can control the tornado known as 'Dixie' ya know!" Andee added, giving Allen a high five.

"I'm at my aunt's for the week." Squeaks said as she wrapped her arms around me in a big welcoming hug.

"We found him M' Lady!" Kin said pushing up his glasses.

"It was Lykie's idea to simply meet with the others so you had to open but one door." Kon said as they trudged through the open portal.

"Thanks for including me, Louanna." DeLainey said then hugged me. "I have been really worried about you." He moved a runaway band of hair from my eye and smiled. Looking in his dreamy eyes I could clearly see there was concern there. "I didn't know that you and your friends were like me."

"We're just people, just like everyone else" I found that I couldn't look away from his eyes, like he had me in a trance.

"Well, then I must be like you then." He laughed.

"No one is like our Lou." Lykie said "She's who our kind has waited for for over two thousand years."

"She's very special." DeLainey said and smiled as he joined the rest of the gang.

ArDonna came into the room where we all stood "Before you all embark on your quest; I have something for each of you." She said.

She took out a small wicker type basket and placed it on the table in the corner. We all gathered around her to see what she had brought. Squeaks held my hand refusing to put any space between us.

"I have woven each of you a conk vine protector." She reached in the basket and took out a small braid like band and held it up for each of us to see.

"Indeed this will be of great use." Kin beamed at his sister "Our minor fawn has given us a truly useful commodity. ArDonna, you have done well."

She looked at Kin and Kon and beamed a huge smile at them. Their approval must mean a great deal to her.

I picked up one of the braided bands ArDonna had made. "What are 'conk vine protectors'? Remember that most of us are not from this realm." I laughed and looked at the three Speritalz "They're really pretty ArDonna."

"Thank you, M' Lady." She took out a conk vine protector and gave one to each of us. "Would you like to explain these to them, Lydian Guardian? There are words and phrases that I would not know how to translate; it would most likely just confuse them instead of inform them." She looked shy at having to make request.

"Of course, M' Lady ArDonna, these will serve us well, and please call me Lykie when I am in this form."

"As you wish Sir Lykie."

Lykie shook his head but didn't comment on the 'sir' part. "Ok everyone, a conk vine is special in a lot of ways. For one: it glows in the dark. Not like the glowing bands you wear at the community gatherings such as Fairs, concerts, and such. A woven conk vine will be more like what you know as a spot light or a flash light."

"So we won't need flash lights? I packed some and extra batteries." Allen said

"I'd keep the flash lights, the conk vines will help them last longer. Another reason that they are good is . . ." he looked at ArDonna and she smiled. "If a conk vine is woven with a . . ." he stopped and tried to think of the right word to describe what he was trying to say. "A sister vine, they will talk to or call out each other." Lykie said

"Toy companies would love to get ahold of talking wrist bands." DJ mused.

"You got a copy on me, Buddy?" Andee said to his bare wrist

"10-4 there buddy I copy... cccc" Alan answered

"Cut it out you guys!" Dixie snapped.

"I'm sure they would, Devaine. But they are not going to talk per say. I guess the best way to tell you is to simply show you. Does everyone have their conk vine protector on?" Everyone tied the conk vines around their wrists

"You don't have one on, Lykie. Do you want me to tie one on for ya?" I asked him and felt bad that he had to have someone to do it for him.

"If you don't mind, Lemoya. Like a collar, around my neck please."

I leaned over and fastened the conk vine around his neck. Tight enough to not fall off but loose enough not to choke him when Lydian shifted back.

"Thank you for saying when and not if."

I hugged him then kissed his head and got to my feet.

"Now, first thing's first. Let's make the room dark. Put out all the torches and close the door." Lykie instructed.

Everyone scrambled around putting out candles and extinguishing all light sources. The instant the last drop of light was gone from the room it was instantly filled with a honey colored light.

ArDonna's smile was so bright and big that I had to hug her again and thank her.

"There is no need for thanks, M' Lady; I enjoy the craft and am pleased that they will be of use to you on your journey." She said

"Breaker one-nine, breaker one-nine, I need a 10-20 on a Smokey, anybody copy? Come back . . . ccccck" DJ was holding his wrist up to his mouth and talking into it like a trucker on a C.B. radio on one of those old '70 shows.

"Hey he stole our bit!" Andee whined

"Much to do about BOYS!"

Everyone laughed at their shenanigan, even Pixie gave him a reprieve on a head thump.

"I do wonder about that boy." Lykie said about DJ. Then turned to Squeaks "Would you like to help me?"

"If I can, yes."

"Take your thumb and rub your conk vine. Say 'I need help'. Walk over to the door before you do it, away from the others." He winked at her.

Squeaks went over to the door and turned to face Lykie. "Do I say it in any special way?" she didn't like being the center of attention and spoke so quietly you had to strain to hear her.

"No little one, just say it and rub the vine, it will be fine."

"I need help." She whispered and rubbed the vine.

Her conk vine began a slow flashing not unlike Morris code. All around the room the other vines started making a sound, like a low hum.

"Hold your conk vines away from the direction of Frankie and then aim them at her." Lykie instructed.

I held my wrist away from where Squeaks was. The vine seemed to grow quieter and the light seemed to dim. When I turned my arm back at Squeaks the light once again grew strong and the hum intensified when it was aimed at her exact location.

"These things are like 007 homing devices or something!" DJ mused

"In a way, yes, they are, DJ." Lykie said. "In order to 'turn off' the conk vine in need of help, someone with a sister vine simply has to touch the conk vine that is in need, like this." He walked over to Squeaks and rubbed his nose on her conk vine. All of the vines stilled and quieted and once again took on their honey colored glow lighting the room once again.

"Whoa! Look at this!!"

I turned to see what had gotten Andee's attention. I found both Farmers were M.I.A. once again. I saw a strange color in the air where I had just seen them standing; like a ripple on a lake at sunset. I wasn't sure if I was the only one who could see the color so I didn't mention it.

"These conk things make everything really clear and bright when we do this." Andee said "Can you see it; see where we are?"

"Not exactly 'see' you but I can sorta sense where you are though. There's a disturbance in the energy around you." I said

"I don't see anything." DJ groused.

"I don't either, just nothingness like always." Pixie added.

"I can't see anything either, Lou. Just hear their voices." Squeaks said quietly

"As the True Weaver, your powers will be stronger than the other's. Then when we add in the brand on your neck and back from Adnama; in this realm, there is no way to know the degree of your abilities." Lykie said

The Farmers 'popped' back into the room. Once again in their bad Charlie's Angels pose.

"You are so goofy. Don't you know that there were three angels? Ya need to have another person to do it right." Pixie laughed.

Life Weaver

DJ ran over and added his pose in with theirs. (It was truly sad how bad they looked trying to get that pose right.)

"Sorry to be the party pooper, but we are on a time table guys." Lykie said "Let's get everything packed and ready to get this journey under way." He looked at me, "We now have six days left."

At the mention of the 'time frame' the mood in the room changed. Everyone seemed to be avoiding eye contact with the 'condemned to die' person, aka me. Who could blame them? I mean what do you say to someone who only has six days to live?

Six days... I thought. How odd it was to be packing for a trip that I may not survive. This would prove to be no normal 'camp out' with my buds. There were no Smores or hot dogs where we were going and if all want as planed we'd come out the other end with me well, Lydian back, and Leah safe and sound; if not, dirt nap for yours truly...

I could already feel the changes in my body from the poison. My arms and legs felt heavy and hard to manage. I packed up everything in my back pack and 'suited up', trying to not show how each movement seemed to drain me of energy. Once I thought about how tired I was it seemed to intensify and make me even more sluggish. Like when you don't know you have to go to the bathroom until you stand up then you realize you have to go NOW!

"Where are we going, Lou? No one has really given us a real answer to that." DJ said as he slipped his back pack on.

"To the castle of winds to seek an audience with the white sorceress, Kaeli VonLunar. We are hoping that she will be able to give us answers to the poison in Lady Louanna and our Lydian guardian. She is the oldest and wisest of our allies." Kin informed as he donned his small green bed roll and checked his note pad like this was an everyday thing here.

DJ looked at me and raised his eye brow in puzzlement.

"What he said." I laughed "I'm just goin' with the flow, my friend."

"Well lead on and we shall 'flow' right along with you." DJ laughed and bowed as I walked past him. An 'ouch' announced that Pixie had popped him again. For the bow or just 'because she could' I don't know but I grinned and headed out into the great wide open with a gang of the strangest misfits I had the pleasure to call my buds following right at my heals.

The group was in good spirits; there was laughter and camaraderie it felt like a weekend camp out we had gone on so many times over the years we've known each other. The main thing on my mind wasn't the poison trudging around in my veins; it was Leah, she should be with us. This time last week she would have been, but things had changed and now on top of everything else . . . we had to save her as well as Lydian and myself.

Well on the bright side, at least we had something to do and we were together so whatever came next we would face it just like we had faced everything up 'til now… as Buds!

I wasn't going to give into this overwhelming cloud of doubt and gloom that had settled over me. I had six days to find a fix for everything that was now on my plate trying to slide off. I was going to do what Papa had always told me to.

"All you need to do is worry about the next breath you pull into your lungs… no problems, no stress, just the next breath. All else will fall into place if you simply concentrate on just the next breath." It was solid advice. Papa made everything easy for me to understand.

"Much to do about take a breath and survive."

With my buds at my side I knew that I was going to make it through this. We would save Leah and get this poison out of me, Lydian would be able to shift again and maybe even make it home in time for dinner. A girl can dream, can't she?

Dreams and Things

It dawned on me as we made our way through the maze of halls that I had been deep below the ground while here. It was cool and comforting so I hadn't even thought about the 'where' of it. We walked for quite a while before I could see light in the distance; it was a huge change from the warm glow of the candles and flames that had lit the home of the Speritalz

It felt good to be going out into the sun again. The smell coming in on the air reminded me of the breeze on a beach; salty and fresh like the ocean itself.

When we made it out of ArDonna's home or "indar" as they call it, I was shocked at the sight that met my eyes. Hundreds of Speritalz stood around smiling and waving, waiting to see us off. They were in every direction feathering out from the opening we now stood in.

"Much to do about, I didn't know there were that many shades of green."

Kin, Kon, and ArDonna walked proudly with their heads held high and each was wearing a huge smile; greeting everyone we passed and introducing the "True Weaver" and the T-Weaves. They walked slow as to give any who wanted to speak to me had the chance.

It was really cute and made me feel a little humble that they felt so honored to be with us. 'Now introducing the True Weaver and the T-Weaves on what is possibly their farewell tour, buy your tickets while they last.' The thought made me kinda giggle to myself.

"Your thoughts are so interesting, Lemoya." Lykie laughed... darn Vulcan mind thingy... a girl needs to have a thought now and again that's all her own.

"We represent the lollipop guild, the lolli..." DJ started only to be *'bonked'* hard in the back of the head by Pixie's tiny hand. "Dang it Dix, you're gonna give me brain damage if you don't stop doing that." He crossed his eyes and staggered sideways causing Pixie to giggle.

"No danger in that, *Meathead*. That big ole head sounded hollow when I thumped it." She tapped it with her knuckles again and 'tutted' with a look of mock sympathy, "Just as I thought . . . empty!"

"How can so much **mean** be in such a . . ."

"Don't say one word about my size DJ! I kid you not!" she warned

"Beautiful package." He finished, grinning like a baboon in a mud hole.

"Um hum." She showed him her fist but was unable to hide her grin.

We had gotten to the edge of the little town and stopped. Kin and Kon; still wearing perma-grins and looked as though they could walk on air; stood waving at the crowd. Cheers broke out all around us. Every face held a smile and I could see some of the Speritalz in the back jumping up and down trying to get a better look.

"Much to do about, a great way to start off a quest."

"This is where I must leave you M' Lady." ArDonna smiled up at me with huge green eyes holding back a well of tears. "I will think of you on every rising. By the grace of Adnama, I hope to see you soon and see you well." She hugged me then turned and hugged Kin and Kon and walked off with her head bowed down, without looking back.

"Fawns are so emotional." Kin said wiping his eyes under his glasses and trying to hide his actions. I smiled at his attempt to hide his emotions from the rest of us, but I was happy he loved his sister so much.

The sky was beautiful. A mystic blue with a silver sheen that made it look like it was covered in plastic wrap. Large plants resembling small trees were strewn around the edge of the border and a slight breeze blew keeping the temperature very comfortable. (P.S. No wet armpit stains for me on this trip.)

I took a deep cleansing breath and started walking again. It felt like the way I needed to be going. So I just kinda walked. The scenery was so beautiful. Mountains or what looked like mountains stood tall off in the distance. Large meadows speckled with amazing smelling and very colorful flowers could be seen for miles and miles. Small creatures that could pass for birds flitted about; their golden transparent wings and tiny bodies that kept changing color was something a bird could never do. I walked on an on admiring the majestic sight that was this realm for what seemed like quite a while.

"Does anyone know which direction that we're supposed to be heading?" I finally asked

"We are following you M' Lady." Kon answered and smiled.

"ME!?" I gaped at him, stopping dead in my tracks. "I don't know where I *am* let alone where we're going. I can't get us to the castle of the whispering winds or whatever."

"Castle of Winds, no whispering involved Lemoya." Lykie laughed. "And you should follow where your feelings lead. Adnama is your guide; have faith that she will lead you true."

I rolled my eyes but continued walking. I will never know *why* they think I know this stuff. Plastering "**True Weaver**" on my be-hind does not an atlas make! I didn't just turn sixteen and suddenly gain GPS, realm wide, in my brain ya know. For the love of Uncle Billy's two toed rooster; I get lost trying to find the food court at the mall and there are signs with directions posted everywhere. My mind was once again a jumbled up mess.

After we walked for a while I suddenly stopped and turned to the group. "We can still use magic here, right? I mean was it when we stepped out of the cave or is there a sign that says "No Magic past this point" or something?"

'Yes we can still use magic M' Lady, and I do not believe there is a notice or sign of any kind. Why do you ask?" Kin asked pushing up his glasses and looking puzzled

"Don't over analyze what I say lil man, not everything is to be taken so literally.' I laughed and retrieved the weaving wands from my back pocket. I closed my eyes and let my hands have free reign; they began to whirl and twist in the air. Feeling the wind blow and the ground fall away from my feet I began to speak.

"Our time is short, we must make haste.

The destiny is a sacred place.

A sorceress spell is woven tight.

It blocks the magic on our plight.

A door to where the block begins.

To shorten our quest to the castle of winds.

I could taste the blood trickling from my nose *again*. My feet returned to the ground as nausea swarmed me driving me to my knees. Once again I found myself wrenching and heaving as my insides fought to become my outsides; and let me tell you, it is not a feeling I recommend . . . to *anyone*.

"Here Lou." Came Squeaks' soft voice. She placed a small towel in my hand and brushed my hair out of my face. "I have bottled water in my pack, if you need some."

My throat felt raw and painful, I couldn't speak so I simply nod my head at the suggestion of the bottled water.

I closed my eyes to try to stop the whirly twirly ride I was on but felt the cool bottle in my hand. I turned it up and took a big swig to rinse out my mouth then took several long gulps to quench my over parched throat.

When the nausea passed I opened my eyes only to slam them closed again. The light was like daggers slicing through my eyes.

"Here, maybe these will help." De said putting a pair of sunglasses in my hand. "Your eyes are watering pretty bad, Lou." He reached up and wiped the watery evidence away.

I put on the glasses and was glad to have the extra eye protection.

"Hang on." He said, taking something from his pack. "This will help too."

He held up a ball cap then threaded my hair through the opening in the back and pulled the cap onto my head; the bill of the cap added extra shade around my eyes. The bitter sting of the light had lessened and I could once again see. I smiled at him and looked at the opening floating in the air in front of us.

Kin and Kon had already gone through the door to inspect where it led.

Taking a step proved to be a chore in itself. I stumbled but found De there instantly with his arm around my waist helping me hold myself upright.

"I got you Lou, just lean on me if you need to." He smiled at me and I looked into his eyes. (FYI: Big mistake) those ice blue eyes made my already flippity stomach dance a little jig. Now add that lethal half grin . . . Geesh! How's a girl supposed to think straight I wondered.

Everyone went through the portal, once Kin and Kon gave the 'all clear'. I turned and looked at it. The thought of going through that whirly twirly flip flop again was not high on my list. I grumbled "Oh close already" my voice sounding broken.

The opening began to shrink and then disappeared. As tired as opening it had made me, closing it was going to put me into a comma I thought. So I was grateful for the surprise.

De walked me over to a fallen log; *well it looked like a fallen log*, and helped me sit down. I began to sway and DJ handed me a snack cake, causing Pixie to giggle.

"What? It is loaded with sugar and she needs the energy." He said sheepishly

"A snack cake? That's your answer to what she needs?" she sat down on the ground and drank a bottle of water all the while grinning at De who was still holding on to me.

"I think I need some of that medicine Doc." Allen said, pretending to stagger.

"Me too, we usually get sick at the same time." Andee lied coughing and' passing out' in true theater style.

DJ took out several snack cakes from his backpack then took the Farmers 'vital signs' and scratched his chin. "Take two of these and call me in the morning." Laughing he tossed Squeaks one and opened Lykie one. De had given Kin and

Kon each one and we all sat quietly snacking on a sugar rush. It was a good distraction and it seemed to get us all back in good spirits.

As the day waned on my body became more and more lethargic. My breathing became labored and every step, every movement of my body seemed to cause me some kind of pain, but I trudged on and tried not to slow down the group.

It had been hours since we had had the snack cakes when I heard Squeaks' stomach growl. I wasn't sure how far we had traveled but I knew it was time to stop and rest for a while.

"I think we should take a break and grab a bite to eat, any ideas?" I asked

"Perhaps we should find a place to settle for the night, M' Lady. Darkness in this area is unsafe for travel." Kin announced.

"Are you familiar with this area, Kin?" Someone asked.

"Indeed, tis a place to be avoided if possible. Darkness in this place is when . . ."**things**", I believe you call it *"hunt"*. We should find a fardal to stay in until the next rising." Kin said as he looked around nervously.

"Fardal . . . What are fardals?" I asked

"Those tree-like things that are growing around here Lou; they are called fardals." Lykie said "The older one's flat tops that will hold us up away from danger and make it less likely that we get attacked by a predator; I don't want to be a meal to anything." His voice filled with laughter.

"I vote for fardals. I don't want to be a snack for some beastie thing." Pixie said and looked around to find DJ

"Nothing's gonna snack on ya, Dix. I won't allow it." DJ winked and flexed his pecks.

We searched around for a suitable fardal to camp in and finally settled on one. Slowly one by one everybody made their way to the top. My heart went out to Lykie as DJ picked him up, fireman style, and climbed him safely into the high canopy. Lykie is an ancient being, born and bred to protect; not be carried by a human because he is unable to shift and move on his own.

My turn to climb, and as tired and worn as I felt I was silently praying that I made it up to the camp site.

"Can I help?" I turned to see De's ice blue eyes boring a hole in me. "You seem to be moving kinda . . . slow"

(I hate that he had noticed. I guess I hadn't hid it quite as well as I thought I had. I'll have to be more careful from here on.)

"Sure, Thanks." I said, taking his outstretched hand. "These fardal things are really weird; Small at the bottom and bigger as you go up. They kinda look like an upside down Christmas tree."

"The tops where there should be leaves seem more like green fur of some kind, its really thick too. I bet this is where all the gnomes get their clothing material." De laughed.

"Speritalz." I corrected. "They're not gnomes, they're called Speritalz; and I bet you're right about the clothes thing."

When we got to the third layer of the fur like fardal; we saw it is where everyone had gathered. I searched the crowd for Lykie and found him over to the side, talking to Kin about something.

It felt strange knowing that he had been jealous of DeLainey before yet now he seemed to not care that he was close to me . . . helping me . . . touching me . . .

With that thought he turned his head and looked right at me.

"You think the strangest things Louanna."

"So you can still talk to me this way."

"I try to give you the space you need Lemoya. You have a lot riding on you; I do not wish to add to your list of troubles."

"You are not trouble to me Lykie . . . well when you hog the bed you are." I laughed

"Hog the bed?" he laughed "Well at least I don't snore like you do"

I could feel the caress he sent with his thoughts; like fingers skimming the edge of my face. I closed my eyes and thought of Lydian.

"Much to do about, being confused."

I'm not sure what Kin and Kon had made everyone to eat (*Probably best not to know*) but it was good.

We all got our sleeping bags and made choices where we would spend the night. De put his down close to where I was. I wished he'd move, as tired as I was I just knew I was going to snore. Not a real dude magnet.

"I will be with you Lemoya, you will not snore alone."

Unable to stop myself, I laughed and hugged him tight. "Thanks Lykie. You have always been there for me when I needed you. You are a true friend." I kissed the top of his head.

Nighttime fell quickly; there was no gradual light to darkness like at home, one minute it was light and the next . . . dark. I was grateful for the conk bands; though I'm not afraid of the dark, being in a strange place and not able to see two inches in front of my face is not a pleasant thought. I worried that their light might attract a predator or some kind of beastie with a hunger for 'poisoned meat', but Kin assured us that we were high enough in the fardal canopy that we would not be bothered.

It was cool but not cold and that's the way I loved to sleep. Snuggling into my sleeping bag I stared up at the night sky. The sky was even more beautiful at night than it was in the day. Colors danced across the entire expanse, like the aurora borealis back home. It was going to be hard to sleep with such a magnificent light show overhead. I had to remind myself that we had to get an early start tomorrow and try to force myself not to think about how much time was left.

I felt Lykie stir beside me and without thought I stroked his fur. "The light is the white sorceress' spell; it can be seen better at night." He explained

"It's a wonderful way to fall asleep." I mumbled "It makes it really easy to forget that we're not in Kansas anymore."

"WE'RE NOT!?" DJ blurted out "That must be why my cell says 'no service'. Can you hear me now? No? Well that's because we're in the Twilight Zone." The sound of a thud announced that Pixie had popped him again. "That shoe stinks Dix!" he fussed and threw it back at her.

"Then shut your open trap so I won't have to throw things at you." She laughed

"Are they always like that?" De asked, trying to hide the humor in his tone.

"YES!!!!!" Came several voices followed by a fit of giggles and laughter.

"Your friends are really cool Louanna. I'm glad I got to meet them." De said, drawing my attention back to him . . . and those dreamy eyes.

"Yes, they are pretty cool." I stammered

I turned over and closed my eyes. Looking at him made me feel kinda funny, and not the 'ha ha' kind of funny that people *like* but the funny that makes you feel like ya just jumped out of a plane and realized ya have no parachute.

"Much to do about, being a coward."

Looking in his eyes gave me the sensation of falling into a bright tunnel. I couldn't afford to fall down that tunnel just now; no matter how tempting the ride might be.

I'd just keep my eyes closed and fall asleep sooner . . . yeah, 'cause that's how easy and uncomplicated my life always is. **'Not likely sister!'**

I lay quietly listening to my friends joke and laugh. Then I turned my mind to the night around us. There were things scratching and digging on the ground below us. Footsteps of big beasties and little critters could be heard. A few snarls and a growl or two made me wonder if they could get to us. I had put my faith in Kin and I would not doubt him now. *No matter how creeped out I was.* Regardless of my fears and doubts; sleep came and slowly took me away for a much needed rest.

"We should have found her by now! The female voice screeched with rage. "This *'friend'* is supposed to be someone she *cares* for, yet she has made *no* attempt to come for her."

"She has yet to receive my gift, my dear I feel the proper motivation is what is needed at this time. The True Weaver thinks to elude me by cloaking her magic. She is such a *Consoyta*, her magic is lacking." The male voice was dripping with hatred. "She can hold no true power because she does not wish to be the True Weaver."

"She does not deserve the gifts she has been given. There are others that were passed over so *she* could be given Adnama's grace." The female complained

"Then it is time to give her *my* little gift. I think . . . just a piece will do. I'm certain she will recognize *this*." There was a horrid sound followed by Leah's screams.

My vision had gone blurry, it was as if I was looking at Leah through a thick sheet of plastic, her image was contorted. Her hands were up in a defensive pose. Red was splashed on the plastic and Leah began to scream again.

"Wake up Louanna!" Lykie screamed. It sounded like he was miles away.

"Lou, **wake up**! You're having a nightmare." Squeaks' voice came from somewhere nearby.

I opened my eyes and saw worried faces all around me. Tasting the familiar coppery tinge I started to wipe at my mouth and realized I had something in my hand. Something sharp poked my palm; looking down at what had caused the pain I suddenly felt sick . . . I could not be seeing that in my hand.

I knew what it was as I registered the gasps around me. The earing I had given Leah at Christmas was staring back at me from my palm. Leah had worn these earrings with such pride, she never took them off. Now one of them sat in the palm of my hand staring back at me, covered in blood and still attached to part of . . . **Leah's ear.**

Castle of Winds

I couldn't move. Panic had paralyzed my body rendering it useless. My head pounded with each beat of my heart and my heart was thundering out a fast pace melody.

Someone was screaming, it was a mournful sound; one that would break your heart if you heard it. The screams were woven with pain and anguish. I looked at my friends, desperate to see who needed me; who I needed to comfort, only to realize the horrific sound of anguish was coming from . . . *me*! I couldn't stop the cries. The pain was rolling over me in huge waves. My eyes glued to the "*gift*" in my hand and I couldn't look away from it. Leah's ear, a piece of my best friend had been sliced off and somehow ended up transported from my dream to my hand.

The image of Leah's hands in the air fending off someone would forever be burned in my memory.

This was my fault! I was the cause of pain being inflicted on my best friend. She was hurt . . . because of me. She was scared . . . because of me. All of my friends were now exposed to the elements, facing all kinds of danger . . . BECAUSE. OF. MEEEEEEE!!!

I clutched the offending gift in my hand. It was probably just my imagination, but it still felt warm, like it had just been taken from Leah.

I leaped up and ran to the edge of the fardal tree and threw up. I have been throwing up so much here lately I'm afraid I may be becoming bulimic.

I tried to draw air into my lungs, my head was still spinning and I went to my knees. Leah's cries echoed in my mind. The oily voice that I believed to be Logton, the Grundal holding her, filled my spirit with a hot rage. He would pay for this! Him and whoever that female voice belonged to. He thinks my magic is Consoyta? New? Beginner!?

Ok, so my power is weaker because I don't want to be the True Weaver? Well guess what you vial little stink rat,

"I **AM** THE TRUE WEAVER!" I screamed. "**I** was chosen by *Jequota*. **I** woke the spirit of Adnama. And I **will** find you!"

An electrical charge, not unlike a bolt of lightning, shot from my fingertips and lit up the night sky above me creating a hole in the colors. I rose four feet in the air, the rainbow webs gathered; the air around me became turbulent. I felt a stirring deep inside that beckoned meto set it free.

"Great spirit of the light,
I call on thee this very night.
Your gifts in me I now embrace'
I take it all, with most haste.
True Weaver is what I now claim,
Adnama's gifts, in me remain."

My voice seemed to boom across the night. My emotions were a tangible force in the air. A tingling down my back let me know that the tattoo had grown. My skin began to glow and shimmer, the rainbow webs attached to my skin and I seemed to absorb them.

I could hear *everything*. My buds' heartbeats, breathing of creatures unseen by me. My eyes began to burn, forcing me to close them. After a moment I opened them to find I had a raptor-like vision. I knew the poison was still inside me, I could hear it traveling through my veins and eating away at my insides, it almost had a voice I could hear as it traveled and destroyed tissue and organs inside me.

No one spoke. Everyone just seemed to be transfixed on me. I remained in the air looking down at them.

"I am the True Weaver, I have been chosen by Adnama and from this moment on, I accept what destiny has in store for me." I announced. Hot pain shot through my body, causing me to nearly black out. I embraced the pain and opened my mind to the sensation as my body took in Adnama's energy.

I could see my body below me. It was bent over backwards, floating. There was light shining down on me like a giant spotlight had been aimed on me. It looked so bright and hot that it should have been burning my skin . . . but it wasn't.

Looking around I saw my friends shielding their eyes from the intense glare of the light. I wanted to watch and see what happened but a pull seemed to have me and was drawing me into the light.

I couldn't see anything but white. Bright sparkling white light reflected off every surface. It was tingly and strangely comforting.

"Louanna Teelf?" a female voice said, penetrating my skin.

I stood there squinting my eyes and looking around. I didn't respond to the voice. I didn't have my henky feeling so I knew I wasn't in any kind of danger but I still did not know who was speaking to me.

"Louanna Teelf?" the voice said again

"I am Louanna Teelf."

"You have summonsed me here. I see you have accepted the gifts offered you. The True Weaver power is embedded deep within you, little one."

"Who are you?" I looked around but still saw no one.

The edge of the light, darkened and I was left standing in a circle of light. I could see a shape approaching from the shadows but still could only see movement. A woman in a long flowing crystal white gown entered the circle. She was the most beautiful woman I had ever seen. Long wavy chestnut colored hair surrounded an oval face with almond shaped deep green eyes. A short pugged nose and what I always called, Elvis lips. Her smile was breath taking. She reached out and took my hand, covering it with both of hers.

"Tis a pleasure to meet you True Weaver." She said. "We have anticipated your arrival for a very long time." She smiled brightly.

"Thank you, but who are you?"

The green in her eyes shimmered and her smile brightened. "I am she who you have summonsed. As Adnama fills your earthly vessel with power and abilities, your spirit has come to me. You do not wish to feel the pain that now racks your body." She took a deep breath and rubbed my cheek. "The poison is progressing I see."

"I mean no respect to you, I have asked a few times with no answer, but as you have not answered me I have to wonder and since I am not the most trusting person these days so I have to ask you again . . . **who are you?**"

"The fire burns hot in you, Louanna." She sighed and waved her hand, dimming the light. "My name, My Dear, is Kaeli VonLunar; and as I have stated, you summonsed me here."

"Much to do about, needing to watch my smart little mouth!"

My eyes bulged out; this angelic looking woman in front of me was the white sorceress!? A female Merlin! I had just got snippy with someone who could zap me into a yellow bellied three eyed toad frog!

She laughed making her already beautiful face glow even more. "Your guardian is right about you, you do think the strangest things."

"You can read my thoughts like Lydian does? Well, isn't that just great!?" I mumbled

"I can do a fair many things, young one. And I can assure you that the population of *yellow bellied three eyed toad frogs* will not increase this day."

I had to laugh, her smile was contagious. "So, am I in Xela?" I asked

"No young one, this is the castle of winds. Your spirit is here. You came seeking answers to a great many things. Your guardian is inflicted?"

"He is just one of many that are suffering because of me." I grumbled, feeling childish.

"The spell on the gateway . . . very ingenious. Had another tried to use the special portal you set for your Speritalz; it would have meant their death. His actions were only directed in saving you, a noble offering." She waved her hand and a crystal bench appeared; one of the symbols of the Jequota carved into its surface. "Please . . . sit." She sat down and patted the bench beside her.

"Can something be done that will help Lykie Shift again?" I blurted

She beamed a telling smile at me. "What would you have me do, Louanna? What wish do *you* make for your guardian?"

I don't know why but I felt like there was hidden meaning imbedded in her question. This particular conundrum needed thought. I didn't want to do more harm than good.

"I think I'd have him answer that question. This is his life we are talking about and it should be his choice."

"Indeed." She got up and walked around me; checking out every angle of me. "I feel you are not aware of all that you hold inside. There is greatness set for you True Weaver."

"I have accepted . . . no . . . embraced the True Weaver in me. I have to go after the Grundal that has taken my friend." I closed my eyes and the image of Leah's ear came rushing in. I choked back the bile that rose and fought to breathe.

"This Grundal, he is the one responsible for the poisoning?" she asked

"I believe so, yes." I grew angry as I thought about Leah and Logton. The wind began to blow and stir.

"Control your emotions, True Weaver. There is no Grundal here. I can help with your guardian. His sacrifice was one of loyalty and love. His devotion to you is unyielding; he knew the consequences of his actions yet chose to enter the forbidden portal."

"He knew!? He knew he would lose the ability to shift . . . to be whole, if he entered that portal?" it felt like I'd been punched in my stomach. He knew . . . he knew that he would be unable to shift and be trapped as a . . ."

"Yes Dear. He did indeed know the result of his actions. He chose to go through that portal, to save . . . you."

Guilt flooded me. A heaping helping of guilt covered in humiliation with a side of *'this is all my fault'*.

Kaeli laughed softly. "The way your mind works." She smiled sweetly at me. "This is not your fault. He is a Lydian

Guardian and therefore his path . . . his chosen path, is to protect you. He *loves* his job." She grinned.

"Can you make Lykie whole again?"

"No."

"But you just said . . ."

"I said I can *help* you with your guardian."

"You are making my head hurt." I snipped and rubbed at my temples. "Can Lydian be whole again?"

"Yes"

"Can you make him right?"

"No" she lowered her gaze and looked at me.

"Then who do I have to go see to get this fixed?" I was getting tired of the mind games. My head was swimming and sorceress or not, I was tired of her playing hop scotch with the answers.

"No one." She stated and stood up. "You are the one who wove the spell and no one, not even I, can reverse magic that has been spun by another."

"I don't know how to fix this, sorceress."

"Yes . . . you do." She placed her hand on my shoulder. "The knowledge is there inside you. Just as the spell itself was there so shall the reversal be."

"I also need to find Leah and Logton and fix all of this other stuff that has gone Bonkers Gazoo because of me." I sounded exasperated and quite a bit like a small child.

Her image wavered "You are in need of rest, True Weaver." I tried to focus on her. "I will come to you upon the next rising when you wake."

My spirit was pulled backwards. The edges of my vision blurred and I began to spin around and around then everything went black.

"Louanna?" the sound of my name caused my eyes to snap open. My band of T-Weave misfits stood around me looking down at me, each face showing concern.

"Hey guys." I said and sat up.

"You were out of it for a long time." De said "We thought that you may not come back to us this time."

"I'm sorry everybody. I didn't know what was gonna happen when I said that. I just felt like I had to say it." I looked at Lykie "I saw Kaeli Von What's her face. She said she's gonna be here at the next rising . . . whenever that is."

"That would be when you wake, True Weaver." Kaeli's voice said.

All eyes turned to see Kaeli standing just outside our circle; her smile as pleasant as before. Her brilliant green eyes sparkled in the light.

Kin and Kon fell to their knees and bowed their heads down in a show of respect. Both Speritalz mumbled something under their breath.

"My dear Speritalz, please rise, that I may thank you for your devotion to our new True Weaver." Kaeli said softly.

They stood and looked at her with wide eyes as she gracefully bent at the waist, lowered her head and bowed to them.

I smiled and looked at Lykie who stood head down in a show of respect to the two Speritalz.

"Do not think your service has gone unnoticed, guardian. Your family has served well the lineage of True Weavers." Once again she bowed at the waste and lowered her head in a show of respect.

Kaeli then turned to my buds and smiled brightly. "Your devotion to the True Weaver is an inspiration. She chose well for the Court of Brethren." She looked at DeLainey and paused then turned to me and spoke.

"Your change is very noticeable, True Weaver. Energy seems to be emanating from you." She looked deep into my eyes "There is something . . . else, for a later date I think." She smiled "I think the quest you are on has with it a time table, and you have to speak to your guardian." Every eye turned to me.

"Much to do about, being in the hot seat."

"Lemoya, is there something wrong?" Lykie looked at me in question then Kaeli and then me again.

"There's no . . . problem, Lykie. She-"I gestured to Kaeli, "She says 'I' can fix your shifting problem."

He stood there, had I not known he was alive I'd have sworn he was a stuffed dog. Then he breathed and looked at Kaeli. "Is this true Sorceress? Shifting can be restored to me that I may once again be whole and able to be the warrior needed by the True Weaver?"

Kaeli knelt to his side and smiled lovingly at him. "Tis indeed true guardian."

No one spoke. We all just stood there and let Lykie digest the news. I knew as the white sorceress Kaeli must know what she was saying . . . I must be able to fix this somehow.

I had accepted the gifts of Adnama and my place as the True Weaver but my actions had been made out of anger and hatred for a Grundal; had my actions fueled my desire for revenge? Would that change my magic to evil or bad because my decision was made in anger? I don't want to end up as the **wicked witch of the west** because I wanted Logton to pay for what he was doing to Leah! The image of "Surrender Louanna" smoky across the sky popped in my head.

"True Weaver, your fears are unfounded and in such an odd array of thought." Kaeli said softly "Magic is neither good nor evil it simply *is*. It is the intent for which one uses the magic that taints its essence either dark or light." She looked around and spoke to everyone. "Energy feeds magic; if you draw energy, such as each of you do, then you will have a stronger more concentrated magic. Grundals become consumed with the plight for power; that obsession will eventually consume their very essence, leaving them empty and hollow inside. They believe the possession of Jequota, even one with a slumbering spirit cloth, will somehow restore the honor and power they once yielded. But they have long since aborted that from their lives it cannot be returned to them with magic or any act in any of the many realms.

"Yes, but I only wanted these powers to get back at Logton for hurting my friend." I admitted, feeling shameful for the truth about myself, hoping my friends wouldn't judge me too harshly for it.

"Little one, you see only that which you wish to see. Feel no guilt; you accepted the gifts of Adnama as is your right, your destiny. The power is already yours. A Grundal seeks to take that which was never meant to be his. Only a Weaver can possess a Jequota and only the True Weaver can awaken the spirit cloth to reveal Adnama there in." Kaeli rubbed down my hair then her hand froze on my back. Her brilliant green eyes sparkled in the light. "You are more special than you believe yourself to be Louanna Teelf."

I simply smiled and felt uncomfortable at her words . . . I'm just me . . .

"My Lady Sorceress, tis a most humbling honor to be in your presence." Kin said to her as he bowed.

"Leafkin, I am honored to meet you and your twain, Leafkon. You have done well in your job as Speritalz to the True Weaver. May the fates keep you and yours forever safe." She bowed to the two Speritalz again causing them to turn a deep crimson red.

"She's really pretty." Squeaks said as she took my hand

"Yes, she is. Kaeli, White Sorceress I'd like for you to meet my buds, they call themselves the T-Weaves." I smiled. I walked Squeaks over and stood by the group.

"I would love to meet the T-Weaves." Kaeli walked over to meet everyone. (Minus Leah)

"Devaine Johnson, but friends call me DJ. Glad to meet you." He held out his hand and took Kaeli's.

"Dixie Styxx, but friends call me Pixie or Dix. I'm honored to meet you too." She followed DJ"s example and shook Kaeli's hand as well.

"I'm Allen and this is Andee Farmer. No, we aren't twins; we're just both really good looking." Allen laughed.

"Yeah 'cause God was like, "Man . . . that is one good looking person. I need to make another one" . . . and bam; here I am." Andee gave Allen a high five. (What can I say, they are who they are.)

"My name is Frankie Hylt" was all that she said. She spoke very quietly.

"We call her Squeaks because that is about as loud as you will ever hear her speak." DJ scuffed up Squeaks' hair and winked at her.

De looked at me in questioning. I guess he still wondered about his placement among our group. I smiled at him and gave a small nod that he too should introduce himself.

He walked over to Kaeli and bowed down, took her hand and placed the back of her hand on his forehead. He closed his eyes and spoke. "DeLainey Landon, M' Lady Kaeli, I am humbled to be in your presence."

She smiled down at him. A sparkle in her eyes spoke volumes as she looked around at each of us. "The T-Weaves are honored in my eyes." She did a small curtsy and lowered her head towards all of us.

It was very humbling to have such a being; one that could yield such power and held unknown knowledge, bow to you.

"And this is Lykie, my guardian, but I don't have to tell you that." I smiled

"I have not had the privilege of meeting him. I did know your kin, Lyden; he was a great guardian, loyal and true to a fault. His service to the True Weaver was unsurpassed by service to all he cherished." Kaeli said.

"I should only hope to be half the guardian that Lyden was. His name still demands the utmost respect amongst our kind." Lykie said.

"If he was anything like Lykie . . . he was wonderful!" Pixie said and hugged Lykie tightly.

We all stood around talking to Kaeli; letting her get to know us. DJ flexed his muscles, earning a 'pop' in the head from Pixie. The Farmers discussed which was stronger of the two. That led to . . . you guessed it, a wrestling match. (PS; I could have *died* of embarrassment.) Kaeli seemed to enjoy their antics so I just shook my head and laughed at what they were doing like I always do.

Finally I spoke up. 'Ok guys, not that the sorceress Kaeli sees for herself that most of us are certifiable and should be institutionalized; we need to get Lykie back to full guardian status so we can rescue Leah. Our six day time frame is growing shorter by the minute." I looked at Pixie, hoping I'd not get 'bonked' for the *short* term.

"We don't have six days Lou." Squeaks said softly.

"I know that baby, we used one of the days just getting here, I should have said five days but I don't want to count the hours and minutes." I smiled at her

"M' Lady; that was not her meaning." Kin said

"When Adnama gave you the full strength and all of the True Weaver gifts; it took quite a toll on your body." Kon added "We thought you were gone from us. Even with us giving you the dottle berry tonic; your body grew paler as you lost blood and energy."

"We only have two days left Lemoya." Lykie summed up.

"Much to do about, **SAY WHAT!?**"

Time Moves On

I couldn't react like I wanted to. I don't think that 'True Weavers' curl up in the fetal position and suck on their thumbs while crying for their Mommy! Our five days were now two days... it wasn't going to change anything to get miffed about what I couldn't change. (The next breath...)

"Well then, all the more reason to get this done and go save our friend." I said sounding a lot braver than I felt. "Our new friend, Kaeli says I can fix Lykie . . . so I will." I looked at Kaeli "So how will I?"

"As True Weaver, you will just know how. Close your eyes; you accepted Adnama and she is deep within you, let her guide you." Kaeli said.

I did what she said. I closed my eyes and tried not to think about there only being two days left. **Focas**! I told myself. I looked deep inside myself for the answers. I could hear the hum of voices but they were far off in the distance. I saw a bright light, bright and blue. It was bright but didn't cause me to look away. It felt comfortable and welcoming.

"You have come a long way, True Weaver." said a voice or several voices; all overlapping one another and at the same time talking down in a fifty gallon drum. It was beautiful . . . and creepy.

"Are you Adnama?"

"We are."

"We? Is there more than one Adnama?"

"No child. We are Adnama. We are all powerful and all knowing. We are where all things come and where all things go. We decide who is worthy and give gifts accordingly. You are worthy to be the True Weaver Louanna Marie Teelf."

"I need to undo what has been done to my guardian."

"He sacrificed all to protect your life. It is honorable that you wish to repay the debt."

"Is this poison going to kill me?"

"Yes."

"Then there is no hope for me?"

"You must find the being that made the offending chemical or you will surely die."

"How do I fix Lydian and how can I find Logton?"

"Follow thy heart True Weaver. The answers are there."

The voices faded and the light dulled and disappeared. I opened my eyes and looked around. I was floating in the air and the wind was stirring all around. I looked at Lykie and pointed in front of me then retrieved the Weaving wands. Without thought I began to move them. Rainbow webs gathered and energy began to pulse through me.

"Your heart beats true, strong and fair.

You sacrificed without a care.

The pain received going through the rift,

Took from you a sacred gift.

Reverse, reverse, reverse I say

Reverse the spell I spun that day.

You are not a dog nor are you man.

By Adnama's gifts, you are full Lydian."

I took both wands and pointed them at Lykie. The rainbow webs shot from the tips and wrapped around every inch of Lykie; raising him into the air.

"Syaw ladna wonnai drauga naidyl erauoy"

(You are Lydian guardian now and always, backwards)
I spoke loud and clear, repeating the words several times. Lykie's body floated to the floor. He lay there panting like he had run for a long time. Kon tore off a layer of the fardal top and laid it over Lykie.

We all stared at each other. I wondered if the spell had been reversed. I heard the familiar popping sound that said it had worked. Looking at Lykie I saw his fur growing in reverse, going into his skin instead of out. His head bent and twisted changing shape. Paws curled and reshaped becoming hands and feet; suddenly Lydian was where Lykie had just been. He just lay there . . . unmoving, with his long hair covering his face.

I looked at my crowd of friends old and new. My heart beat so loud and strong I was sure that they could all hear it.

Lydian started to stir, first a little then he moved and sat up. He threw his head to the side flipping his hair out of his eyes revealing his handsome face . . . my I have missed that face!

His lopsided grin said he had caught my thought. "Lemoya, you have done it! You have made me whole once again. I will be forever in your debt." He wrapped the green fur-like thing around his waist like a towel after a shower then tied it together with a nearby vine.

"Much to do about, you Tarzan, me Jane."

He walked over and pulled me into a big hug. I had forgotten how good it felt to have his arms hold me. I didn't want him to ever let me go.

"Welcome back." DJ said "I was getting tired of being the best looking guy here. Don't get me wrong, some are *fair* looking." He winked at De "but being the *best* looking guy is really taxing on a guy's nerves."

"Best looking!?" Pixie snapped "You can- **not** be serious!?"

"Denial . . . one of the first signs that a gal is swooning over a guy."

"SWOONING!? OVER YOU!? You are an even bigger meathead than I thought you were. Pixie said and popped him in the head.

DJ scooped Pixie up and twirled her around, laughing. "I'm your big ole meathead though."

After a few minutes of laughing at the two of them, everyone turned to look at me.

"So, what's next Lou?" DJ asked "What do we do now?"

"We find that little snot stain, Logton and save Leah. Getting Leah outta there is our primary goal." I said simply

"I doubt that Logton will just hand her over to us Lou." DJ said "Not to mention the fact that we don't know where they are or how we can find them."

"It's not gonna matter if he gives her to us or not, we're getting her. He messed up big time when he sent me his little gift. He was dealing with Louanna Teelf, teenaged girl before. From now on he will be dealing with the True Weaver and she won't be alone." I said

"T-Weave powers, activate! Oh yeah!" DJ said

"We got your back, Lou." Pixie chimed in

"Apart we are bad . . . together, we are un-stop-able!" the Farmers added

"So what do we do now Lou?" Squeaks asked

I looked at their smiling, trusting faces. They had utter faith . . . in me. Faith that I'd get us through this big ole mess. I don't want to let them down. But to be honest . . . I do not have a clue how we were gonna get to Leah, beat Logton and save my hide . . . in two days.

"I guess the first step is to find where the lil snot stain is. If we can find where he is holding Leah, we can come up with a plan to either sneak in or charge in with 'guns-a-blazin'." I said

"I think you should look to the caves on in the Eenok Mountains. There has been a disturbance in the energy there. Most likely a cloaking spell has been used for hiding deeds that would not want to be discovered. Would you agree?" Kaeli asked, looking at Kin, Kon and Lydian.

"It would indeed be a great place to start, M' Lady" Kin said as he scratched down some notes on his pad and pushed up on his glasses.

"How subtle is the disturbance, Lady Kaeli?" Lydian asked

"It is well hidden. I don't think any level of magic could detect it." Kaeli looked at me "Louanna, I'd like for you to try to hone in on the location of Logton." She leveled her gaze on me "I must warn you; however, you must at no time alert him to your presence there. What I ask of you is an advanced form of magic however with Adnama's power so strong in you, I feel you will be able to do this." She smiled sweetly

"What do I do, I mean how do I find him and not let him know that I'm there? I just got these powers and I don't know what I'm doing with them." I said, sounding whinny and childish. It felt like they had just set me to drive in a banged up race car and expected me to take off and win the race... I wasn't sure if I could even get the car started!

"Seek the guidance of Adnama, and then follow where she leads." Kaeli said

I took a deep breath and closed my eyes; thinking I do this an awful lot here lately. *"I need to find Logton."* I whispered.

Suddenly I was flying over the fardal trees. Giant boulders and beautiful landscape were spread out below me. I felt like a fog, airy and weightless on a mountain side.

I floated freely, letting my spirit go where it was led. I found myself floating by an opening in the side of the mountain; its location was obscured by fallen fardal trees. I made sure to make a mental note of all my surroundings so I could relay the information to the others.

I entered the cave; once inside I could feel an ominous presence in the air. Even being in this 'fog-like' form, I knew that moving with caution was a necessity. I could not disturb the energy and alert Logton that I was here.

Inside the cave was nothing like it had been outside, out there it felt like I had been floating; but in here it was more like trying to swim in tar. I knew I wasn't breathing but it still felt like I had a pillow, (old, moldy, mildew ridden pillow) over my nose and mouth.

> -Keep calm. Keep your heartbeats normal.
> No thoughts. Ride the energy to its origin.- I
> told myself.

I continued to ride the vile energy; not shifting or directing it, just going wherever it led. Several times the energy back tracked and 'retraced' its steps and then would go in a different direction. Logton was being very cautious about keeping his location hidden.

***WHOOP…WHOOP…WHOOP…
Henky feeling alert!!!***

I didn't react, everything in me screamed to 'stop' and 'go back!' I struggled to keep my heart beat in sync with the energy flow and I stayed to the course I was on.

As I rounded the corner I heard voices ahead. The flow of energy stalled and began to circle around an opening in the cave wall. Orange light moved and shifted beyond the opening; giving the impression of little beings dancing around an open fire.

"I DON'T KNOW HOW SHE DID IT!!" Logton bellowed. "There was no trace of energy that could have been followed to me from that ear I sent. She should not have been able to find me."

"Is there no explanation to how she did it?"

The sound of a slap followed by Leah's cry of pain said she had been struck again.

"Her friend will pay for the True Weaver's arrogance." He snapped. "Get out of my sight! The mere sight of you sickens me."

Another slap and Leah's cries echoed off the wall. My heart ached for her. I wanted so much to go in that room and zap him with some spell. It took all the control I had to continue just riding the energy and not reacting to what was going on.

As the flow of energy passed by the crack in the wall I could see Leah, sitting in the corner; still covered in dried blood. The bruises were all over her; some new and others going yellow and green at the edges. No matter how long I live; I will never be able to explain just how badly I wanted to rush in there and get her and bring her out.

She took in a sharp breath and slowly looked at the opening. Squinting and trying to focus the only eye that was not swollen and bruised in my direction then she looked in Logton's direction.

"Lou . . . Lou, are you here?"

My heart broke! My best friend could sense me near. She knew I was close but I couldn't help her; not even offer her a small measure of hope.

"Lou, Please . . . HELP ME!!"

The energy began to sort of 'unwind' itself. I began to back track my path in and out of the taverns. I noted where the pits and traps were so we would be able to avoid them when we came in to rescue Leah.

"What are you doing!? Logton snapped "Are you trying to speak to her?" Leah's cry filled the air and soaking into my, now transparent, body.

I pulled back and away from the vial energy and headed back to my body. I pulled rapidly until I could feel my body close. Before I could focus on what was going on, I was back inside my body.

The now familiar coppery taste told me my nose had bled again.

"I guess using my gifts makes that poison have a lil hissy fit." I laughed and wiped at the trail of blood . . . then hit the floor. Blood gushed from my nose and I grew dizzy.

-I will not pass out! I thought-

The edges of my vision became blurred and I gasped for breath.

Lydian put his arm under my right side and De took the left side. Another time . . . another place . . . this would be quite interesting. But here . . . now? I was humiliated. "True

Weaver" my fat fanny! More like "True Sissy"! I can't even stand up on my own. (Insert sad face here)

The tension between Lydian and DeLainey felt like a vice on my head. I wanted to tell them to "Lighten up!" but took the coward's way out instead.

"Pixie? Squeaks? Can you guys help me, it's kinda a girl thing." I smiled at Lydian and De as sweetly as I could manage.

"You little coward!" Pixie laughed and handed me a wet towel

"You better know it, Sista!" I mumbled then washed my face and neck.

"Why is she a coward? I think Lou is the bravest. It was the bravest to go looking for that Grundal." Squeaks said defensively.

Pixie laughed and took the towel from me. "Looks like it's time for you to have 'the talk' with our young Frankie." She hugged Squeaks lovingly and went to refresh the towel.

"The talk? What talk? I just wondered why she called you a . . ." Squeaks looked at Lydian and De who were shooting darts at each other through their eyes then looked back at me . . . them . . . me. . . color flooded her cheeks. "Oh, it's boy stuff." She said.

"Don't worry baby, it's not "That" that. Just boys being silly ole boys." I smiled at her. She returned the smile and hugged me.

"The poison's grip on you seems to be strengthening M' Lady Louanna." Kin said as he handed me a goblet of dottle berry tea. "This will help and should not make you sleepy." Eyeing me over the top of his glasses he blinked Back tears. "I know our time grows short to retrieve thy friend."

I was thankful that he didn't say "Until you're pushing up daisies" or whatever weird name the called flowers here.

I smiled and took the tea. "Thanks Kin. We will find her in plenty of time. I have the best help." I turned the goblet up to my lips and drank the entire contents in two gulps. –I really like doddle berry tea-

After a few minute I felt more like 'me' again. I told everyone what I had seen on my 'spirit journey'. What I heard and felt. No one spoke; I'm not sure they even breathed.

"With only two days left, we need to come up with a really good plan, execute the plan and get Leah out of there safely."

"And," Kon added "Find the antidote for the poison that wreaks havoc in the True Weaver's body. You are also a priority Lou." He smiled at the informal 'Lou' he had called me.

"Well, and then there's that." I said, winking at him.

"True Weaver," Kaeli interjected, reaching for my hand. "If I may . . .?" She took my hands and then looked deeply into my eyes.

"Wonkot deeni tahwl aevere yesd nimym hguorht"

She spoke these words three times and stared deeper and deeper in my eyes. I felt like she was looking at my soul.

"What are you saying?" I asked when I finally found my voice again. "Is it another language? My Papa said those exact words to me once when I was in Xela."

Kaeli smiled at me. "He is your spirit guide, little one. It does not surprise me that he would know this particular spell." When I still looked like she had sprouted a horn from the top of her head she rubbed my face and went on. "It is not unlike the spell you set on your guardian. I simply said the words backwards while I looked in your eyes. It is like watching what you saw" I said. "through my mind's eye reveal what I need to know" and I saw your trip to Eenok Mountain."

From the troubled look on her face, she had also felt my pain at seeing Leah with the knowledge that I had to leave without helping her.

"My Lady Kaeli, the Grundal Logton was a very powerful Speritalz. From all the knowledge we have gathered over time and what I have seen with my own eyes; he may just be the most powerful Grundal in existence." He lowered his voice and looked around nervously, as if not to be over heard. "His power grows as well as his anger at an alarming rate."

"I fear you may be right Leafkin. As I am not familiar with the darker side of magic's embrace, I may be of little use to you with his particular techniques in wielding." she sighed

"Your knowledge of magic will be a huge asset to us Kaeli." I said "You yourself said that magic is neither good or evil it is only the wielder; so the magic is the same it just uses different strands to achieve its purpose."

"Maybe the Nivlem holds the answers to these paradoxical insoluble." Kin turned to me and the T-Weaves "Difficult problems" he explained. I guess I should have paid more attention in realm class and I'd of known what that was.

Before I could respond to what he had said I was slammed with a Henky feeling.

"HIT THE DECK!!!" I yelled and dove to the ground.

Without questioning, everyone followed suit.

An ear splitting screech like the whale of a banshee, came thundering towards us. I looked around trying to find the source of the noise but my eyes settled on Kaeli. She was mumbling and moving her hands in the direction of the horrific disturbance. There was a crashing boom announcing that something had made contact with the spell she had cast trying to slow down the projectile. Searching the sky; it only took seconds to find out what that 'something' was. A boulder, about the size of a riding lawnmower, covered in red, orange, and yellow flames was screaming through the sky, straight at us!

Without conscious thought I grabbed the weaving wands from my back pocket and began to move my hands in zig zags, circles, and loop-de-loops; they had seemingly taken on a mind of their own. Instantly the rainbow webs and wind made their grand appearance all around us. I looked at Kaeli and noticed her hands were moving in the exact patterns mine were. She had been casting another spell so the only thing I knew to say was, "Shield us!" Kaeli said the words as well and our voices seemed to echo out across the sky. (I couldn't help but think "*Spells in stereo.*")

A clear shimmer, like the surface of a bubble in the sun, formed over our group just as the fire ball struck. PS it was defiantly __no__ bubble! On impact, the 'bubble dome' seemed to absorb the fire boulder's blow. Ripples were sent over the entire surface and the fireball was sent tumbling to the ground; knocking over and destroying everything in its path. Everyone inside the 'bubble' was safe and completely unharmed; though I think several of us needed a diaper change.

Friends in Strange Places

No one spoke. We stood there staring silently at each other with the knowledge on each face . . . we had almost just died!!!

"Is everyone ok? Appendages all accounted for?" I asked. "Extremities intact?"

"I think I need some clean bloomers." DJ said, fanning his behind. "'Cause I think I soiled this pair."

"You wouldn't be alone in that one DJ." De said and laughed

"What was that?" Squeaks whispered, taking my hand for comfort.

I looked down at her sweet face; her huge blue-green eyes and scarlet red hair shinning in the sunlight. I couldn't help but think that she looked so much younger than she was when she was frightened or alarmed. With her being so smart and having so much book knowledge; I often forget just how very young and innocent my sweet Squeaks actually is.

"I don't know what it is baby. Are you ok?" I hugged her tightly to me.

"I am now." She said squeezing me back and smiling up at me.

"What *was* that?" I asked, directing the question to Lydian.

"I hope I am wrong, Lemoya, but I think that is an ettabird egg." He answered grimly.

Lydian turned to Kin and Kon, mumbled something inaudible, then he shifted into Lykie form and the three of them bounded over the edge of the fardal tree to the ground below.

"What's an ettabird?" Pixie asked

Kaeli stepped forward and answered. "They are large birds; usually controlled by someone or something holding their essence stone." She looked at us seeing the "ERRR-UGH" in our expressions "An essence stone is a palm sized growth on the beak of a fledgling ettabird. If you can find a young ettabird and take the essence stone; you can direct or control the ettabird until you die or choose to release it."

"Are ettabirds mean?" Squeaks asked nervously

Kaeli smiled at her sweetly. "That depends on the driver, little one. The one holding the essence stone essentially determines the path of the ettabirds demure." She explained seeing the questioning look at the 'driver' comment.

"It wasn't sent. You may come down if you wish." Lydian sent the message to everyone.

"I wanna see that etta egg thingy." DJ said. "Come on Dix, let's go see it."

Pixie sighed like it was a big aggravation but the twinkle in her eyes said she was as excited to see the egg as DJ was. "Whatever Caveman. Let's go see the thing so you don't have a hissy over it." She said

The Farmers fell in line behind, following them to the ground.

"Can we go see it too Lou?" Squeaks asked

"Much to do about, how can you say no to that sweet little face?"

"Baby girl, if you wanna go see a big ole ettabird egg . . . we'll go see a big ole ettabird egg, you don't need my permission."

"Thanks Lou." She said and hugged me tightly again. Her face was lit up with a bright smile.

I knew if I said I didn't think we should or if I simply said 'no' she would have stayed right there with me, even though she didn't need my permission to go or do anything.

The ettabird egg was one weird lookin' thing: A large, bumpy, orange, rock-looking thing that had white slashy lightning bolt cracks all over its surface. I'm sorry I'm speaking so technically but I want you to know what the thing looks like. It was embedded about a fourth of the way up the side of the egg into the ground and still on fire.

"Funny looking thing, isn't it?" Andee asked

"Not as funny looking as your face is." Allen laughed.

"Smooth." Andee said, raising his eye brow. "You do know that we look exactly the same . . . don't you?"

"Ha! I'm much prettier than you are."

"Did it hurt?" Andee asked

"Hurt!?" a confused look crossed Allen's face

"When you hit your head and went Bonkers Gazoo! Anyone with eyes can see that I am the looker of the two of us."

Allen jumped on Andee and a "Farmer scuffle" started. Everyone laughed as the two Farmers tried to 'best' each other. They rolled and scooted all around on the ground 'oomphing' and 'ouching' all over the place as they pushed and shoved, each trying to best the other but neither seemed to be able to get the upper hand.

From the corner of my eye I saw Squeaks; still standing by the egg staring at it like she was hypnotized. I didn't reactor acknowledge it, simply watched her and silently prayed that I didn't get a henky feeling. I sent out my senses but felt no danger to her so I didn't *'freak out'* looking at her strange actions.

She stood there staring at the egg, an intense expression on her face. I could see her eyes had begun to change color and started to glow. The blue was completely gone and the green had taken a neon look to it. Henky feeling or not, seeing my sweet Squeaks looking like that had me worried. No one was going to put a spell on my Squeaks! When I got close to her I could see sheen of tears in her eyes.

"She's scared, Lou." Squeaks' voice was so quiet I almost couldn't hear it.

"Who's scared, baby? What are you talking about?" I looked around nervously.

"The little bird." Her voice quivered with sorrow.

"What little bird? What are you talking about Squeaks?"

She closed her eyes and sighed. "I never told anyone this; I'm already such a freak as it is, but I can talk to animals. It's kind of like the way you talk to Lykie." She wiped her eyes and looked at me. "I have always been able to do it and never told anyone about it. I was afraid that people would think I was weird . . . or weirder than they already think the 'freaky little kid in high school' is. I have been able to 'talk' to animals I think all my life; they sort of 'find' me."

"I would have never thought you were weird, baby. Surely you knew that?"

"I have kept this a secret for so long, I just never thought about telling you. I never really think about it." She returned her gaze to the smoking ettabird egg.

"You said the bird was scared; what did you mean? What is it scared of?"

"She didn't grow right in her egg. She has a deformed wing. She doesn't think she'll ever be able to fly and she is in pain." The quiver had returned to her voice.

"Can you talk to her?" I looked at the egg and then back at the Farmers where they were still rolling around on the ground; grateful they were holding everyone's attention.

"Yes, I have been talking to her since we got down here and I heard her crying."

The egg started to smoke, a low hissing sound came from it that drew the attention of the rest of the group.

"*What* in the name of aunt May's missing left sock was that?" DJ asked, walking up to my side.

"Is that thing *alive*!?" Allen asked.

"*She is not a thing*! And **yes**, she *is* alive!" Squeaks snapped

"She!? The smoking rock is a girl?" Andee asked

Squeaks narrowed her eyes and gave him a stern look but didn't comment; turning her attention back to the ettabird egg. I saw the neon color return to her eyes and knew she was talking to the infant bird.

The egg stopped moving and a crack appeared in its surface. A thick green substance came oozing out of the crack.

"It's ok, come on out." Squeaks cooed

"Everyone move away." Lydian said "This creature is most dangerous. Get back in the fardal until we have destroyed it."

"NO!!" Squeaks yelled "Please, don't hurt her! She is only a baby and she's hurt." She turned and looked at me, tears streaming down her angelic face. "Please Lou, don't let them hurt her. She is really scared and alone . . . PLEASE!?"

She did that "sad cat eye" thing to me and my heart melted. Squeaks never asked me for anything, she had just asked me for something and I was going to do everything in my power to give her what she asked for.

"I'll do what I can baby. But you have to promise me that if she turns out evil you won't try to stop us from getting rid of her. Can you promise me that?" I asked

"Thank you, Lou. And yes, I promise." She hugged me then turned back to the ettabird egg, calming the fledgling inside.

I looked at Kaeli, "You can . . . control it can't you?"

"You know the answer True Weaver; your power is nearly as strong as mine. It is only your knowledge and experience that are lacking." She raised her hands and chanted a spell to protect us should the Ettabird be dangerous.

A loud pop followed by a hiss drew my attention back to the egg. (It was open) everyone got quiet, staring at the bird that had just exited the egg. It was about the size of a collie dog, the color of coffee with cream in it. Its huge yellow eyes looked at each of us its beak was shaped like a hawk beak. It must have been the essence stone that protruded from the top of the beak, just behind the nose holes.

The bird was covered in the green goo from inside the egg. She stood to her full height and shook, like a wet dog shakes to get rid of the excess water. I barely had time to close my mouth and eyes when I felt myself being covered in ettabird goo.

"Much to do about, Eww!"

Squeaks walked over to the bird "Be careful Frankie, ettabirds are very dangerous." Lydian cautioned.

Squeaks didn't respond, she just eased closer to the bird and held out her hand to it. The bird eyed Squeaks, turning her head and blinking thoughtfully, like she was sizing Squeaks up. The bird then looked at the group of us, stopping on each face then she returned her gaze to Squeaks again.

After about five minutes of silence the bird leaned her head down and scratched it's face with it's very long talons; hooking one of the claws on the essence stone, ripping it off. She picked up the stone and raised her head, looking around.

"No one move." Lydian hissed "Ettabirds don't like being controlled and will fight to the death to protect their essence stone. She will attack us if she thinks we are after it."

With the stone glistening between her beak's razor points; the bird continued to stare at us. Her attention kept returning to Squeaks.

My heart skipped a beat when the bird took an attentive step in Squeaks' direction. Leah was in danger because of me. I will not allow anything to happen to Squeaks too. Everything in me insisted that I protect her but when I made eye contact with her she shook her head very slightly, indicating she knew what I was about to do.

The bird walked slowly up to Squeaks, it was about a foot away. The goo it had been covered with was nearly dry. The feathers on its head looked like dreadlocks hanging down around her face. She turned her head sideways looking at Squeaks. My heart was in my throat; that razor sharp beak was mere inches from my baby Squeaks' face.

----- If that bird hurts her; we're having fried chicken for dinner ---- I thought.

The ettabird turned her head and dropped the essence stone in Squeaks' tiny palm. Then it nipped the end of her finger causing it to bleed.

"I'm calling her Etta." Squeaks said, beaming at the bird.

Etta nipped her gimpy wing causing it to bleed and Squeaks rubbed her bleeding finger on it, mixing their blood. "I belong to her now." Squeaks said smiling at Etta.

Etta rubbed her head on Squeaks and made a noise like a purr.

"*That* . . . **was** . . . **amazing!**" Kon said. "Ettabirds are known for protecting their essence stone. That one . . . took it off . . . and **gave** to the small human Frankie." His eyes so large they were about to pop out of his head.

"Are you ok?" I looked at Squeaks. "Your hand is still bleeding there kiddo."

"She did a blood exchange with me, Lou. It is a big honor for an ettabird to do that. Now other of her kind won't bother me. They will smell her blood in me and will know I belong to her." She looked down at her hand and smiled.

I tore a strip from the bottom of my shirt and tied it around her hand. Sensing something at my side I turned and found myself looking into a pair of bright yellow eyes.

"Don't worry Etta, I would never hurt her. She's my girl." I said it but didn't feel so strong looking into those questioning eyes.

"As odd as an ettabird, willingly, giving up their essence stone is; I still feel that you need to know about them." Kin said

Ok, to save you the long and boring lecture of all there is to know about an ettabird and its behavior; I have edited it down for you...PS, you're welcome.

1) Ettabirds are controlled by an essence stone that comes from its beak.
2) Ettabirds are vicious.

3) Ettabirds will fight to the death to keep the stone from someone possessing it.
4) They can hibernate inside the stone.
5) They are virtually indestructible because they can respawn to where their essence stone is and will emerge from it around a day later.
6) The ettabird is the only thing that can destroy an essence stone.

There were a few more," Bla... Bla... Blas" and one or two "Du, du, du, du, dus" but you get the jest of his little talk.

"She will defend you at all cost, Frankie." Kon said

The T-Weaves all gathered around Etta and we started getting to know the newest member of our little gang.

Kaeli came over to where I stood and put her hand on my shoulder. "You must look into your heart to find the way to defeat Logton. Have the faith in yourself that others have found in you." She put a gold necklace around my neck. "This will allow you to travel through the magic boundaries I have placed here." She kissed my forehead and she was gone.

It felt strange without her there. I guess I shouldn't have simply assumed that she was going to go into battle with me. You know what they say when you assume something...

The next few hours were spent by making plans and coming up with different strategies; and we now had only two days left to get it all done. Even if I didn't make it out of this alive; I was darn sure gonna make sure Leah got out safe.

Even thought Kaeli had given me a means to use magic here, we still didn't want to alert Logton to our presence. Being afraid that he might feel the pull or shift in the energy, we decided to walk. After seeing my memories, Lydian said it was under a day's journey to the caves. Now let me see if my math is right . . . 2-1=1 . . . wow, I was hoping that I was wrong; but we're cutting this short on time . . . my time that is. (Sad face)

I found my strength waning with every step as time passed. Every moment that passed seemed to be harder for me to get my body to cooperate and function properly. I didn't even want to think about how hard this would be for me without the doddle berry tea.

It must have been noticeable to the gang because Squeaks said that Etta wanted to carry me; not a time for silly pride, I accepted the offer and hopped aboard the Etta Express. Riding was much better than walking and now the group seemed to have picked up a little speed. I had no idea how slow we were traveling until I was on Etta and we could actually move. I guess my attempt to hide my weakness had only fooled me. My Buds had seen I was struggling and they had simply altered their pace rather than mention it.

The instant that we crossed over Logton's magic bearer; I knew, we all knew. The air felt thick and your skin just felt . . . unclean like a vile film had coated your entire body and was trying to smother you. The air had stopped stirring, no creature seemed to move or flutter around, and even the sounds that had been following us from around the area, all stopped and only an eerie silence could be heard.

"Ok guys, this is it. If anyone has second thoughts, now is the time to speak up." I said, trying for the last time to offer everyone an out before it was too late.

Eight pair of eyes stared at me, practically unblinking, but no one spoke. One by one each of them held out their hand and gave a 'thumbs up' sign. They were in it for the long haul and I knew none of them was about to tuck tail and run. We were Buds 'til the end.

"Alrighty then . . . it's a go." I looked at Squeaks. "Baby, since we don't know much about Etta's magic, I think it might be best if we leave her here."

I could see the conflict in Squeaks' eyes. She wanted to protect the 'baby bird' but she wanted to be with me at the same time. She sighed and nod her head in agreement.

"We can't use *any* magic on this side of Logton's barrier. I'll walk you back to where I can't feel the magic shift on the other side and you can, umm, explain it to Etta so she will know what we are doing." I said gently, I knew the bird was important to Squeaks and I didn't want her to think she wasn't important to the rest of us, I knew she understood it was only a precaution to keep us all safe.

"If Frankie will allow me," Lydian said, smiling down a Squeaks "I'd be honored to assist her in this task; I too can feel the magical line and can get her and her new special friend past the danger zone and back."

I looked at Squeaks, took in her big blue-green eyes, now shrouded in sadness. She shook her head giving the 'ok' but didn't say anything. The two of them walked off, I felt like it should be me helping her. She was still so young and this was probably the hardest thing she had ever had to do. Lydian had placed his hand on her tiny shoulder and was talking very low and comforting to her as they walked off together.

"Much to do about, feeling like a *bad* big sister."

After about six minutes, Lydian and Squeaks came walking back. Her sweet little face was streaked with tears but she was laughing at something they were talking about. (Just when I thought I could think any higher of my Guardian, I found out I was . . . WRONG!)

"Etta shrank, like Jell-O in reverse and 'poofed' into her stone." She said and smiled. "She is right here in it now; but I told her not to try talking to me because I'm pretty sure that is magic and Logton would hear it." She was holding out the essence stone beaming a huge smile at me like a child presenting a painting to their mom.

"Good thinking baby girl." I pulled her into a hug. "We don't want that little butt nugget, Logton to get wind of anything that will give away the fact that we are here. I don't want him to get his hands on any of us; and that includes Etta!"

DJ raised his hand, like we were in class and he wanted to get the teacher's attention.

"Yes, DJ, you need to go potty?" I joked

"Naa, I'm wearing my pull-ups for that. I's just wondering . . . how on earth; even though we're not on earth, but how on earth are we going to get in there where Logton is without him knowing? If you can't use your magic right now that kinda puts us at a disadvantage."

I looked at all of the trusting faces that surrounded me to know what to do and how to get us through this ordeal and I smiled and said "Like this…"

I wrapped my fingers around the necklace that Kaeli had given me and told them to all gather 'round and lock hands. "Make sure that you are all connected to each other then make sure you are in contact with me."

Everyone did as I had instructed and then we stood there, all eyes on me. I sure hoped I was right about this. The thought had just left the runway of my brain when I felt a pull in the pit of my stomach. Pulling and pushing at the same time. I closed my eyes and silently prayed that we would be where we were supposed to be to get inside Logton's fortress.

The pull slowed then stopped; I opened my eyes and saw that we had been transported just outside the entrance to where I had seen Logton holding Leah.

"Kaeli said the necklace would shield us inside her bearer; I took a shot that it would help us get here."

"I'm glad to see you are beginning to trust your gifts. Adnama chose wisely in you, Lemoya." Lydian whispered in my ear.

Painful Revelations

Standing just outside the cave the temperature dropped about ten degrees. When I felt a different shift in energy I knew we were close to his hiding place. We had gone over the plan and it was solid . . . I hoped.

"Everyone knows what they're to do, right?" I whispered. "Don't hesitate to use the conk band if you get in a jam. It's what they're for."

My friends all shook their heads and separated into their groups.

Lydian was with Squeaks. DJ was with Kin and Pixie. The Farmers, De and Kon were together; consequently leaving me as a team of one.

"Much to do about, how it feels to be in a pressure cooker."

Think! I told myself. You are not Louanna Teelf, you are the True Weaver and you are not alone. Go Deep, find the True Weaver, and set her loose on that little butt nugget, Logton. (Thanks Ms. Rhone.)

The feeling inside the cave was worse on my skin than it had been on my spirit fog. It was almost a tangible substance, and it was alert and seemingly scanning as well. It was more like a being than a feeling; that in itself made our progress slow. Added to the fact that several times I went down a passage, I knew to be wrong; so I could cough up blood without my friends knowing. Our progress was not advancing as I had hoped and I was literally running out of time.

My head was pounding and I was fighting for breath . . . Time was defiantly running out. Even with the help of the dottle berry tea, keeping this knowledge from my buds was becoming a real challenge. I knew in my heart that each one of them knew but I was grateful none of them said it out loud.

I suppose that travel as energy or spirit, made the trip seem shorter because the distance into the cave's labyrinth seemed to be taking twice the amount of time as before. Time we didn't have to spare. I didn't have...

A wave of nausea swept over me, taking me to my knees. Wrenching repeatedly until I threw up a large pool of blood; and what looked strangely like raw chicken liver.

"Much to do about, G-R-O-S-S!"

"Here, Lou. Let me help you." DeLainey said, wiping the ick from my mouth and chin. "Maybe you should sit down for a minute and catch your breath."

"I can't, DeLai... De; we have to find Leah." I said quietly. "We're running out of time."

"We're with you. But you still have to take care of *you*." He whispered.

He rubbed his thumb along my jaw, and then tucked a stray band of hair behind my ear. I felt a stirring in my stomach; that wasn't related to barfing. He got a twinkle in his eye and then planted that adorable lopsided grin on his face.

"You're lethal with those eyes and that smile, ya know." I joked then coughed up more blood.

"I'm glad you think so," he laughed; then once again, gently wiped my mouth free of 'Lou Goo'.

"We should keep moving." Lydian said, pulling me to my feet . . . away from De. "Are you up to this, Mia noja?" He was walking me far enough from where De stood; that there could be no physical contact between us. If I didn't feel like *"warmed over death"* this would seem really sweet . . . Now? . . . Not so much.

*"You don't have to go all **alpha wolf** on me."*

I knew I had made a mistake the second the thought left my head. Using my magic caused blood to come out of my nose and the air around us stilled.

"He knows I am here." I whispered.

"I believe you are correct." Kin said, attentively looking around.

"Okay. We planned for this, guys. If Logton found out we were here . . . plan B. good luck everyone." I barked out the order and people began to scramble.

Lydian wasn't crazy about not being on**, *team Louanna*,** but I had insisted that he stay with Squeaks. He could protect her. She is still so young. I can't lose her and Leah.

"Be careful, Mia noja" he whispered. "Should you have need of me . . ." He ran his thumb along my jaw, looked at me for a moment, then turned with Squeaks and walked away; not looking back. My heart felt heavy. I didn't want him to leave me. I couldn't . . . no! WOULDN'T let anything happen to Squeaks, and Lydian would be her best bet at safety. (*But he wouldn't be with me.*).

"I am *always* with you, Lemoya" He sent a caress with the thought, making me feel safe.

"Are you sure you don't want me . . . I mean need my skills with you?" De asked, bringing my attention back to him.

"We all have our instructions, DeLainey. Thanks for the offer; but, we stick to the plan." I smiled at him weakly.

"De." He corrected quietly. "And I was just *hoping*." He leaned over and kissed my cheek. "A guy can hope ya know." The lopsided grin jumped to his lips and his eyes sparkled.

--- Enter butterflies, Stage left. --- I'm becoming such a girlie girl.

I watched as my buds walked off together, all in different directions; until I was standing there . . . Alone. *Maybe I should have rethought the line up in this game.* I laughed; game . . . a game of life and death, played on an unfamiliar playing field, with unclear rules, and an undetermined amount of players. I sure hope I can respawn to my last checkpoint if I die . . . hey, a girl can hope too.

We thought that the groups were a good idea. If one group got taken out, there would be others behind it. I thought this our best chance to get Leah out of there. And my buds all agreed, each taking on a specific task.

I couldn't think about them or what they were doing. We each had a job to do, now, it's my turn. I took out my Weaving wands and looked at them; sticks, really. Just twigs picked up at random. But in the right hands, *MY* hands, they could yield magic.

I took out the small towel that Squeaks had insisted I keep handy, and tucked it under my conk band. I took a deep calming breath, closed my eyes, and let Adnama guide me. Opening my eyes I saw the rainbow webs forming and felt the wind around me began to stir.

The call of violence has brought me here.
The pain it caused, I have endured.
What you sent out was aimed at me.
I now send back, with strength times three.
REVEAL . . .

I jammed my hands into the air in front of me and saw an electrical charge leave my fingertips. I knew the moment the spell had struck a blow. The air grew more turbulent and the feel in the cave became more ominous. Logton screamed in agony as he was hit by the spell.

I found myself again on my knees, heaving and wrenching in pain. Logton's scream had felt like razors slicing through my brain; like shards of glass were stabbing the back of my eyes and the now all too familiar, taste of copper, once again filled my mouth. "Get up, Louanna!" I growled at myself. Struggling to my feet, I retrieved the small towel and cleaned my mouth.

The plan was coming together nicely. I put a tail on the spell and would be able to find Logton easier. I'm sure I now had his **full** attention. He will know where I am and *hopefully* not pay attention to the others as they make their way closer to where he is. I just have to keep his attention on me.

Walking had become difficult. It felt like my brain was made of sludge and I had to fight the urge to throw up nearly every second.

I took out the Weaving wands and quickly wove a spell of protection; it looked like a large bubble had encased me. I was becoming familiar with the way the wands moved. I knew that Logton would retaliate for the spell I had hit him with and it would be soon. Just as I had the thought, my henky feeling warned me and I instantly crossed the Weaving wands over my chest and braced for the impact. A huge ball of blue flames came blasting its way down the hall straight at me.

My protection spell took the brunt of his spell; but, it did make contact with me knocking my body backwards into the air, burning my skin, and taking my breath. I landed on the ground several feet behind where I had been standing. It felt like acid had been poured over my skin. I quickly grabbed the towel Squeaks had given me and shoved it in my mouth to stifle my scream . . . and I **DID** scream!

"That's fine, you little fungus; just keep your attention focused on me." I said when I found my voice again. I got to my feet and started to make my way to where Logton was waiting. I stumbled down the dark hall. Even with the torches lit, it was still a dark place. The sound of water dripping through the walls seemed to be my only companion. I took out some of the dottle berry tea and drank it quickly; hoping to relieve some of the pain that now racked through my very essence.

After traveling quite a distance in the labyrinth of tunnels; my conk band began to blink and hum. One of my buds was in trouble. I slowly held my arm up and began to turn. It was no surprise that it got louder and faster in the same direction that Logton was in. My heart felt like it was made of lead and unable to properly function. It was having so much trouble beating. Now I'm responsible for two of my buds getting hurt, I thought.

"Much to do about, this True Weaver junk stinks!"

I took a breath to steady myself. Losing my focus would do no one any good. I have to remember why I'm here and stay on course. I found myself once again weaving a spell of protection around me; it seemed to take all the energy I had left. Logton had sent a few spells that vibrated the protection bubble, but nothing as strong as the first one. I didn't retaliate; I didn't have the strength, but didn't want him to know that.

Screams . . . Mournful, pain laden, screams reached my ears; causing my blood to run cold. Unable to tell whose they were only made it worse. I knew one of my buds was being hurt or tortured.

Standing just outside the room or cell; *which seems more appropriate in this case*, I tried to calm myself. Logton's hatred came pouring out of the room; like waves in the ocean. He knew I was there and he was ready for me. The feeling of despair saturated my skin.

"Come in, my dear. We have been waiting for you; dallying in the hallway shows poor etiquette." Logton's greasy voice seemed to wrap around me as he spoke.

It took a great deal of concentration to keep my heart beat at a normal pace once inside the cell. The scene was so horrific that I wanted to cry. Along the walls strange beings were shackled, all in different stages of torture. On each face the look of defeat was clear to see. The corners held large stone chalices filled with flaming oil. In the center of the room, Logton had fashioned himself a large marble throne; where he sat staring at me. Scattered around the room sat small medal cages and within them were . . . some of my buds.

"True Weaver, at last we meet. Tis an honor" Logton said. "The festivities have started without you, I'm afraid; but do not fear, I have saved the best entertainment for *you*." A cruel smile slithered across his ugly little face; I noticed the entire left side was blackened. I couldn't help but think I had done that and smiled to myself. He raised his goblet and took a drink from it, never taking his eyes from me.

"Nice place you've got here, it seems like a nice place to bury you in." I said and smiled sweetly.

He raised his eyebrow at me over his drink. "To shay" He said and raised his glass to me in mock salute at my statement. "Would indeed be a grand resting place, But tis not *I* that shall use it in that manner; Tis **thee** who will die here this day . . . True Weaver." He returned the goblet to the small table beside his seat and leaned forward, lacing his fingers together. His beady little red eyes seemed to bore a hole through me. I braced myself for his attack.

"Now, my Dear, you do not think this historical event will end so soon, do you?" He asked. "Why, you have just arrived and we have yet to get acquainted." He sat quietly for a moment; seemingly thinking. "I think a reunion is long overdue here." He finally said.

He got up from his throne, smoothed back his greasy red hair, and straightened his little brown suit. Then he looked around the room. "Go retrieve our *special guest*." He said to a large, bear like, creature that was chained to the wall. He then waved his hand and the chain fell to the ground. The bear thingy simply left the room without further prompting. "Broogs are quite useful; when they are properly trained." He said. "They are most unpredictable until then."

I started to comment, but the sound of feet scuffling, made me pause. Looking towards the noise I saw the Broog return . . . with **Leah**.

She looked so battered and bruised. She stared at the ground, but I could see that her eyes were red and swollen. Beatings? Crying? I didn't know. She looked nothing like she did the last time I saw her.

The Broog yanked on the chain shackled to her wrists, causing her to wince in pain. She looked up to say something, saw me and stopped.

"Lou! You're here." She spoke quietly, her voice sounding dry and raspy.

"You're my best friend. I had no choice. Are you ok, Leah?" I asked

"You have no idea how much better I am; now that you're here." She said.

"Aaaah, a blessed reunion." Logton sneered. "My heart is truly touched."

A moan drew my attention. There was movement in the cage that held Allen and Andee. They were tied back to back and unconscious, but they were both alive. And it sounded like one of them was waking up.

"Much to do about, **RELIEF**!"

"I was worried that you wouldn't come." Leah said then slowly walked to the cage where Kon's body lay in a lifeless heap. He was covered in blood and one of his arms looked as if it had been chewed off. "Are these your friends?" She asked quietly.

"Yes." I said, keeping my eyes on Logton. "They came to help rescue you."

"Somehow I doubt that." She sniffed. "I'm sure they came to help you get better."

"Well, that too." I laughed, fighting the urge to throw up again. "Our main goal was to rescue you."

"You should have worried more about yourself and not me, Louanna."

Something about the way she said *Louanna* and not Lou made my henky feeling kick in. I took my eyes off of Logton and looked at my best friend. She stood there; smiling at me, holding Kon's conk band. She no longer looked tired and frail. She stood straight and not slumped over in pain.

"What's going on, Leah?" I asked the question, I was afraid I didn't want the answer to.

"What *is* going on here, Louanna?" She snapped. "I thought by now *you*; being the, all powerful True Weaver, would have figured at least *some* of it out. And you were the one they all called the smart one. It was always, Lou . . . Lou . . . **LOU**! Even the sound of your name makes me sick!"

I could only stare at her. My mouth hung open in shock. This was Leah, my best friend! We had shared everything together since we were in kindergarten. She looked like my friend; sounded like her, but this couldn't be her.

"What happened to you Leah? What did *he*," I gestured towards Logton, "do to you?"

"*He*? No, Louanna, He didn't do this. **You** did." She swung her arms around aiming them at me; a force flew at me, knocking me to the ground. "Our father gave all the gifts to you; gifts that are rightfully mine!" She swung her arms again driving me into the wall. A cracking sound and a jabbing pain in my side told me I was now the proud owner of a broken rib. (Or two)

"I had to sit back silently, year after year and watch you in your perfect little world, surrounded by love and protection; while I was beaten and abused because I wasn't good enough!" She was screaming so loud that spittle was flying out of her mouth.

"I didn't ask for any of this, Leah. You know that."

"Oh shut up, Louanna! I have watched you with people, manipulating them 'til you get your way. "Oh Papa" was all it took and little Louanna got whatever she wanted." She turned and sneered at me. "I took him from you, ya know. He was getting suspicious of all the 'little accidents' that kept happening to you. He even tried reading my thoughts. For what good that did him." She said, more to herself than to me.

"So you killed him, you killed Papa?" My heart felt like it was in my throat.

"Death is too good for that nosey ole goat. I simply . . . sent him away." She laughed.

"What do you mean 'sent him away'? What did you do, Leah?" I snapped

"Well, being the **True Weaver**; I suspect you'll figure that out on your own." She looked at me with a smirk on her face. "Then again, you really aren't that quick on the up take, are you?"

My blood was boiling. It felt like I was fighting for every breath and to spite it all, I missed my friend. Leah had been my best friend for as long as I could remember. We had always been more like sisters than we were friends. This can't be happening.

"You said **our father**. What did you mean by that?" I asked, but didn't want to know.

"You caught that did you?" She laughed again. "I suppose I should tell you; it looks like you won't be with us for much longer. And you do have the right to know . . . Dear sister. Our father was an Elder; he and your mom were never married. Sort of makes you a bastard like me, doesn't it?" She laughed

"Get on with it." I snapped. I may have to listen to her but I didn't have to let her enjoy it so much.

"Tut, tut, Louanna, stories will lose their audience if they are told improperly." She said, smiling at me, a cold, evil, calculating smile. (*I was not impressed.*) "It is prophesized that the True Weaver would come from the union of an Elder and a woman with Weaver blood. Subsequently; Elders have become, magical prostitutes, bedding anyone with Weaver blood. They couldn't stop there; they would even bed human women, though not all of the humans made it." The pain in her voice was clear.

"My Mom was pregnant with me when she met dear ole Larry. She died having me and Larry blamed me for her death; apparently, he actually loved my mom and hated me for her being taken from him. He never let me live it down; and you know how he **rewarded** me for it."

For a bleak second, she once again looked like my lifelong friend, when she noticed me looking at her; she changed her facial appearance back to the cold hard face she seemed to prefer now.

"One night I lay in the park; after Larry had slapped me around for an hour or so; a man approached me and introduced himself. He said he was my father." Her nose flared at the memory. "Foolish child that I was; I got my hopes up, and believed all my troubles were over. My real *daddy* had come to take me away from Larry and all his *touchy feely* friends. Then "dad" gave me a small box. It was so pretty and . . . the only gift anyone had ever given me. He smiled at me and told me to open it, so I did."

"It was a Jequota. That's an awesome gift, Leah." I said.

"SHUT UP! I know what it was; though I didn't at the time." She snapped. "When I opened it, I looked at him and smiled. He looked down his nose at me like I was some form of vermin, just like Larry does. He simply said he still had hope in *Louanna*. Then he just poofed and was gone." Her voice was laced with pain, anger, and hatred. "I was four years old, my mom was dead, my stepdad didn't want me, and it seemed that neither did my *real* dad. But all was not lost; that was when something wonderful happened." She turned and smiled at me.

"**I** found her." Logton spoke up, drawing my attention again. "Her anger was so powerful... a sweet enticement. I could do no other than find its source. And what a wonderful find she was; young and magical and so full of rage. It was as if Adnama had placed her in my hands."

I didn't know what to do or say. I simply stood there and stared at them. I wasn't sure what they were up to but I wasn't so foolish as to let my guard down.

"After Logton told me about the magic and *what* I was, I didn't feel quite so bad . . . I had a friend." She smiled lovingly at Logton.

He smiled back at her. The smile didn't quite reach his eyes however. Was Leah so starved for love that she had fallen for his gaggle of lies? He saw her one true weakness and was using it against her. I didn't think it possible to hate any one being as much as I hated him.

"After we found you, Leah here, befriended you. It made keeping track of your whereabouts so much easier." He smirked at me.

"So we grew up together." Leah went on. "Every day you rubbing your wonderful life in my face; pitching me a scrap now and again from your table of plenty. Do you remember your broken leg in the seventh grade? Your accident on the teeter totters in the fifth grade?" She faked concern. "I did that. Logton was teaching me about magic; *you* didn't even know that you *had* magic and I was already casting spells." She cut her eyes at me. "You, the *True Weaver* didn't have a clue."

"Why didn't you tell me, Leah? If there was a problem we could have fixed it together. We were friends." I whispered.

She stared at me; like I'd grown a horn out of my head or an extra eye on my forehead. She shook her head, as if to clear it, and went on. "So time passed and we grew up. One day at school I noticed those little vermin, in the window, trying to communicate with you." She looked at Kon then at the conk

Life Weaver

band in her hand and smiled. "When I told Logton, we broke into the school and . . . fixed the problem. Remember the windows and mirrors at school? I did that. I tried to get you out that night to throw suspicion on you; but little goody two shoes was in for the night." Her voice dripped with sarcasm.

"Seems like a lot of trouble for nothing, Leah. They got to me anyway." I said

"Yes, and isn't that just great for you, *True Weaver*?" she laughed as she looked at Kon's body, lying in the cage.

I wanted to lash out at her; to end this once and for all, instead I just laid there. I knew there was a battle about to take place and I needed all my strength.

"Regardless of how this has come about; you do show remarkable skills." Logton said, bringing attention to the red whelp just below his eye. I could feel the waves of hatred rolling off of him.

"I'm not sure how you managed to strike Logton but; rest assured, it won't happen again." Leah hissed. "I can feel the poison flowing through you, Louanna. Are you in pain?" Once more she faked concern for me.

"I'm fine, Leah. Thanks for your; umm, **concern**." I said sweetly.

I could feel the buildup of energy around me, the battle was about to start. The rainbow webs had started to gather, and the wind was changing; becoming a more familiar breeze to me.

Leah and Logton swung their arms, sending a huge ball of fire in my direction. I quickly sent duel streaks of electricity at them. I hit dead center, driving them to the ground; my quick reactions had caught them by surprise; giving me only seconds to move to safety. I jumped behind one of the stone challises and went to my knees. I became warm, as if a heated blanket had been thrown over me.

True Weaver, I have limited time with you as this cloak will not last long. Use your talents as a way to defeat your enemies. Trust in yourself and know; you are not alone.

The voice came from inside as well as around me. *"You are not alone.'* It had said. I can't think about what has gone wrong; I have to look at the big picture. Slowly I got to my feet and took a slow steading breath. Weaving wands in each hand I opened my eyes. Leah and Logton were looking at each other, disbelief on their faces, that I had attacked them so swiftly when they were sure I was out for the count.

"Very good, True Weaver; it would seem we have under estimated your abilities. This round goes to you, it would appear." Logton said, his voice laced with uncertainty. "Now that I see you have been holding back; I must bring forth my *'A'* game."

He raised his hands; at once the creatures on the wall were set free. *Now would be a good time for some of that 'not alone' stuff the mystery voice was talking about.* There was an out pouring of movement as the beasts began to roam around the room.

I stood still and refused to give way to my fears. I had been placed in this position for a reason. True Weaver . . . that is something special. I will NOT die here today. I let my hands move as they wanted to; without conscience thought they were casting a spell. "Protect" I whispered, seeing a Vail fall over my fallen friends as I spoke.

"We are here, Lemoya" Lydian whispered. "Do not alert them. When our plan starts you will have but one chance at getting him. You can do this, Mia noja."

I wanted to cry with relief; the sound of that voice in my head, left me feeling much stronger than I really was.

"**This has gone on long enough!**" Leah yelled. "**Now you die, Louanna!**" She swung her arms upwards to curse me.

"*NOT YET*!" Logton screamed, turning to look at me.

Everything in the room froze; the look of horror on Logton's face, forever etched in my mind, as he saw me strike the final blow in our battle for life. He bowed to me and dissolved as the spell meant to kill him passed through the mist he had become and hit Leah square in the chest. Everything took on the feel of one of the old movies where people moved in slow motion and it felt like I was running in mud.

Leah stood there looking at me; shock etched across her face. Slowly she went to her knees. Her body seemed to fold in on itself, as I finally reached her side, she fell to the ground. I wrapped her in my arms and held her close. Unable to stop them; tears flowed down my face, soaking her hair.

"Leah, what have you done?" I choked out.

"Lou? How has it come to this?" She asked through ragged gasps of air.

Tears streamed from her eyes. There was blood oozing from her mouth and ears. My best friend was dying; and I had killed her. I wiped the blood from her mouth.

"I just turned sixteen. I can't lose you. You're my best friend. We're gonna start dating and call each other with dirty questions." I whispered.

"How can you call me your best friend? I tried to kill you, Lou. I don't think that qualifies me as friend let alone best friend." She said, coughing blood down her front.

"Well, that *is* a bad thing; I'll have to ground you from sanctuary for a week for that." I said, feeling my heart break. The sparkle she once held was fading before my eyes.

"I don't think I'll be at sanctuary any more, Lou. I'm not leaving this place . . . alive." She looked up at me and I saw so much sadness in her eyes.

Leah convulsed and went limp in my arms. My body was cold; I knew I was quickly running out of energy. I shook her, "Leah, don't leave me!" I screamed. She opened her eyes and smiled at me; taking something from her pocket, she dropped it in my hand. "See ya on the flip side, Chickadee." She whispered, took a ragged breath and was gone. That was Leah, no long good byes, just click, and it was over.

I was lost. I sat there on the ground holding the shell of my best friend, my half-sister, one I had never really known and cried. My head pounded and I knew I was about to pass out again, but I couldn't muster the energy it would take to care. This had all been for nothing. Logton had gotten away, Leah was dead, and I was about to join her.

I heard movement behind me, but didn't bother to see what the grim reaper looked like. I wrapped my arms around Leah's body, closed my eyes and welcomed death's final blow.

Keeping Promises

I woke in the field of Xela, it was familiar and welcoming. Lying there on the grass, I stared at the crystal blue sky above and relaxed. My body was no longer in pain. I no longer had to see my friends hurt or dying. This is a good place to be. . . . So why did it feel so wrong?

I finally sat up, expecting pain but none came. A gentle breeze caused the tall grass to sway and dance. There were no more nightmares, no more suffering; only peace could be found here. This is a good place to be . . . So why did it feel so wrong?

"Papa?" I whispered, looking around the sunny field. "Are you here?"

The snap of something breaking, caused my blood to run cold. With all that had happened; this calm could very well be another trick that Logton had put into play. Slowly I turned and searched for the source of the noise. A deer and fawn stood quietly watching me from the edge of tree line. I smiled to myself and wondered if they were the same pair I had seen from one of my earlier visits to Xela.

I began walking, in no particular direction; just reveling in the ability to do so. When we are well, we take what we do every day for granted. It is when an ability has been taken; then returned to us, that we realize it is a *privilege* and I was enjoying the privilege of walking without pain.

Time had taken on new meaning for me. I enjoyed each moment that I had; though to be honest, I don't recall how much time had passed. I found myself under the large tree Papa and I had once sat beneath and smiled at the memory.

"This place is so peaceful." I mumbled, sitting down and closing my eyes. I found that the endless waves of stress were no longer bound to me. I could now relax.

"Don't fall asleep, Lemoya."

My eyes snapped open. Papa stood before me with his arms crossed over his chest and a huge smile plastered across his handsome face. I leapt to my feet and was instantly rewarded with a grizzle hug. The smell of pipe tobacco and cedar engulfed me.

"Papa, I have so much to tell you." I said.

"Do you?" He laughed, pushing me back and eyeing me suspiciously. "Well then, I shall have to listen."

I told him the whole story; I just rambled on an on barely pausing for breath. Papa sat quietly listening to every word. He never acted or reacted to any one statement; just listened to me jabber. When I finally stopped, he smiled at me.

"That's quite a story Louanna, and you told it very well." He said quietly." It seems however; there are pieces missing. Some of the things in the tale were; I fear, relayed to your friend incorrectly."

"What do you mean, Papa? The prophecy was told and repeated to me just as I told it to you. My father was the same as Leah's." I said the words, but still couldn't believe them.

"The prophecy does speak of the True Weaver being born of the Elder and Weaver blood lines. But, it also foretells that she would be born under an Autumn Moon at the stroke of twelve, by; and this is the most important part, ***a union***, of Elder and Weaver. Your father was indeed married to your mother. They were very much in love Louanna, never doubt that. The farce that was given to your friend, was one invented to fuel her anger and bring about someone's twisted scheme."

"She believed what she told me. I could see the pain in her eyes." I admitted.

"I am sure that she did not relay to you an untruth, Lemoya; merely the version she had been told. She longed for love and acceptance, a need that was easily manipulated. She was alone and venerable; and for those who wish to concur, she was merely a pawn to be used and discarded when her usefulness was gone." He looked at me, sadness etched deep with in his eyes. "We must try to not judge your friend too harshly. Do you understand Mia noja?"

"I think so, Papa. It's one of those "outside the box" things, isn't it?"

"Yes. That is precisely what it is little one. Our lives are not contained in a box. We each have a destiny to fulfill." He said.

"So what do I do now, Papa? Is there a light that "Beams me up" or do *you* take me on?"

He looked at me with a puzzled look on his face. "I'm not sure I follow your questioning, Lemoya. What beam would you put up that I must take you to?" he asked.

I laughed then plucked a blade of grass to play with. "Now that I'm dead, do I become someone's spirit guide, like you?"

He stood quietly for a few minutes then smiled at me. "You are not dead, Louanna; though, it would appear that you gave it your best try. You are as you were before, simply in a deep sleep. I'd venture to go as far as to say you may be in a comma. Your mind was in; I believe you call it, overload, and needed to sort out all of this."

So I wasn't dead. Well, that was a good thing . . . Right?!

"I have to go back, don't I?" I asked more to myself than to Papa.

"You don't *have* to do anything Lemoya. But are you asking *should* you go back . . . I believe you are the only one who can answer that." He picked a blade of grass and chewed the tip.

"Logton got away, Papa. There are things I still have to do; I can't just walk away. That would mean Leah's death, your being here; it would all be for nothing. I told Adnama that I was accepting the gifts of the True Weaver. That means I accept the responsibilities as well." I looked at him. "But this poison is still in me and that little butt nugget got away so I have no cure." I felt like I was again four years old griping about taking medicine.

"Louanna, you never fail to bring me laughter. The way you phrase things is truly inspiring." He got to his feet and my heart ached as I realized he was preparing to leave. He stretched and breathed in the fresh air. "I love the place you chose for us to meet. It is just as I would have imagined *your* Xela would be."

"Are you leaving me, Papa?" I asked and fought back tears that tried to escape. The pain in my heart was nearly taking my breath.

"Never Lemoya, I am always with you." He leaned down and kissed my forehead. "But you are leaving. Your body calls to you; and you can do no other than answer the call."

I got to my feet and threw my arms around him.

Papa . . . My port in a world gone mad. He said nothing, simply stroked my hair as I cried. I didn't want to go back to the pain and sorrow. This is a good place to be . . . but staying would be so wrong.

I inhaled his unique smell. Holding him close, I found myself unable to let him go.

The life I'm now in is so out of control, chaos seems to be the only thing I can depend on. But here in this place with Papa holding me, everything seems to be right. Now I have the unhappy task of walking away and returning to the pain and suffering again. (Lucky me!)

"Lemoya, not all in your life is pain and suffering." Papa said "You have wonderful friends and family who love you. Look at what your T-Weaves have gone through for you. It was all done out of love."

I knew he was right. My buds had been willing to walk through all the mud and muck that now filled my life, just because they wanted to help. I couldn't dwell on all the negative things when there were still so many positive ones to concentrate on.

"I know your right Papa. I hate being such a baby about this. I have a lot to be happy and excited about."

A wave of nausea fell over me causing me to pull away from his arms.

"You are getting close to waking in the other plane, Lemoya." He said gently. "I want you to promise me that you will fight, Louanna. Fight to survive and to follow the path that Adnama has laid before you. Even when the path leads in a direction you would rather not travel."

The sky drew my attention as it began to darken. Ominous looking clouds rolled in the distance.

"Is there danger coming, Papa? " I asked

"Danger always lingers on the edge of life, Mia noja. But no, those clouds are your doing. Your subconscious is trying to force you to leave; subsequently, making your paradise less attractive." His smile was bright and genuine; just as he was.

"Then I guess it's time for me to go Papa. I can't keep *me* waiting forever." I laughed

He wrapped his arms around me once more for a grizzle hug. "Just remember that you are only *one* person, Louanna. Follow your instincts as they will be guided by Adnama and will never lead you astray."

I closed my eyes as I felt the warmth of his lips press against my forehead; then found myself alone sitting in the field once again; the smell of tobacco and cedar filling my nostrils. A single tear escaped and ran down my cheek. Wiping my eyes, I got to my feet feeling the return of the aches knowing I was going back.

Pain racked over my entire body. My eyes were closed but I knew that Xela was long gone. I felt strong arms holding me and could tell I was being carried; but the pain that now dominated my mind prevented me from caring.

"Is she going to be ok?" Squeaks' voice came from just right of my head.

"I'm sure she will be little one. She is much stronger than you think." Lydian said. The rumble of his chest by my head told me he was who now carried me.

I felt a touch on my head; a tender, loving touch that said Squeaks wasn't so sure he was telling the truth. It was gonna hurt like crazy; but I had to let her know I was alive. I mustered all the energy left in my reserve, and opened my eyes.

The sharp intake of air said she saw me.

"Oh Lou, I'm so glad you're alive." She smiled but tears rolled down her sweet little face; breaking my heart.

I wanted to speak to her and ease her troubled mind; however, all I could manage was a weak smile and I was forced to reclose my eyes. The pain of opening them was more than I had anticipated and now I found myself fighting the urge to throw up. Once again retreating into myself, the only place left for me it seemed.

"Lemoya, I knew I had not lost you. My heart can once again function properly." Lykie's voice caressed my mind.

I couldn't respond I simply snuggled closer to the safety of his chest. I could feel the tension of my buds coming from all around me; but I couldn't find the strength to confront them. I simply withdrew and hid from then pain.

"What about this little guy? He's not looking so hot right now." DeLainey asked. And despite the consequences; I opened my eyes and looked at him.

Kon's seemingly lifeless body was cradled in DeLainey's arms; making him look like a small wounded child. It made me want to comfort him. I could see the bandages covering the torn or gnawed off arm. He was pale and nothing at all like his cheerful little self.

"He is stronger than you think Mia noja. He will not perish so easily. Speritalz are a strong breed of creatures." Logton said, drawing attention to me. I felt several pair of eyes fall on me.

Each face was covered in scrapes and bruises that were going yellow at the edges; but their eyes still held hope. That above anything gave me strength. They had not given up on me . . . or on themselves.

"Dang, Lou. It looks like you have no shame when it comes to getting a guy to carry you around. Tut . . . tut . . . What a diva you have become." DJ smirked.

"I'm sure Lydian would have carried you if you'd of asked him to. There was no need in all the frou-frou." Andee said. He elbowed Allen in the ribs and grinned.

"Yea, Lou. There was no need in all of this; just to get a guy to tote you around like some *damsel in distress*." Allen added.

It felt good to hear them tease me. It brought a kind of normalcy to a very unmoral situation.

The sound of three simultaneous, "OUCH's and OOW's" said that Pixie had; not only popped DJ for his little joke, but now the Farmer's knew the wrath she yielded. I couldn't contain the laugh that bubbled up and spilled out.

"Don't worry Lou, I got your back." Pixie laughed.

"Yea and she got my front." Allen replied.

"And my side!" Andee joked.

"Serves you right." She said. "Lou has had enough badgering and doesn't need the commentary from three realm Stooges."

I could hear their good humor bantering but could not manage to stay alert. My eyes drifted down and my mind fell into a semi stupor. The voices of my friends carried me along as much as the strong arms that held me. Each laugh or gesture of humor seemed to relax my mind and bring about calm.

"You are indeed blessed True Weaver. The ones you chose to share your life with have an unyielding faith in you. You have chosen well for the Court of Brethren. I give to you this gift."

I knew now that it was Adnama who spoke when I heard that voice. Instantly I was engulfed in a sea of warmth; pain was replaced with a feeling of peace. I opened my eyes and saw that my buds had been touched by Adnama's gift as well. Though battered and bruised; it was clear on each face that the pain was lessoned or gone entirely.

In DeLainey's arms I saw Kon stir and open his eyes. He looked disorientated and confused but he was alive.

"Welcome back Stump." DJ said. "Bout time you woke up from your; much needed beauty sleep."

Kon looked at DJ then at each face surrounding him, stopping on Kin. They simply stared at each other; whether they were unable to speak or simply too shaken to try, it was clear they were truly relieved to see one another.

"Don't call him "STUMP" you Neanderthal! He nearly died and you cut jokes about his losing part of his arm?!" Pixie snapped. She was unable to hide the sparkle in her eyes at DJ trying to make Kon feel like he was truly one of us.

"Look, he has a stump now where an arm was. It just seems to me that we should get it over with and just say the inevitable; besides, he kinda looks like a stump." DJ joked.

Kon wiggled the little bloody nub up and down then; a mischievous smile crossed his lips. . "Stump seems appropriate." He said.

Unable to stop ourselves; we all laughed.

Several hours passed and we stopped to camp for the night. Once again I found myself high in the safety of a fardal tree, surrounded by my buds.

"So, what happened when I, umm, took my little nap?" I asked.

"It was the epitome of cur-azy! All those bear things started running around slamming into everything. They knocked over the cages we were in." Allen said. "That's when I got out and Pixie untied me."

"I had been on the roof of the cave, if I crawl really slow; I can pull a chameleon stunt and blend in. Logton never even knew I was in there." Pixie chimed in.

"And then all the animals just sort of calmed down and began foraging through the rubble for food or something." Andee said.

"That part was me." Squeaks said happily. "I told the Broogs that we were not there to hurt them. Logton had told them they needed to protect themselves against us, that we were there to enslave them. Etta was a big help, they saw how I cared for her and she told them of the True Weaver and how they were lied to." She looked at Etta and smiled, running her hand over the caramel colored feathers. Etta seemed to purr at the gesture.

"Then everything froze. You were knocked out cold; and you looked dead. A bright light popped up in the center of the room and a ball of blue fire-like stuff floated about three feet from the ground and hovered here. A voice; or I think it was a voice." DJ said; his voice filled with awe. "It came out of . . . everywhere."

"It was like a voice and a feeling all rolled into one." DeLainey said. "It made me feel safe and warm. Each word felt like a caress; she said we were her children and she was proud of us."

"It was Adnama." Kin supplied. "She was here with us. We were witness to her great power. The fact that we serve the True Weaver and give honor to Adnama gives us favor in her eyes. Few have ever had such an honor." He sounded so humble and proud.

"She is how we were able to help you, Lemoya. When Leah left, she placed in your palm a small pendant. It is called a Life pendant; it is one of four such treasures. The content of the pendant is what is now driving the poison from your body." Lydian said

"So in a roundabout and twisted way; Leah tried to knock you off then gave us your cure." DJ said.

Hearing my lifelong friends name was painful. She had been manipulated and lied to. I know we are responsible for our own actions but when the facts we are given are lies and cause behavior we would not respond to in other circumstances, are we truly responsible?

Logton was the monster here. Leah's death was his doing and on his hands.

Lydian placed the small pendant in my hand. It looked like it was made of warn gold and shaped like a tear drop. A large emerald was held tightly in its center. The sides were ruffled like the edge of a pie crust and on one side there was a small clasp. Turning it over I saw on its back, two double-ended arrows; bent to look like parenthesis: the sign of the Life Weaver. I ran my finger along its surface; reveling in its beauty. Slowly I eased the clasp open and looked inside. It was empty.

"There was a small seed inside that pendant when we opened it. Then that voice told us to place it under your tongue. We did and you took in a deep breath; it was ragged at first, but as we started out of the labyrinth of tunnels you began to stir a bit." Squeaks said.

I closed the pendant and looked at it again. Leah had given this to me. Even as hot as her hatred had burned, she still felt love for me. Logton thought he had her wrapped tightly in a web of anger and hate. His plan had been well orcastraighted. But her true nature, the real Leah had still been inside doing what she had her entire life . . . fighting to survive.

We sat in the top of the fardal tree going over the fight. Logton had known he was losing and had run like a rat from a sinking ship. I took out my Jequota and opened it. A whoosh of air blew out and everyone turned to see where it had come from. I placed the life pendant inside Jequota and watched as it seemingly melted into the cloth. For a moment I was nervous that I had lost it. Retrieving it I saw that it no longer looked like worn gold; but was now glistening like it had just been made. The emerald shone brightly sparkling in the sunlight. I replaced it in the Jequota and again it appeared to disappear.

"It is here for you, True Weaver. Jequota takes into itself that which belongs to it. The life pendant belongs in the Jequota of the True Weaver; as do its sister pieces. You have done well in your plight."

I looked around the group and could tell they had all heard Adnama's voice. It wasn't my accomplishment alone. Each of them had contributed in one way or another. This was a T-Weave victory.

"You look really tired, Lou." DeLainey said quietly.

"I am tired DeLainey, but I'll live. How 'bout you, you make it through that mess ok?"

"De, are you ever going to call me De? " He grumped. "Yes, I made it through ok. I froze time a few times and helped keep things going at a slow pace. It's not really a big deal. I'm sorry that you lost your friend. It is clear that you cared for her a great deal."

That was an understatement. I loved Leah like she was my sister, or even closer. We were like two halves of one whole, I felt alone without her.

"I do care for her a lot, De. She was more like a sister than a friend. She has been fed lies for years and was so desperate for love, she believed all the lies Logton fed her. Thanks for helping us; it was really sweet of you. You hardly even know any of us yet you risked your life to help, Thanks." I looked at him and smiled. Those deep blue eyes sparkled and shined. My heart seemed to skip a beat, or three. Instantly the lopsided grin spread across his face and I looked away.

What? I told you I was a coward when it comes to guys. DeLainey Landon is lethal and he knew it; the fact that he had just followed us into this mess without questioning why, simply made him more attractive.

Everyone sat talking to each other over the events we'd gone through. Laughing at things I knew had scared them. My mind returned to the last time I had seen Leah. How had all of this horrific stuff happened? I was feeling better; still weak, but better. Leah had given me the means to heal, yet it was my misguided spell that had ended her life. My heart was so heavy with sorrow.

"You cannot blame yourself for what happened in the cave, Lemoya."

I looked and saw Lydian standing a few feet from me. I motioned for him to sit by me.

"It was all so unnecessary." I whispered. "Leah would have never done all the things she did had Logton not fed her full of lies. She believed he was a friend to her but all she ever was to him was something to be used." The words were choked out and I felt the sting of my eyes as tears fell down my face."

Lydian put his arm around me and pulled me into a much needed embrace. Quietly I cried, deep, mournful, sorrow-laced tears. I couldn't stop the flow and wasn't sure I wanted to.

Was I to blame? Could this have been stopped? Questions I'd never know the answer to flooded my mind. I'm not sure how much time passed as I cried out the loss of my best friend. I found my tear reservoir had gone dry and I had no more to give. With my head still buried in the comfort of Lydian's chest I managed to say "Thank you."

"You have never needed to thank me, Lemoya. I was born to serve you. It is my duty, my *honor* to be here to comfort you." His hand stroked my hair and he played with the ends as he spoke. "We need to get some sleep and try to get everyone back home tomorrow."

Home . . . it seemed like a lifetime since I had been there. I suddenly found myself homesick.

I wanted to weave a passage to ArDonna's home but I was forbidden to use magic. So we walked. By the second day we were enjoying the trip and everyone was back to their old selves again.

Allen and Andee were wrestling around, DJ was cutting monkey shines, Pixie was popping them when she deemed it necessary, Squeaks was telling Etta all about this and that, De and Lydian were playing alpha at each other towards me. Kin and Kon were picking berries and laughing at the shenanigans going on. Life had returned to normal . . . or as normal as it was for us.

When we finally got to the villa where the two Speritalz lived we decided to leave them and I was at last granted permission to weave a passage home.

Taking out the Weaving Wands I felt a bit strange. I closed my eyes and felt the wind start to blow. Opening my eyes I saw the rainbow webs gathering and I began to weave.

"Home has been so far away,
We cannot wait another day.
A passage is needed for those who roam,
Open for us a doorway home."

In front of me a tear appeared in the air, then a passage became clear and on the other side my back yard was plain to see.

"I never thought I'd be so glad to see your house, Lou." DJ said

"Me either. Let's go before some new challenge pops up." Allen laughed

One by one my buds went through the door. Squeaks hesitated as she looked back in the direction of the Villa where she'd entrusted Etta to the care of Kin, Kon and LaDonna.

"She will be fine, little one. The Speritalz will take great care of her and she will be here when you wish to come back and visit her." Lydian said, seeing the worry on her young face.

"Could we really come see her sometimes, Lou?" she asked, looking her young age.

"Of course we can baby. We will not just abandon her here, she is yours." I looked at Lydian and thought how I'd feel if I had to give him up.

"Much to do about, not gonna happen!"

Everyone went through the portal and I closed it.
"Well I have a lot of explaining to do." Allen said
"What do you mean?" I asked
"We have been gone a week or more. I'm sure we are all in a lot of trouble." He answered.
"You don't have to worry about that." De said and smiled at me." I slowed time here. We have only been gone for about one day. I didn't know how long this would take so I left us some "playing room" in case we were gone for a while."

I looked at him and smiled. "That was really good thinking, De. Thanks!"

"It's nothing, but you're welcome." He turned around and did a funny gesture with his hands. "Everything's back on its right time now."

Back on track, I thought. We had lived through this nightmare and had lived to tell the tale. It would be a long time before any of us wanted to leave again.

I heard the screen door to the kitchen slam and knew mom was on her way to greet me. Before I could speak she wrapped her arms around me and we fell to the ground as she held on to me tightly.

"I'm ok, Mom. We're home now." I squeaked out.

"I have been so worried. I didn't know if I'd ever see you again.' She cried.

Lucy wrapped her arms around me. "Don't you worry us like that again, Louanna. We have been going crazy worrying about you," she said quietly.

"I'm fine, guys. We made it home safe and sound." I looked at my buds and smiled.

"Now we just have to find Logton and stop this from happening again." Lydian said

"You can try to find me True Weaver. But you will fail to do so. I will not be so easily found for our next battle. You have the pendant but I still possess the life ring. You have not won yet."

I looked at the happy faces of the people around me; joy was all I could see. Logton had spoken only to me. He wanted me to know we were not through playing his little game of cat and mouse. I didn't react to his statement. We had earned this reprieve and I wouldn't spoil it for everyone. Logton's greasy voice had slipped into my mind and mine alone. I knew the battle was far from over but for now we won't have to think about what's to come...

www.ingramcontent.com/pod-product-compliance
Lightning Source LLC
LaVergne TN
LVHW041626060526
838200LV00040B/1459